Mike Hutton is the author of three previous novels. In addition to writing he has a life-long interest in early twentieth-century British art, and is a part owner in a National Hunt racehorse. He lives on the borders of Northamptonshire and Leicestershire.

THE VICE CAPTAIN

Mike Hutton

Book Guild Publishing
Sussex, England

First published in Great Britain in 2005 by
The Book Guild Ltd
25 High Street
Lewes, East Sussex
BN7 2LU

Typesetting in Baskerville by
Keyboard Services, Luton, Bedfordshire

Printed in Great Britain by
Athenaeum Press Ltd, Gateshead

A catalogue record for this book is available from
The British Library

ISBN 1 85776 902 3

Prologue

Exposing family secrets can either prove extremely painful or strangely therapeutic. In my case both emotions jostled with others no less potent. As I learnt more about my parents, my moods lurched from love and tenderness to outright shame. So why have I chosen to share this exposure with such an extended audience? Well, much of my career has been dedicated to uncovering other people's lives on my television chat show – now it's my turn.

PART 1
THE CAPTAIN'S SON

My father was hanged at Pentonville Prison in February 1954.

I was only a small child at the time. Within a year my mother had remarried, anxious no doubt to lose the shame attached to his name. Marcus Searle became my new father. My real father, as far as I was concerned. I was a teenager before doubts started itching at the back of my mind. It was a further ten years before I learnt the truth.

The marriage of my mother to Marcus must have been one of convenience. She thought she was gaining respectability. He financial security. He was right. She was wrong.

Certainly it was Marcus who most easily fitted into our leafy, suburban London lifestyle. My mother was too exotic a flower. Foreigners were still viewed with suspicion then. They must have appeared an incongruous couple. Marcus had the looks and bearing of an upper-class Englishman. He wasn't. By profession he was an actor. None too successful, although he had appeared on the West End stage in supporting roles. He was tall, slightly stooped with thinning blond hair that he dyed as the years progressed. He had the palest of skins. He avoided the sun whenever possible. The slightest exposure left him red and blotchy. During the summer, he hid under a wide-brimmed panama. He was a vain man. His dress was foppish, and he always stood out in a crowd. Although his clothes were of good quality and well cut, because he was colour-blind they often clashed violently. He never learnt that stripes and checks rarely sit comfortably together. He bought ties and cravats in Burlington Arcade whose schools and regiments he had no right to represent. He was a born impostor. He was also utterly charming. In those early days, I was proud to call him my dad.

Post-war Britain was dour and bleak. We, though, lived in considerable comfort. Power cuts may have been annoying but food rationing and petrol coupons were for others. We ate lavishly and the Armstrong Siddeley was in constant use. I remember long queues outside food shops, but it was rare for my mother to join one. We were cossetted by staff.

Our house was set well back from the road, opposite the common. Approached down a winding gravel drive, it was of substantial construction and mock Tudor in design. Bridie, my nanny, lived in the main body of the house. Her bedroom and private sitting room overlooked the common and the woods beyond. I loved Bridie and continued to visit her long after she left our employment in my teens. This was when the financial implications of my father's heroic spending finally dawned.

Miguel and Maria lived in staff quarters, a separate building, tucked behind the kitchen. Miguel acted as gardener whilst his wife did the shopping and housework. A local woman came in to cook evening meals, and the Spanish couple would serve at table when my parents entertained.

The interior of the house reflected the diverse taste of two people who appeared to have nothing in common. My mother appreciated antique furnishings at a time when generally they were little sought after. She would regularly disappear for whole days, apparently attending auctions. Her purchases tended to be of huge pieces of Victorian furniture, which reminded her of her childhood Normandy home. Heavy tapestries were also snapped up, giving the rooms a rather gloomy feel, partly offset by her love of garish porcelain. As a child I really disliked her taste, but many of her early purchases sold for hefty prices as financial crisis bore in on us years later.

Marcus was a 'G Plan' man. Modern furniture. Vernon Ward prints and flying ducks beside a York-stone fireplace was his mark. His interest in books was confined to *Wisden*. Cricket was his abiding passion, and he acquired every copy dating back to the nineteenth century.

Between the two, there was no meeting place. They each had their separate sitting rooms. It wasn't long before they had separate bedrooms too. Being young, the significance of this was lost on me.

By the time I started school, Marcus was already spending less time at home. Unable to secure parts in the West End, he joined a touring repertory company. Whilst theatrical 'digs' couldn't compete with the comforts of home, they offered other exciting advantages. Chorus girls and even some leading ladies fell under his spell, helped no doubt by the amount of money he was able to lavish on them. As I grew older he would sometimes involve me. Sitting in the members' enclosure at Lord's, nursing a glass of good claret, he would introduce me to his new leading lady. Tall and languid or blonde and bubbly, they would soon tire of watching the boring game and, linking arms, would walk with me in the shade of the giant stands. Men tended to step aside for us, doffing their straw hats. I sensed these women's glamour. They were desirable even then, well before I reached puberty. Innocent desire, but nonetheless potent. I would arrive home and enthuse about my day. I never mentioned 'the leading ladies' to my mother. It was sufficient for Marcus to tell me she wouldn't understand. Besides I didn't want to hurt either of them.

Of my mother's passions I could only guess. She seemed so sad in spite of the comfortable lives we led. Nervous also, as if at any moment all the advantages she enjoyed would be snatched away from her. Each night after supper, she would sit alone drinking brandy. Sometimes this would lighten her mood and I would hear her singing. The songs tended to be melancholy and some evenings, unable to sleep, I would find her in tears. Then she would cuddle me on her lap and talk of her childhood in France. This was the only retrospection she allowed herself. I knew she had moved to Paris in her teens, but that is where her recollections ended. No amount of prompting would prise information from her.

'My life has been so boring,' she assured me. Increasingly I doubted it.

Marcus made up for my mother's reticence. He never read me bedtime stories. Instead he would thrill me with talks of his wartime experiences as a bomber pilot. The sorties over Dresden and Berlin. Of being shot down in the Channel. I never tired of his accounts of appearing on Broadway with Marlene Dietrich. He had also starred in a film with James Cagney. Strangely my mother was forever interrupting him, her accent thickening with anger.

'Stop filling his head with rubbish,' she would shout. I thought she was being very unreasonable. Her outbursts only postponed his accounts and he would carry on unabashed.

In time I found out that asthma ensured that he

8

had been unable to serve in the war. The only time he had left the country was on a day trip to Calais. Somehow, the revelation that none of his stories were true didn't diminish them in my mind. I didn't need to be told my father was being untruthful. He was such a poor liar. His shocking memory guaranteed that. He would forget he had supposedly been a pilot and reinvent himself as a submarine commander. The more fanciful the story, the more I enjoyed it.

My mother had too much time on her hands. She had no real interests. She listened to the wireless, particularly to the popular music of the day. We had a rather grand gramophone, on which she played endless dance-band music. Sometimes I would catch her dancing. Then she seemed to have shed years. Unaware I was watching, she would gyrate her hips in time to the music, eyes half closed. Mostly, though, she devoted her waking hours to interfering with the staff's duties. Menus discussed with cook would be changed three times before the food arrived at the table. Then she would complain it was overcooked, or a sauce was too thick, or a soup too cold. Cooks were dismissed and new ones appointed. The English, she declared, were barbarians, the worst cooks in the world.

Maria agreed, but her efforts were dismissed as peasants' fodder. So eventually my mother began to cook herself. After a faltering start, her confidence increased. She had found a new focus for her life. My father even began staying in for supper, before leaving for 'his club' or an imaginary rehearsal.

From as early as I can remember, my mother spoke to me in French. For a time I muddled the languages, speaking a kind of gibberish. Marcus became particularly irritated that we could exclude him from the conversation.

'For God's sake, speak to the boy in English,' he would complain.

I didn't realise that financial pressures were already beginning to bear down on the family. Miguel and Maria were dismissed, amongst much acrimony. A part-time gardener was appointed, and Nanny took on the role of housekeeper. Our increasing financial frailty had yet to enter my father's consciousness. Despite our reducing staff numbers, Marcus once arrived home driving a sparkling new Jaguar. This caused a huge row between my parents. I thought my mother was being unreasonable. I spent hours sitting in the car, pretending to drive it, breathing in the intoxicating smell of the soft leather seats.

The visit from a serious-looking accountant led to the withdrawal of a joint bank account facility for Marcus. He was allocated a small monthly allowance. His trips home became more intermittent. He devoted his visits to trying to extract more money from my mother. The rows became quite frightening. Then Marcus played his ace card. He sought a divorce. I never discovered on what grounds and at the time I could think of none, but she capitulated. Her already declining financial stability was halved. Marcus even took possession of the G Plan furniture.

We struggled on in the house. The garden was no longer well tended, and paint peeled off the windows and garage doors. My mother channelled all her hopes for the future through me. It was a somewhat claustro-phobic upbringing. She fussed about me playing sports which she considered dangerous. She embarrassed me by asking that I be excused boxing, which was a major sport at my prep school.

I was not particularly academic, and sport was one of the few activities I excelled at. The other was drawing and capturing a likeness. I developed a cartoon-like style, picking out key features and enlarging and distorting them. I specialised in lampooning the teachers. It made me rather popular with my class-mates, but infuriated those who were trying to inculcate some kind of knowledge into my unreceptive brain. My mother was determined I should have the very best education and a variety of private schools were contacted. She employed a succession of private tutors and with their guidance I managed to scrape into one of London's leading boarding schools. My early days there were fairly miserable. I was unprepared for the sexual advances of a number of prefects and my house captain.

Slowly it dawned on me that I showed little physical likeness to my 'father'. Unlike him my hair was dark and curly. My mother encouraged me to wear it long, accentuating my girlish features. I was short for my age, and my skin darkened quickly on exposure to the sun. Doubts began to form in my mind, but I attributed my looks to being more like my mother, who was dark and petite.

I must have been about fourteen when my mother's sister arrived unannounced. Cécile became flustered. Minette was outrageous and I thought she was very exciting. She had long dyed-blonde hair that constantly flopped over her highly painted face. She tended to wear tight-fitting, low-cut dresses and high platform shoes. Her cleavage, to a boy of my age, was deeply exciting. Bridie decreed her to be a tart. My mother

11

seemed inexplicably concerned by her arrival. Conversations were conducted in French, so urgently and at such speed that even I found them hard to understand.

The day after Minette arrived, my father appeared. I had only seen him a couple of times since the divorce just over a year before. He went into overdrive with Minette, openly flirting with her. Now I understood these two had one thing in common. They wanted money. Needed money. Marcus had cash-flow problems. Business ventures were taking longer to take off than anticipated. A loan was all he required. My mother ushered him into the hall. I heard him thanking her profusely. The money he promised would be returned shortly. I watched him walk down the drive, a hunched rather sad figure. There was no sign of his Jaguar!

By the third day of her stay, my opinion of my aunt Minette was beginning to change. She was no longer bothering to be charming and ebullient. The conversations with my mother had become hectoring and threatening. My mother was tearful and apprehensive. I wanted to confront Minette, but Bridie urged caution. I heard Minette quite clearly threaten Cécile that she would open up the whole can of worms. She would tell me everything. Standing on the landing, I struggled to hear what was being said. My mother was crying, and it was only Minette's voice that carried.

'Ten thousand, you stuck-up cow, and you won't see me again.'

Now my mother's voice rose in anger. 'You're mad. Where can I get that kind of money?'

'Don't you kid me, bitch. I know the sort of bread he left you.'

The door which had been left ajar was pushed shut and their conversation became a mumble. Unable to contain my curiosity I crept down the stairs and held my ear to the door. They were still arguing. Minette had dropped her demand to eight thousand, but her language was even more foul and menacing. I felt my hair being twisted and I was led off to the kitchen by Bridie and given a lecture on eavesdropping. Later that evening Minette left. She was all charm again. She kissed me, saying what a handsome boy I was and she pressed a ten-shilling note into my hand. My mother had been crying, her mascara smudged. I felt like a traitor. The figure eight thousand kept swirling in my mind. Eight thousand what? Francs surely, not pounds? What was it about my mother's past that enabled Marcus and Minette to be given money she could ill afford? I knew for the moment at least, I couldn't ask her.

I only met Marcus once more after he called that afternoon when Minette had crashed into our lives. He took me to lunch at the Strand Corner House. My memories are of a motley gypsy band and, bizarrely, of an outstanding lemon meringue pie. He was quite watery-eyed, as he told me how much he loved me. His fortunes seemed to have taken an upturn and he wore a smart new suit. He had arrived carrying a number of Harrods carrier bags, which he left in the cloakroom, along with an expensive cashmere overcoat. I tried to get him to tell me about old times. How he had met my mother? Had he been over to see her family in France? He was evasive. He was no more forthcoming than my mother. Abruptly he called for the bill, not even waiting for coffee, to which he was something of an addict. He embarrassed me terribly by kissing me goodbye, insisting he would be in touch in a couple of weeks.

He never made contact. Not with my mother either as far as I am aware. I did once catch sight of him, many years later. He was amongst the crowds outside Waterloo Station. He shuffled. His clothes were stained and threadbare. He wore open-toe sandals, with no socks to ward off the cold. His feet were red and raw, caked with grime. He clutched a can of export lager, and a half bottle of whisky protruded from his jacket pocket. I went over to speak to him. He had a haunted look. His eyes didn't take in his immediate surroundings. Every few yards he would stop and stare around aggressively. He swigged from the can spilling most of the contents down his old Harrovian tie.

'Bollocks!' he screamed, staring through his alcoholic mist to see if he was getting any reaction from passers-by. Then he laughed uncontrollably for a few seconds.

'Fuck you all!' he roared, his voice even now preserving something of the cadence perfected on stage. To my shame, I hurried to catch my train. I never mentioned my encounter to anyone.

Now it was time for Bridie to leave us, amongst many tears and much soul-searching. The house was sold during the Christmas holidays, and I helped my mother pack in readiness for our move. She had rented a shop, with a flat above, in the Finchley Road. She had decided to open a pâtisserie and seemed genuinely excited at the prospect. I realised that our financial situation must have gone into freefall. Most of the antiques my mother had acquired were sent off for auction. Between them, my parents appeared to have squandered a fortune. Now, though, my mother was

14

less apprehensive about her future. She had forged a new attitude, adversity bringing out the best in her.

Just weeks before we moved, Minette reappeared, without warning as before. Again she was ushered away by my mother, this time out of earshot. She left within the hour, but I had the impression that my mother had paid her off. Why?

A couple of days later a visitor arrived in a chauffeur-driven Bentley. He was thickset, dark and swarthy. Expensively dressed. His arrival seemed to totally unnerve my mother. The colour drained from her face. Ignoring me, he took her quite roughly by the arm and led her into the living room. He exuded a sort of menace I had not encountered before. Following them I demanded to know what he wanted.

'Get lost, sonny, this doesn't concern you.' His voice was high-pitched for such a tough-looking man. The accent was difficult to place. Foreign certainly.

'Xavier, please!' She was shaking with fear. 'Jamie, leave us now.'

I hesitated.

'Sod off!' I had never heard my mother swear. It was quite out of character.

'Who are you?' I persisted.

'Go!' he barked, moving towards me. I scuttled from the room. Watching him leave ten minutes later, as he climbed into the powder-blue Bentley, I saw he was older than I had realised. Now, as he was picked out in a shaft of sunlight, it was obvious that he dyed his hair. The chauffeur helped lower him into the passenger seat before the car glided down the drive.

'Who was that?' I demanded.

Cécile seemed distracted. 'It's none of your business,'

15

she said, but as an afterthought she added, 'If you really want to know, he's my financial advisor.'

I didn't believe her.

The unease I felt following the visit was still with me as I packed my possessions into cartons, in readiness for our move. Much that I had collected as a child was discarded. We were about to make a fresh start. Somehow our move assumed an added significance in my mind. I felt protective and wanted to be of more use to my mother. I sensed she needed my support, but in some undefined way my protection too, but against what I was unable to guess.

Bored with my own half-hearted packing, I wandered into her bedroom. Moving through a sea of clutter, I saw her standing outside on the unmown lawn. She looked quite frail, staring out over the garden, which had become weed-strewn and uncared for.

Turning, I noticed a pile of photographs on her bedside table. Inquisitive, like most youngsters, I collected them up and sitting on the bed studied each in turn.

The first captured my mother, aged perhaps seven or eight. She stares unblinking at the camera. She holds on to an ornately carved chair. Her hair, straight and black, falls to her shoulders. She wears a smocked pinafore over a high-necked woollen dress. Her stockings are coarse, and the ankle boots she wears button up at the side. She is a serious little girl, standing so still. You sense she is holding her breath. Next are a couple of sepia prints, taken on a French beach. In the first she is little more than a toddler. Already serious, she stares almost accusingly, her bucket and spade discarded at her feet. The next shot appears to have been taken on the same stretch of sand, with the vague outline

16

of a promenade in the background. She is much older, probably in her early teens. She appears to resent the intrusion of the camera. She is sulky and sultry. That uneasy age, part child, part woman.

Next a complete change of scene. I stare with added interest at the black-and-white shot. A group of young women smile provocatively. They are all smoking. One holds an absurdly long cigarette holder. A young Minette blows a kiss towards the camera. She wears a dress cut so low that her breasts are almost entirely visible. Next to her, I am shocked to see my mother. She sits on a table that is cluttered with empty glasses. She wears a tight skirt with a slit up the side, which reaches to her thigh. Her legs are encased in fishnet stockings, which are fastened to frilly suspenders. The whiteness of her flesh is accentuated by the gaping skirt. On her feet she wears the highest of heels, drawing the eye back to the shapeliness of her legs. She is being outrageously provocative, her face creased in a look of mock ecstasy.

I felt a sense of unease and tossed the photo aside. The next was a formal portrait of a British army officer. He has a good face. Young, probably in his early twenties. His hair is cut regulation-short and is Brylcreemed. He has a rather jutting jawline. He smiles self-consciously for the camera. I turned the photo over, expecting some inscription identifying him. Nothing. The reverse is blank. Then another shot. The same man, but older. Pictured with him is Cécile, my mother. He is dressed in black. A polo necked sweater under a loose-cut suit. His hair is longer, but well groomed. His jawline gives him a look of self-assurance. She, by contrast, appears nervous. The photograph has been taken in a bar or club. They sit at a table covered

17

in a crisp damask cloth. He holds her left hand, extending it towards the camera. The light catches the triple set diamonds. A champagne bottle rests in a bucket at his side, whilst in the fluted glass she raises, bubbles sparkle.

Suddenly I noticed that newspaper cuttings had fallen out onto the bed. I started unfolding a faded copy of the *News Chronicle*.

The slap to my face is ferocious. It propels me sideways.

'How dare you!' she screamed. 'You fucking little snooper!'

I was dumbfounded. More swearing, fouler than anything I'd ever heard. I tried to calm her, but the stream of abuse continued. She was out of control, eyes bulging. She hurled a lampshade at me. Confused and upset, I retreated to my room. Then I heard her crying. Sobbing. I didn't go to comfort her.

We duly moved into our new home in Swiss Cottage. The shop was sizeable. Professional ovens, fridges and counters were installed. A crazy Hungarian was employed to help with the baking and two part-time assistants to serve in the shop. The flat above was comfortable enough, although it felt very cramped after living in a large rambling house. The living room was a reasonable size, but the kitchen, bathroom and two bedrooms were tiny. Our few remaining pieces of furniture overpowered our living space.

My mother's outburst was never mentioned. I think the record player she bought me soon after we moved in was by way of a peace offering. I became a day boy at school, which was a huge financial saving. I completed my A level exams, but my results were not as good as had been predicted. I was turned down by the university of my choice, and it was only after much persuasion that I was allowed to apply to attend art school. Most of these had acquired a reputation for rather wild behaviour and my mother didn't approve.

I suppose I really rather fancied myself as an artist. I grew my hair and began to dress outlandishly. Girls started to show an interest in me, but although I might have felt I looked the part, I was awkward and gauche in their company. I enrolled at St Peter's School of Art in Bayswater. Modern art in all its various forms was much in favour. My tutors pilloried me for my traditionalist style. They thought I was condemning myself to a life of painting fat businessmen and minor politicians. Certainly their influence brought a lighter touch to my work, and it even drew some tepid praise. I was therefore astonished to win the Silver Prize for a painting featuring my mother, serving in her shop, in my final year. I was approaching my twenty-first birthday. It was time to leave home.

The principal of my college called me into his office to inform me that Jean-Paul Arneau had been one of the judges who had awarded my prize. He had been impressed by my work and was willing to offer me the opportunity of studying under him in his Paris studio. He was the leading French portraitist of his generation. I was hugely flattered. My mother supported the decision. The shop was doing well, and I think she wanted more space to live her own life. She also didn't approve of my latest girlfriend. Valerie Watson was a first-year student at the college. We had been going out together for about six months. She had become increasingly intense and possessive. Crazily, she talked of marriage.

Our relationship was becoming claustrophobic. She even resented me having a 'boys' night out at the pub. News that I was off to France produced a reaction that I thought hysterical. She even threatened to follow me to Paris.

With a wicked smile, my mother handed me two ten-pound notes and suggested I took Valerie somewhere memorable for our final date. Rules is one of the most attractive restaurants in London. Valerie, however, was in no mood to be impressed. She picked at her food and cried so much that diners at nearby tables stared at me accusingly. I was furious with her. She continued sobbing, pushing her plate aside and refusing to drink her wine. Casting my napkin down, I left her and sought refuge in the toilet. Slowly climbing the stairs, I paused to glance at the rows of photographs that lined the walls. They were mostly of film stars, writers or sportsmen. Each was autographed with a flourish. An unmistakeable face stared out at me. Standing next to the American actor George Raft was the army officer from my mother's photos. He looked rather older than when he was pictured with my mother drinking champagne. He looked hard and fit. Unlike the famous actor, he wasn't smiling. He was holding a hand out towards the cameraman as if he didn't want the moment recorded.

I sought out the head waiter in the hope he would be able to identify the man. He was unable to help. The photo was taken before he joined the restaurant. He found a waiter who had worked at Rules since the war. He told me the name was on the tip of his tongue. It wasn't. He hovered, expecting a tip. Returning to my table I found Valerie still weeping.

I spent two years in Paris studying, eventually acting as studio assistant to Jean-Paul. He was an amusing and inspirational master. During my final year, I was even allowed to have some direct input into his work, though this was mainly confined to backgrounds. His much-admired painting of Maurice Chevalier was partly my work, with Jean-Paul in effect reversing our roles, devoting himself to the elaborate background. However, I was unable to capture the star's twinkling eyes, and his bony hands, with their prominent veins and age spots, completely defeated me. I still had a great deal to learn.

On my return home, I found that my mother's shop continued to do relatively well. Another pâtisserie had opened up a few hundred yards down the road and had poached a couple of my mother's staff. She was a poor employer. She paid the lowest wage she could get away with and expected unstinting hard work and loyalty in return. She was convinced all her employees were cheating her. I would have hardly blamed them if they had been.

My mother had aged alarmingly since I had been abroad. To me she had always appeared attractive for her age, but now her weight had soared. Too many cakes and pastries. Her face had coarsened. Only her legs remained shapely, but now seemed too thin to accommodate her burgeoning body.

For a time on my return I stayed with her, occupying my old room. Increasingly I felt the need for my own space. I found a rather dingy room on the top floor of a house just off Mornington Crescent. It was transformed when I cleared a thick layer of green paint from the fanlight and whitewashed the walls. It made an ideal studio. Unfortunately I had to live in it as well. Each morning I woke up to the smell of white spirit and a sore throat. I looked out on the same sea of roof tops and chimneys that Walter Sickert and Charles Ginner had done years before me. I was convinced the omens were good. Now all I needed were a few commissions. Money was already a problem. I did manage to get a short write-up in the *Evening News* about my apprenticeship with Jean-Paul. I was convinced this would lead to a stream of enquiries. Instead I painted my landlady and the manageress of the local launderette. They were both thrilled, but I was beginning to doubt if life as a portrait painter was such a good idea.

My landlady took the call. I was at the pub, and Ethel came to find me. My mother had collapsed and had been taken to University College Hospital. She had suffered a massive heart attack. Irrationally, I had been convinced that coronaries were confined to men.

She looked ghastly. I touched her face. Her skin was damp, cold to the touch. Her eyes were open, but she showed no sign of recognition. The young doctor told me, with classic understatement, that she was rather poorly. That the next twenty-four hours were crucial. I couldn't take it in. She was far too young to die. I tried talking to her, without making any contact. There was so much I wanted to tell her. Even more that I needed to ask. I sat with her all through the night, listening to the cries and snores of the other patients in the ward. I held her hand and stroked her forehead before dropping off into a fitful sleep. I was wakened by nurses wheeling trolleys and the sound of tea being prepared in the kitchen. A West Indian nurse suggested I went home to change and have some breakfast. Instead I found a workman's café off Tottenham Court Road. I picked at a greasy fry-up, and washed it down with a mug of strong, sweet tea.

Returning to the ward, I saw the screens were round my mother's bed. I presumed they were washing her. Then I noticed the staff nurse walking towards me. I knew from the expression on her face – my mum was dead.

The cremation was sad and poorly attended – just a few neighbours and a couple of customers. As the electrically controlled curtains closed to hide the coffin, I became aware that someone behind me was leaving. The vicar was still intoning some final prayers.

Outside I stood in the autumn sunshine thanking those who had attended. My attention was drawn to a chauffeur-driven powder-blue Bentley, as it glided towards the exit. In the back seat I recognised the hunched figure of the rather threatening character who had called on my mother, all those years ago. He leant back as if anxious to avoid eye contact with me. Beside him sat a young woman, perhaps in her early thirties. She had jet-black hair that fell to her shoulders. She looked familiar, but I couldn't think why.

That night I went back to my room. I didn't feel ready to face the shop and my mother's flat. Lying back on my divan, I mulled over the past, as we all tend to in times of grief. I was uncomfortable and reaching into my back pocket I found I was lying on the cards the undertaker had removed from the floral tributes. I flipped through them without much interest. Formal messages from neighbours and friends, and one from the staff at the pâtisserie. Then a plain white card whose inscription had me holding it under the beam of my bedside lamp to make sure I had not misread it. It was written in French.

Mamam, I miss you already
All my love,
Nadine

I felt guilty that I didn't grieve more. For a couple of days I was upset and depressed, but then the weather changed. Pathetic, I know, but true. It heralded the longest, hottest summer on record. Perhaps I was in denial, but my lack of emotion really underlined my immaturity. Years of love and caring pushed to the back of my mind, purely by the sight of legions of pretty girls walking the streets of London.

The capital shed its grey skin and reinvented itself. Tables with parasols invaded the normally cold pavements outside restaurants and coffee bars. Crowds spilt out of pubs, clasping glasses in sweaty hands. Roads melted and the parks were lined with reddening bodies, snatching a few minutes away from sweltering offices. Normally tight-lipped Londoners started talking to strangers. The old grumbled about the intolerable heat and humidity, whilst the young chattered because they felt a new sense of liberation.

In winter, I reckoned the women of London hardly warranted a second glance. Shrouded in heavy, unflattering coats, sullen-faced, they trudged through the fog

24

and showers. Now, miraculously, they were transformed. They walked with a bounce, hair shining, legs tanned, temporarily released from restricting tights. In contrast, the men under forty looked ghastly. Their hair was worn uniformly long. They sweated beneath fitted shirts, with enormous collars and wore ridiculous flared trousers. I couldn't stand it. I had my hair cut really short, my black curls left on the tiled floor of a Cypriot barber's in Camden Town. I then bought the entire stock of smocks from a strange shop run by a huge Czechoslovakian woman on the Bayswater Road. Cotton for the summer, with wide dolman sleeves. The winter design was of a heavier material and secured round the waist with a sash. The trousers I chose were baggy, jodhpur-like, and the outfit was completed by tight-fitting calf-length boots. I was convinced I looked every inch a bohemian. In hindsight I cringe.

When I eventually did pay a visit, the shop was looking sad, untidy and grubby, with little choice on offer. The manageress, whom I only knew by sight, was aggressive and yet shifty. Rightly she wanted to know why I hadn't been in touch. How was she supposed to know what to do? The pâtisserie cook had left, and she reckoned she had shown initiative by buying stock from a wholesaler. She was vague about turnover and banking arrangements. She had been paying herself and the assistant out of the takings. I was being done, that much was sure.

Upstairs the flat was dark and musty, whilst outside London shimmered under another cloudless sky. Wandering through the rooms I was struck by how orderly everything seemed. My mother had never been particularly house-proud, and yet it was as if she had tidied the flat in anticipation of someone she was trying to impress. Maybe she had some premonition about her failing health and wanted to leave her home in perfect order, worried as ever about other people's opinions of her. I was conscious that the flat seemed to have been cleared of anything that related to her past. Even family photographs had been removed. I began to think someone had been in the flat before me, but as far as I knew I was the only one with keys. Certainly the shop staff didn't have access. Her desk, too, was exceptionally tidy. Normally papers and invoices spilled out of half-opened drawers or were scattered over the floor. Now each section contained paperwork relating to the shop systematically filed in alphabetical order. Catalogues from trade exhibitions were neatly stacked. There was no sign of a will or of the photographs and newspaper cuttings I had discovered just before we moved to Swiss Cottage. There was, however, correspondence relating to the lease on the property. The work had been carried out by a firm of lawyers in Highgate. I rang them on the off-chance that they might be able to help. I was put through to a Mr Waterfield, who much to my amazement immediately confirmed that my mother had indeed lodged her will with him. I was given an appointment for the following week.

Wandering into my mother's bedroom I felt a sense of her presence. I opened the wardrobe and stared at the row of her familiar clothes. Here nothing seemed to have been discarded. Dresses I remembered her wearing when I was a young child were crammed in between more recent purchases. I picked a black cocktail dress from the rail which she had loved before she had put on weight. I caught a glimpse of myself in the wardrobe mirror looking incongruous as I stroked the black satin material. It was then that I was overwhelmed by a tidal wave of grief. Throwing myself on her bed I clutched the dress to me. It retained a vague lingering smell of her. For weeks I had kept reality at bay, but now the barriers were down. I howled, wretched and ashamed at my own fecklessness.

Andrew Waterfield could only have been a few years older than me and yet he talked to me as if I were a child. He had the annoying habit of repeating everything he said, whilst peering owlishly over heavy-rimmed spectacles, I still left his gloomy, cluttered office with a feeling of euphoria. I was overwhelmed by what I thought was a vast amount of money that I had inherited. Today it would seem quite paltry, but back in that boiling summer, it was enough for me to purchase the top floor of a Georgian house just a short stroll from Regent's Park, with partial views over the canal.

Once more my immaturity asserted itself. I couldn't spend my new-found wealth quickly enough. I bought an MG sports car before I had even learnt to drive. I was an appalling driver. I failed my test three times. When eventually I was allowed on the road by myself, I crashed with monotonous regularity. The furnishings in my flat were influenced by the taste of whichever passing girlfriend was around at the time. The result was an embarrassing mixture of Indian carved furniture, ethnic rugs and a huge Victorian four-poster bed. I even allowed the walls to be lined with vile Dalí prints.

It was a mess and so was I. The only purchase I made which I still have was a superb antique easel. But I didn't paint. I'm afraid to admit I had only one interest, which was dictated by a seemingly endless supply of testosterone. My thoughts were confined to seduction. Stupidly, I was quite indiscriminate.

The steamy summer ended as abruptly as it had begun. Autumn somehow passed me by. Winter closed in, and it was only then that it dawned on me that my flat had no heating. There were no radiators and the old tiled fireplaces had been blocked off. Life suddenly didn't seem so great. I was already running short of money. My car was back in the body shop, and my latest girlfriend, whom I actually really liked, had ditched me. I was depressed and overcome by a sense of lethargy. I had been feeling off colour for a while. I realised I had been running off to the toilet every five minutes or so. I was even waking in the night three or four times, desperate for a pee. It was hurting too. I wouldn't mention this normally, but two unconnected events conspired to shake up my life on the same day. The first a sore and weeping cock and the second a letter from Harvey's Bank concerning a deposit box held in my mother's name.

That morning my cock took precedence. I was too embarrassed to contact our family doctor who had known me since I was at school. Instead I went to a skin clinic on the Waterloo Road, which I had seen advertised on the Tube. Confidential treatment was apparently assured. The clinic was housed in a scruffy Victorian building, with lines of scruffy men seated on plastic chairs awaiting their appointments. My immediate reaction was to leave, but instead I joined the queue and avoided all eye contact. A rather jolly bald-headed man sitting next to me informed anyone who cared to listen that he had syphilis. He seemed to be proud of it. I was mortified and prayed that I hadn't the same problem. At that moment I would have signed a pledge to sexual abstinence for life.

My thoughts were interrupted and I was led into a small consulting room. A tall bored-looking doctor and a lumpy nurse of uncertain age viewed me with obvious distaste. I was instructed to drop my ... there was a hesitation before trousers were mentioned. My jodhpurs were certainly not being greeted with universal acclaim. My cock which had jutted and thrusted with great enthusiasm throughout the summer was a shadow of its former self. It was raised with some difficulty on a wooden spatula held by the nurse as the doctor beamed a light at the source of my discomfort. Irony was obviously the doctor's strong suit. He suggested I took a sabbatical for a few weeks.

'Let the girls catch their breath. I suppose it *is* girls you're into?' he queried.

'God, you don't think I'm queer surely?'

They were watching intently as I buttoned my jodhpurs. That's it, I thought. The bloody things would have to go.

To my relief I was informed that a course of penicillin should clear my problem up pretty rapidly. I was so euphoric that it was a couple of days before I remembered the letter from the bank. My lawyers had contacted them as a matter of routine because my mother had once had an account with Harvey's. This had apparently been closed years before, but a safe deposit was still held in her name.

Not only did I discard my jodhpurs for my appointment with the bank, but I also resurrected an old sports jacket from the back of my wardrobe. I even bought a new white shirt and a sober tie for the occasion. Harvey's was a small merchant bank just off Piccadilly. They have subsequently been swallowed up by one of the major banks. Stepping through the doors was like being cast back in time. The sound of traffic outside was completely obliterated. The atmosphere was not unlike that found in church. It was mammon that was worshipped here, though, rather than God. Elderly tellers behind brass grilles spoke in hushed tones to well-heeled clients.

I was escorted to the basement by a frock-coated assistant manager. We passed through a series of security doors to a small room lined with rows of grey-fronted safes. I was seated at a superb Georgian desk and asked to sign sheaves of forms. The reasons for each signature were explained to me, but I scarcely listened, my sense of anticipation now running wild. Was the security box to contain wads of money or perhaps priceless jewellery? Still more identification was required. My driving licence (recently endorsed for dangerous driving). Then my passport. A huge black security guard looked on impassively. With a shaky hand, I turned the key to safe 304. My disappointment was intense. Two rigid cardboard boxes filled the available space. Opening the first I saw it contained numerous exercise books and some desk diaries. The second box was similarly crammed, but on top was a sealed envelope addressed to me in my mother's handwriting. I avoided the temptation to open it right there. The boxes were very heavy, but the security guard insisted on carrying them both upstairs. Outside a uniformed doorman hailed me a taxi.

The letter was written in French and was undated. It was on headed notepaper from our previous home.

Darling Jamie,
    I hope by the time you read this you will be old enough for the news not to upset you. Darling, Marcus was not your father. I think you suspected as much. The contents of these boxes were written by Derek Emms, your real dad. I have often been tempted to destroy the diaries, but after much soul-searching I have decided you have a right to know. I wish I had been brave enough to tell you myself. They tell an incredible story. Derek was an extraordinary but complicated man. You will come to your own conclusions.
    Your memories of me may well be tarnished, as I have done much to be ashamed of. Please don't think too badly of me,
        Your adoring Mamma

I sat shivering. My flat was freezing despite the electric fire I had installed. I was shocked by the letter. My mind went back to the funeral. The woman in the back of the Bentley – a younger version of my mother.

Gingerly I sorted through the contents of the boxes. Each notebook and diary had been thrown in haphazardly, in no particular order. The first I opened was a Boots half-year diary from 1949. The entries were in a neat, educated hand and written in black ink. As I flipped through, I noticed that most entries

31

seemed brief and covered mundane, everyday events. Some weeks had no entries at all, whilst occasionally whole pages were covered. I started arranging the volumes in date order. The earliest was for 1947. As I stacked them into a neat pile, a single black-and-white photograph fluttered to the floor. A stout woman and a pretty blonde child sitting on a mountainside. The child, smiling, holds up a daisy chain. They are dressed in traditional, or possibly national, costume.

I placed it to one side and started reading the first entry. It was almost dawn before I finally went to bed, though it was many years until everything became clear to me.

PART 2

A DIFFICULT TRANSITION

Derek Emms was discharged from the army in the summer of 1946, with the rank of Captain. He had been called up on leaving school, shortly after his eighteenth birthday. Two years later he was recruited into a newly formed Commando Unit and saw action from the debacle at Dieppe to the Normandy landings.

It was whilst on leave a year before the end of the war that he met Mary Dawson, at a party in a rather grand house in Russell Square. There was a mutual attraction. She was a tall, vivacious blonde, surrounded by an eager group of admirers. He was quiet, not seeking attention. Neither was he shy. She noticed him at once. He had the saddest eyes, too old for the rest of his face. He showed just the flicker of a smile, as she broke away from the group of young men who had congregated around her. It was as if he had expected her to. His bearing set him apart. He spelt excitement, maybe even a hint of danger.

They spent two hectic days and one exhausting night together, agreeing to meet on Derek's next leave. Even as she waved goodbye to him on the platform at Victoria Station, he doubted it. He had found her rather empty-headed and vacuous. He did occasionally think of her, but only of her long legs crossed behind his neck and the smell of cigarettes on her breath. She also had been disappointed. Rather than exciting, she found him uneasy company. He never relaxed, and his nightmares, when he had finally drifted off to sleep that night, had woken and frightened her.

There was no contact between them, until a couple of months later he received a hysterical phone call. She was pregnant. It was quite possible that he was not the father, but he didn't question her. He did the

35

decent thing, and married her. The baby was stillborn, and so was the marriage. Both felt betrayed. Derek was convinced he had been trapped unnecessarily. Mary felt deceived. She had been determined to make a good marriage. As her mother constantly advised, 'Don't marry for the money, but don't court where there isn't any.'

In their brief time together Mary had drawn a number of false conclusions. Derek had talked of what appeared to be a privileged upbringing. He had attended an expensive boarding school. His father had been a senior officer in the Great War and lived in a huge Victorian pile in rural Hertfordshire. These were facts that helped placate her parents, who were absurdly impressed by such matters. What he had omitted to tell her was that his education had been grudgingly paid for by his father's older brother, Robert. With the same degree of ill grace, his father had been allowed to lodge in two damp rooms located in the east wing of Mackworth Manor. His father had suffered the double blow of losing both his wife and subsequently all his money during the Depression.

The hastily arranged marriage in Harrow was a sombre and uncomfortable affair. The service lasted barely a quarter of an hour, and the reception at a local hotel was notable only for a salad of tinned salmon and a toast made to the happy couple with pale ale for the men and a sweet sherry for the ladies. When the true state of the Emms family fortunes became apparent, Mary's parents were openly hostile towards him.

The couple saw little of each other until Derek's discharge. Mary continued to live with her parents, although subsequently he learnt she had spent much of the time in London with 'friends'. On his discharge he had little money and was forced to live in her parents' bungalow in Rickmansworth. The atmosphere was poisonous. He wanted to find a job in London, but to his surprise Mary had developed a love of the country. She had returned to her childhood passion of riding, obtaining lifts each week to join in the Cambridgeshire hunt. Derek had no experience of work in civvy street and had no idea what he wanted to do. At Mary's prompting, he applied for a position of trainee manager for a privately owned store group with outlets in the Midlands and the North. He was interviewed at the Savoy by the chairman, Stuart Brunton, and two other directors. He was asked to attend a second interview at the group headquarters in Leicester, this time accompanied by his wife. Within minutes he knew the job was his. Mary fluttered her eyelashes, constantly crossed her long legs and insisted on pouring the coffees. She was brilliant, as she always was in men's company. Each in turn was made to feel that they were the very centre of her attention. The money was poor, but a house was provided by the company. They moved in just before Christmas. It was a stone-built lodge at the gates to Brunthorpe Hall, home to Stuart Brunton. Presumably it was the prospect of the new direction in his life that prompted Derek to start his diary entries. Although spasmodic, they cover seven quite extraordinary years.

The First Diary – 1947

Wednesday, January 1st
First day at work. The store is four miles away. I cycle and arrive red-faced and mud-splattered. Everyone hung over and bleary-eyed, moaning about having to work on New Year's Day. The store is a sea of linoleumed floors, glass-fronted counters and juddering lifts. The Christmas decorations were being cleared away, leaving the place looking under-stocked and overstaffed. Except that is for the senior management, none of whom had turned up. Nobody seemed to know what to do with me. I spent most of the day sitting in an office drinking coffee and pretending to read staff regulations.

Mary is carping about the furnishings in our house. I agree. What isn't cast-offs or threadbare is cheap and tacky. Hardly a great advert for Brunton's department stores. She is on about me buying a car. What a joke! Until I get paid, we can't even afford a second bike. Life in the country probably doesn't seem quite so rosy to her now.

Friday, January 3rd
The fragrant Mrs Brunton paid Mary a visit today with some more hand-outs from the Hall. I mustn't be ungrateful. It has made the place look a little more homely. The trouble is I feel as if we have sold our soul to the company store.

Sunday, January 12th
Spent most of the day in bed. It is bitter outside and the house is damp. The log fire in the living room belches smoke every time the door is opened.

Mary is a stranger to me. We live together, but there is no real contact. Our interests and ambitions are different. She talks endlessly of my being promoted. She imagines a fine country house, sports cars, a flat in London. She must be kidding! I feel drained. I hate the job and most of the people who work at Brunton's. They fall into two main categories – the bullies and the bullied.

Perhaps if we spent all our time in bed, our relationship would be better. Here there are no difficulties. Here we have developed an understanding. We are easy and at ease with each other. There is also a genuine warmth that seems to evaporate when we leave the bedroom. Physically I find her more attractive than ever. I have never been to bed with any girl as skilful as Mary. Perhaps a little too skilful.

She is also a good cook. A strange thing happened tonight. In the middle of supper I broke down. I was quite unable to stop sobbing. I don't know what prompted it. If it had happened an hour earlier, whilst we were still in bed, I think Mary would have been more sympathetic. As it was she flew at me, accusing me of being spineless. I think she might be right.

Friday, January 24th
Today the snows came. Blankets of the stuff. It was so deep that I was unable to cycle to work, so I walked. I staggered in at ten o'clock. Hardly any staff and no customers. The snow intensified. The store closed at three. Abandoned cars and buses everywhere. Hundreds of people stranded. Local hotels and pubs overflowing.

I loved the walk home in blizzard conditions. Once out of town there was not a soul to be seen. I peed

in what I think was the middle of the A6. I forced
myself to run, with the snow up around my knees. It
was a good feeling to stretch myself physically, again.
I have let myself go since demob. From now on I will
work to get myself back into shape. It's probably the
reason why I have been feeling so down recently.

Wednesday, February 5th
More snow last night, but I managed to get to work.
The roads were icy. I am covered in bruises. Where it
is too hazardous to ride, I carry the bike over my
shoulder and run; I'm getting much fitter. I time myself
and set new targets. I think I'm getting quite obsessive.

I'm about to end a spell in the leather goods
department. The buyer is of the old school, complete
with blue-tinted perm. She loves the power she wields.
Poor reps are kept waiting, sometimes for hours. She
views me with outright hostility. She can obviously
sense my heart isn't in the job. To her Brunton's is
her life. How sad! In hushed tones she pointed out Mr
Timothy, the chairman's son, who was doing a tour of
the store. He has just returned from a visit to the
States, where he had apparently spent the war years.
Studying American retailing no doubt. Nothing to do
with avoiding being called up of course. It is amazing
how many sons of the rich and famous continue to
come out of the woodwork. Mr Timothy must be about
thirty. He is tall, tanned and good-looking. He ignored
us as he swept through attended by a group of acolytes.
It was as if we had been honoured by a visit from
royalty.

Our house is so freezing cold, we took supper to
bed. We had layers of clothing on, and the bed is

heaped with coats. Being amorous wearing woollen gloves was difficult, but we managed. I haven't laughed as much for years. Looking down at Mary asleep as I write this (gloves still on), I realise how beautiful she is. More so, when she is unaware of being watched. We are an odd couple, but I think we are beginning to come to terms with each other.

Saturday, February 22nd
The snow has finally vanished. Last night when we went to bed it still lay several inches thick. This morning we have floods. The road outside the house is under water. This has not deterred Mary. She has gone riding. She didn't even wait for breakfast. She has made friends with Doreen Wilford, whose parents' farm is just half a mile away. She's a plump, almost masculine, girl in her early twenties. Her parents are tenant farmers, and no prizes for guessing who owns their farm. In fact Stuart Brunton's family owns thousands of acres locally, together with farmhouses, tied cottages and three village pubs.

I am beginning to doubt the wisdom of opening a joint account at the bank. Since I was paid last month Mary has invested in full riding gear, from gloves to expensive calf boots. Lamps, vases and rugs have also appeared. She insists I am being boring when I question her and keeps mentioning the staff discount we can claim. Ten percent off inflated prices. I've seen the 'mark-ups' the store works on. Besides she has now used up all our clothing coupons and my suit is getting more shiny by the day.

My first Saturday off since I started work. Treated myself. Wandered down to the Brunthorpe Arms. I had ordered a second pint, before it occurred to me

41

that the profits were going to the bloody Bruntons. The beer suddenly tasted flat.

Thursday, February 27th
Letter from the bank. We have gone into overdraft – would I care to call in to discuss the matter? No, I bloody wouldn't, but I make an appointment to see the manager tomorrow anyway.

I am currently working in the bedding department. The manager is Arthur Saunders. At last an independent spirit. He served in bomber command and comes complete with handlebar moustache. It's a relief to find I'm not the only one who can't settle into civvy street. We chatter away in his cupboard of an office, appearing periodically to the shocked looks of the staff. Laughter is a rare sound in Brunton's, but Arthur has a wonderfully sardonic sense of humour. He is also a terrific mimic. I really like the man. We agreed to meet for a drink after work tomorrow evening.

Friday, February 28th
My bank manager is young and understanding. Although I have no collateral, he agrees to an overdraft based on my prospects at Brunton's. He has more faith in my managerial ability than I do. On my return from my satisfactory lunchtime meeting I find a note on my desk, asking me to ring Mr Timothy's secretary. The great man wishes to see me next Friday at 4 o'clock. I have a feeling late Friday meetings with directors are bad news. It's generally known as the 'sacking hour'.

I raise the matter with Arthur later over a drink in a garish city pub, but apparently our Tim is meeting with all the management, even down to my lowly level.

After four pints I rode unsteadily through the rain. I keep trying to tell Mary I am in the wrong job. She certainly didn't want to hear it again on my beery return. She was angry that I hadn't told her that I was going to be late. It was almost in self-defence that I told her that I had secured an overdraft. Maybe a mistake. She cheered up at once.

Monday, March 3rd
We spent the evening listening to the wireless. The fire has stopped smoking. Good. Mary managed to buy me a half-bottle of White Horse whisky. Bad. Not the whisky, that's fine, but she has also bought a complete new outfit for herself. Very slinky and smart. No coupons needed, she said, with a silly grin on her face. Why, I wonder, and how much? I daren't ask. I feel another letter from the bank coming on. Later she lets drop that she has acquired a horse on loan. The saddle and tack, she assures me, are essential and were very reasonable. I was furious. I sat and sulked. Turning away from her I made a great production of listening to the news. She came and sat on my lap. Suddenly I lost all interest in world affairs.

Wednesday, March 5th
The snow is back. Borne overnight on gale-force winds. There are massive drifts, whilst only feet away the road is clear but for a covering of ice. Again I struggled to work on foot. I arrived perished and soaked. Only those who live in the city have made it in. They all think I'm mad except for the personnel manager. She is a rather sad, gangling woman in her late forties. She wears tweed suits and thick brogue shoes. I think

she has taken a bit of a shine to me. Her father was a military man, so she favours those who she thinks 'had a good war'.

A thaw set in as soon as I reached work, but by the time I left this evening the temperature had dropped. A bitter easterly wind carried fresh volleys of snow. Soon there were blizzard conditions. Getting home was worse than some of the endurance courses I have been on. The wind howled and rampaged. It was difficult to see where I was going once I was out into the country. I was pleased when I eventually stumbled to our front door. The house was in darkness. Inside it was freezing, no fire in the sitting room and the boiler out in the kitchen. There was no sign of Mary. I was worried that she was out in such weather. I rang Doreen at the farm, but she had not seen her. As I sat nursing a glass of whisky I was surprised how worried I was. My affection for her has grown. My imagination ran riot and I found myself imagining life without Mary. Before we moved away from Rickmansworth, I think I would have almost welcomed the prospect. But now? Now is different.

As I contemplated ringing the police, the phone rang. It was Mary. She was up at the Hall. She said it was too foul out to trudge home through the snow. Anyway she had enjoyed a divine supper. The house was out of this world. She sounded so affected. I think she was tipsy. I hardly slept, the bed was so cold.

Friday, March 7th
I have my audience with the blessed Mr Timothy Brunton. He occupies a sizeable oak-panelled office on the top floor. Gloomy paintings of his ancestors peer

down. They graduate from coarse features and mutton-chop whiskers, through frock-coated formality to a self-satisfied Stuart Brunton who takes pride of place on the wall behind his son. The girth of those depicted expands in rough relation to the family's increasing wealth. Timothy, though, remains lean. He still has years ahead of him to rectify matters. His heavy-lidded eyes are the feature common to them all. They convey a studied boredom and a God-given superiority.

I had no need to worry about being given the sack. The meeting is a vehicle for him to indulge his ego. He tells me about his plans for the group after his in-depth study of the American market. I try to look enthusiastic, nodding my head in agreement. Out will go the old-fashioned counters, in will come cork-tiled flooring and cash registers. It's a time of opportunity, and he wants me to be a part of it.

On he drones and my nodding declines. Arthur tells me he has given this talk to every manager. Why didn't he get us all together and save his breath?

Finally he finishes. He didn't ask anything about me or my training. As I was leaving, he told me how much he enjoyed meeting my wife, when they were all snowed in at his parents' house. It's the first time his face shows any sign of animation. He obviously rates her higher than her husband. He shuts the door in my face whilst I am still replying. An odious man.

Drinks with Arthur this evening. Same ghastly pub. A few beers with whisky chasers. We are united in our dislike for all the Bruntons. He wants us to have supper with him and his wife next week. Sounds good to me.

Back home at nine o'clock to furious reception. I'm sure I told Mary I was going out. No placating her.

Spent night in the spare room. Same recurring nightmare. Woke drenched and frightened.

Friday, March 14th
I am to be assigned for the next month to the accounts department. I can't think of anything worse. I have now been in almost every department in the store. After the accounts, I have to endure three whole months working on the shop floor.

Dinner at Arthur's. Not a success. He is married to the widow of his rear gunner, who was killed in action. I almost get the impression Arthur is doing penance; as if he were responsible. Maybe he was. Anyway their small house is full of photos of the flight sergeant. His medals and cap take pride of place in a display cabinet that dominates their tiny living room.

Beryl Saunders is small, dark and not unattractive. She seems to do her best to disguise this. She wears no make-up. Her hair is short. Hacked, as if cut off in anger. Her floral frock is surely several sizes too big for her. Her accent is East End. Aggressively so.

Mary had not wanted to come. I insisted. She seems to be under the wing of the fragrant Mrs Brunton. She spends hours at the Hall. They have even taken to riding together. We came by taxi. Mary has a bike, and we could have ridden but she wouldn't hear of it. The women took an instant dislike to each other. Mary, dressed as if for Ascot, is a terrible snob. Beryl is strange though. Her accent became more strident as Mary played lady of the manor. We took a bottle of wine but were only offered beer. Mary's face was a study. She had to settle for water from the tap. Beryl was antagonistic towards Arthur as well, but he didn't seem to notice or react.

The meal was liver and bacon. Mary doesn't eat liver. The atmosphere was crazily tense, although Arthur appeared to be in denial. When he wasn't talking, there was silence. He kept filing my glass, and I drank whatever was placed in front of me.

Eventually we did get a conversation going about our employers. Arthur and I as usual were making what we thought were clever and witty asides about the store and the family. Without warning Mary rose and delivered a withering tirade about our disloyalty. There was no stopping her. From memory she informed me I didn't know which side my bread was buttered and I should choose my friends more carefully. With that insult she collected her coat and walked out into the night. By the time I had made my apologies, she had disappeared. I walked through the slushy deserted streets to the station. There were no taxis.

It was gone two by the time I got home. The house was in darkness. Mary had the key. I hammered on the door. No reply. I slept on the floor in the garage using Mary's new saddle as a pillow.

Saturday, March 15th
When I woke the door to the house was open, but no sign of Mary. Tried to iron the creases out of my shiny suit. No luck. It looks like a rag. I must buy a new one.

Rang Arthur to apologise. He felt it was Beryl who was in the wrong. He said he would tell me about her one day. He sounded uncharacteristically sad.

The evening spent mending fences. Mary had cooled down and had written a letter of apology to the Saunders. Good. However, she insisted that I should

47

be more careful in my choice of friends at work. Not so good. She hinted darkly that Arthur was not well thought of at Brunton's. How the hell does she know? Bad. I started to object. She knows how to get round me. We made love in front of a spitting log fire.

She went to bed before me. I still find sleeping difficult, so decided to read for a while. As I picked the latest Nevil Shute from the bookcase, a letter fluttered down. It was from the bank manager asking me to contact him. I couldn't believe the enclosed statement. What on earth is she up to?

Saturday, March 23rd
A week of continuous blazing rows. The young bank manager, Adrian Davis, is no longer so friendly. I don't blame him. Our overdraft is now approaching what I shall earn in the next six months. Regular payments made monthly from my meagre salary were agreed. I have also closed the joint account. Mary will have to survive on housekeeping money given to her in cash, weekly.

Our screaming matches have intensified. It appears that Mary has joined the local hunt. Her subscription apparently includes tickets for the hunt ball, which takes place at the Hall next Saturday. I protest, but she rants that I have no idea how to get noticed. Why should she be confined to a life of poverty? I am told I am spineless and destined to a life as a shop assistant. Her face was contorted and full of hate. Slamming the door she ran upstairs. I heard her on the phone to her mother. It was only then that it dawned on me that her parents are due up next weekend. I guarantee she has brought tickets for them too.

I have taken to running when I get home each night. I push myself to go faster and further. The physical pain I inflict on myself is preferable to the way I feel about my life at the moment.

Wednesday, March 26th
As I labour over endless columns of figures in the accounts department, Mary is out hunting. She looks fantastic in her gear. Quite erotic. She has spent most of the week helping Cynthia prepare for the ball. She and at least fifty other helpers. They, though, are getting paid. Yes, the fragrant one and Mary are now on Christian name terms.

Cynthia turned up at our door last evening. I swear I could smell her coming. The expensive perfume precedes her. I think she feels sorry for Mary, married to an oaf like me. She is tall, imperious and outwardly charming. Everything is amusing, such fun, or divine. She swears she can hardly recognise the place. She ignores me. I resent her intrusion. I stay seated, reading. Mary looks daggers at me. I am in shirtsleeves and braces. Mary hates them. I only wear them to annoy her. Mrs B. swoops on a small art deco bronze of a ballet dancer. Where has that come from? Another new purchase. It is given the seal of Cynthia's approval. She acknowledges me for the first time with a languid movement of a raised hand. I do struggle from my chair, but they move into the kitchen muttering quietly.

When Cynthia eventually leaves, Mary lambasts me for my rudeness. She is right, of course, but I can't seem to stop myself. Lying on the narrow divan in the spare room I feel wretched. I am assailed by debts and a job I hate. I have a wife I desire, but really don't even like. I think seven years in the Forces has institutionalised me. I miss the companionship, the trust we had in each other. Maybe I even miss the danger. I am now locked into a banal existence and I can see no way out. If I was unattached I could do whatever took my fancy. I feel I was trapped by convention. Marriage seemed the only honourable route when Mary informed me she was pregnant. Now convention dictates that we make the best of things. We have made our bed and we must continue to lie on it. I'm sure Mary is no happier than me, but I feel emasculated. I have a feeling that life is going to get worse before it improves. I know it is. The social climbers from Rickmansworth arrive on Friday. Surely a night for a couple of beers with Arthur.

Friday, March 28th
The dreaded in-laws have arrived. My booze night with Arthur was cancelled. The look in Mary's eye warned of retribution. I can't stand any more rows. I know when I'm beaten.

Supper was a trial. I had to endure veiled comments about not being able to keep Mary in the comfort they expect for their daughter. Mildred is ghastly, a hectoring embarrassment. Harold is pathetic, although sometimes emboldened by his wife's rhetoric. I was surly and monosyllabic. I went to bed early. I wish I could rise above the loathing I feel for them.

Saturday, March 29th
Another huge row. The ball invitation states white tie and decorations. Medals belong on uniforms, not dinner jackets. I had the three of them shouting at me. Their

rules dictate if you've got it, flaunt it. Eventually I capitulated.

The excitement has been intense all day. Harold has ordered a taxi – the walk up the drive considered to be *infra dig*. I hope he pays.

Mary looks fantastic. A new yellow ball gown cut low, but extremely elegant. I hope it was on the new account she has negotiated for herself and not from the housekeeping money. She has grown her hair. She wears it pinned up for the first time. A new image, she declares. Mildred is still a good-looking woman. Her accent becomes more plummy by the day. Tonight she will be judged and found wanting by the toffs. She holds her knife like a pen. By such small deviations do we English divine a person's true background. Harold is squeezed into his dinner jacket, surrounded by an aura of mothballs. My DJ is relatively new. I should wear it to work. They would hardly recognise me.

Eight thirty – the witching hour. The taxi awaits.

Sunday, March 30th
The drive to the house must be all of half a mile. So we did need a taxi (I paid). It was too dark for me to gauge when the house had been built, but I guess it had been added to by each successive generation of Bruntons. It's huge.

The great and the good were gathered in a milling flock. As we arrived, large chauffeur-driven limousines jostled for position. Staff stood with lanterns to light our way to the marbled entrance hall. There was a fair smattering of pink coats. The women, some squeezed into pre-war gowns, others sporting the latest creations, all seemed united in the need to wear jewellery. Real or false, I couldn't tell. Some, usually the least attractive, were weighed down with the stuff. The most beautiful woman I saw, apart from Mary, looked Spanish. She was tall, olive-skinned and haughty. Round her swanlike neck was a single velvet strand, with a small cameo at its centre.

I hardly recognised anyone. Arthur had told me that requests for tickets were stringently vetted. Presumably we were attending courtesy of the fragrant Mrs B. Within minutes Mary was surrounded by an army of male admirers. Nothing changes, she was in her element. I was forgotten, as were her parents, as she headed for the dance floor with one of the directors who had interviewed me in London. Grabbing a glass of champagne, I ducked away from the in-laws, who suddenly looked like fish out of water. Even Mildred had been silenced by the grandeur of the setting and the braying crowds.

A six-piece band played from a raised platform in the great hall. The stairs to the minstrel's gallery was lined with couples drinking, chatting, flirting. Above them crowds leaned over banisters, staring down at the crammed dance floor. I moved on through the library where there were less people. Everywhere flower arrangements. Huge sprays in jardinières and antique vases. Every few yards were uniformed waitresses, armed with trays of champagne and cordials. A bar in the corner served beers and spirits.

I picked up the sound of competing music, this time not to a set tempo. In a large room at the back of the house was a steel band. Here many of the young were gathered. They were energetic, but uncoordinated in their movements. A small group of teenaged girls giggled, as they peered at the brightly clad band. Perhaps they had never seen black faces before.

I saw her standing quite apart from the crowd. She looked bored, tapping her foot in time to the music. I asked her if she would care to dance. She seemed to take an age to answer. 'Sorry, chum, I'm working.' She was Scottish, not Spanish, and later in the evening I learnt she was one of a team of security workers. Even the landed gentry are not above pinching the odd silver teaspoon apparently.

A huge matron standing nearby grabbed me. How is it that overweight people often have such a superb sense of rhythm? Within minutes we had cleared the floor and a circle formed around us. I cast aside my inhibitions. We cavorted round the room. There were huge expanses of white teeth as the musicians' smiles widened. The tempo increased and we spun like dervishes. I noticed she had tiny feet, which presumably allowed her to move so lightly. To raucous applause, and with reddened cheeks, I bowed deeply as the music finished.

I was then introduced to the jolly matron's husband, who seemed to take a great interest in me. An imposing man with a mop of white hair. He was tall in stature and with the assurance of one used to power. He sported three rows of medals. They clanked as we sought a couple of easy chairs in the library, where disconcertingly the music from the two bands jarred in the background. He questioned me as if conducting an interview. He had spotted a couple of my decorations. I hate talking about the war and dismissed the awarding of them as a lottery (which is what it is). He was also very pressing about my role at Brunton's and seemed astonished at my lowly status. Having managed to tease out my life history, I was dismissed. Quite kindly, but dismissed none the less. His wife grabbed me again as I left the library. This time she led me to the other dance floor. It was there that I learnt that her husband was General Sir Thomas Leverton, no less. Lord Lieutenant of the county and also a non-executive director of Brunton's.

As we waltzed round, I noticed that Mary was still doing her rounds of the board, gazing up into the suntanned face of Timothy. Noticing me, she waved smiling happily. I'm sure Timothy was about to ignore me, but bowed curtly in our direction when he saw who my partner was.

Most of my evening was spent prowling round the bars dotted throughout the house, trying to avoid Harold, whose face shone like a beacon. Free drinks had seemingly converted him from his normal virtual teetotal status. I did manage one dance with Mary. She was slightly tipsy, but I can never recall her being so happy. She nibbled at my ear and wanted to be assured that I was having a wonderful time. With her in my arms and for a moment the centre of her attention, I was. I did groan inwardly, though, when she told me she'd been pushing for my promotion with every influential person she had spoken to. Suddenly she broke away leaving me in mid-sentence. Watching in astonishment, I saw her pluck Stuart Brunton from the top table. He was a willing victim, staring down at her cleavage. Her dress had shifted southwards; moments later I noticed Brunton's hand had also taken a southerly course. As he stroked Mary's shapely bottom, her smile never faded.

By three o'clock in the morning I was ready for my bed. I tried to find Mary. No sign. I knew she would stay to the death – cooked breakfast and all. Mildred was searching for Harold who had gone AWOL. I told her to try the bars. If looks could kill. She went off in high dudgeon.

Walking past lines of parked cars and chattering chauffeurs, I made my way home down the long gravel drive. I was aware of movement amongst the trees. Assorted couples in amorous clinches. The cool air was comforting after the sweltering atmosphere of the dance floor. I was sweaty and a little tipsy. Daybreak was not far off and a strange mist hovered just off the ground, like a gauze blanket. I slipped gratefully into bed and was asleep instantly. Later I was vaguely aware of shouting and crying from below. I drifted back to sleep.

By the time Mary fell into bed, I was aware it was light. She was still wearing her ball dress. Perfume and perspiration mixed are quite intoxicating. Still half asleep I raised the skirts to her dress. She giggled and snuggled up to me. It was only when I woke, just before midday, that I realised that she hadn't been wearing any knickers.

Monday, March 31st
The commotion in the early hours of Sunday morning was apparently caused by Mildred. She reckoned Harold and Mary had brought shame on the family. She was inconsolable. I didn't help by laughing, but she knows I am a lost cause.

Harold had drunk far too much. He had progressed from being happy and harmless to aggressive and abusive. He had made lewd suggestions whilst dancing

55

with the attractive wife of a local doctor and had then taken an ineffectual swing at him as he was led from the great hall. Mildred, who had been alerted to the problem, was then horrified to see him throw up all over the settee where he had slumped. Having pushed him out into the night air, she found worse was to follow.

Seeking Mary for help, she returned to the dance. An auction to aid hunt funds was just concluding, when the auctioneer asked if any lady might offer an item of her underwear for sale. A petticoat, he suggested, might be appropriate. Mary had never been the one to refuse a challenge or to duck the limelight. To wolf whistles she climbed on a table and very discreetly removed her frilly panties, waving them triumphantly above her head. The men cheered, the younger woman joined in the applause; only the older matrons looked on disapprovingly. Mildred was mortified. The knickers fetched ten guineas.

Friday, April 4th
Now the truth. The ball gown was secured with the housekeeping money as a deposit. I demand she takes it back. She can't. Perspiration stains. Besides, everyone knew she had worn it to the ball. I told her no more money. She veered from eye-popping fury to her seduction ploy. For once I was steadfast. Now it appears she has withdrawn all favours. Tonight it's her turn in the spare bed. Slept really well – quite a bonus.

Monday, April 7th
Guerrilla warfare is spreading. Mary is refusing to cook or clean the house. She continues to sleep in the spare

room. I am already becoming bored by spam and tinned pilchards. We solemnly sit at the same table eating from our separate menus. She had lamb cutlets tonight. I pretend to enjoy my slightly burnt fried spam and mashed potatoes (full of lumps). She is infuriating. Tonight she came downstairs wearing just her underwear. I try not to look. She had a smug smile on her face. At the moment it is her cooking that I am missing more than sharing her bed. Will I still feel the same way next week?

Tuesday, April 15th
The strangest day. I was summoned to Stuart Brunton's office. Massive acres of carpet to cross until you reach his desk. More bloody Bruntons stare down from their gilded frames.

He tells me he feels I am being under-utilised. He has been going over my application again, studying my references. He speaks of my leadership qualities. I mumble my appreciation. I am to be promoted, after attending a management training course near Colwyn Bay. Then, following a short spell on the shop floor, I am to act as a relief store manager, understudying for holidays and illness. Providing my progress is satisfactory, within a year I will be in charge of my own store. Why? I'm sure I looked astonished. I have shown little aptitude or even much interest in my training. I have been seriously considering a career move. The trouble is I'm not really qualified for anything. My salary is to be increased, doubling on completion of my probationary period.

At home, the stand-off continues. I hoover. Mary reads, or pretends to, languidly spread over the settee.

She wears her silk dressing gown with the embroidered dragon on the back. I get glimpses of a thigh or cleavage as she fidgets. She is a real tease. I quite admire her resolve. She is pleasant enough. We behave like polite guests in a small hotel. No, that's wrong, she's a guest – I'm staff. I hate ironing. She watches me and smiles. I am conscious I am becoming more crumpled by the day.

Wednesday, April 16th
I admit defeat, I had decided to tell Mary about my promotion. I didn't get a chance – she was going out as I arrived home. I didn't ask where. I don't think she has been up to the Hall since the knickers episode. Perhaps Mrs B. didn't approve.

Fried eggs on toast tonight. They ended up a congealed mess in the pan. Felt quite queasy later. Heard Mary come in about 10.30. Asked if I had enjoyed my evening. She was all giggles and smiles. I'm sure she wanted me to ask where she had been. I didn't give her the satisfaction. Lying in bed I suddenly felt amazingly randy. I crept along the corridor, deciding now was the time for us to make it up. Her door was locked. I tried to win her round. She told me to get lost.

Thursday, April 17th
A truce has been struck. Mary has heard about my promotion. News spreads like wildfire throughout the store. Colleagues' attitudes have changed already. Not Arthur's, though, who thinks I'm a jammy sod.

Mary is claiming that her lobbying has brought about my change in fortune. Could be, but I think it more likely Stuart Brunton was influenced by Sir Thomas

Leverton. Whoever it was, I was told that the business required men of my calibre. I'm not sure Timothy agrees with his father. He was openly hostile when we both attended a meeting today. I do realise I am being given a real opportunity to further my career. I will give it my best shot.

Mary agreed not to spend recklessly. In return, I am restoring the joint account, once my pay increase comes through. Normal service was resumed tonight. I'm not sure which I enjoyed most.

Friday, May 9th
Still keeping to my regular nights out with Arthur. Mary now tolerates this, providing I'm home by nine o'clock. I sense all is not well in the Saunders household. I think he would like to talk about it, but always backs off at the last moment.

Wednesday, May 28th
Mary down visiting her parents. I miss her. We are totally wrong for each other, but whoever said marriage is easy. Back to spam and corned beef.

Sunday, June 8th
We have joined the tennis club. Tucked away from the Hall, beyond the walled gardens, there are two immaculate grass courts. The pavilion with its white picket fence was donated to the village by Stuart's father. Long scrubbed tables overlook the courts, and the kitchen has been modernised and always seems full of ladies, boiling kettles and making sandwiches.

Mary looks very stylish until the ball arrives. She has almost no coordination, which is strange for someone who dances so well. I played some tennis at school, but I am very rusty. I feel rather self-conscious in my Aertex shirt and a pair of my father's shorts that come down to my knees. I saw Timothy Brunton watching me from the shadow of the pavilion. He is singles champion and looks immaculate, all suntanned legs and well-cut shorts. He brought a new girlfriend. Quite attractive in an understated way. She beat Mary in a singles match. Mary declared her to be a mouse. I was beaten by a bald lawyer with a huge gut. My plimsoles are so worn that I could hardly turn without falling over. No excuses, he is a better player than me.

I notice that Tim can hardly keep his eyes off Mary. She does look wonderful. She, however, is setting her sights on his father. She flirts with him outrageously. The old boy is hooked. The fragrant one is not as warm to Mary as she used to be. Perhaps she reserves her friendship for the hunting season only.

Wednesday, June 18th
Dreadful news: Beryl Saunders is dead. The rumour is she committed suicide. Tried to contact Arthur by phone. No reply. Called at the house this evening. The place in darkness. I was annoyed by Mary's response to the news. More interested in telling me she has been promised a new hunter on loan. Mary can be incredibly insensitive at times.

Friday, June 27th
I loathe funerals. I suppose most people do. The coroner kindly recorded accidental death. Beryl had taken an overdose of sleeping pills. Arthur tells me she left a note which he didn't disclose. On a mercenary

60

level this at least ensures that the house passes to him. This would have been complicated by a recording of suicide.

It was a moving service. Several of Arthur's flight crew turned up. I was the only representative from Brunton's. There was a wreath from staff members, but nothing from the directors.

I had long chats with Arthur prior to the funeral. As I thought, Arthur felt a responsibility for her first husband's death. Beryl was devastated. She went from being an outward-going girl to a recluse. She hardly ate and took no pride in her appearance. The marriage had not been one of convenience like mine, but born of guilt. They had been having an affair at the time of the rear gunner's death. Their marriage, a year later, like so many undertaken against a background of war, was fatally flawed. Their guilt was a barrier to their happiness. Arthur was progressively excluded. A man for whom Beryl had previously felt little affection was placed on a pedestal. Even from the grave he exerted a malign influence over them. Finally, Arthur snapped. He was not prepared to live in another man's shadow any more. They had a huge row. She had threatened suicide before. As he stormed out of the house, he had shouted, 'Then bloody well do it.' She obliged. What can you do to comfort a man in that position? Answer: get drunk together. I slept on the floor in Arthur's house, a photograph of George stared down at me from the display cabinet. He had a cheeky smile. What a mess we have all made of our lives.

Mary isn't talking to me. I did ring her to say I wouldn't be home, but still she sulks. Sod her! I think she should have come to the funeral.

61

Friday, July 11th
Arthur tells me that they docked a day's wages from him for attending his own wife's funeral. He has had enough; he is quitting. I quite envy him. I think his relationship with Beryl was destructive. He has reinvented himself. He is smarter and more confident. They should be sending him on this wretched management course that I am starting next week. I shall miss him. Outside the church after Beryl's funeral we hugged each other. Nothing was said. I felt comforted. I think he did too. I have never experienced that feeling with Mary. She is exciting, but hard. Genuine emotions are either an embarrassment to her or taken as a sign of weakness.

Monday, July 14th
By train to the wilds of North Wales. The course is being held in an Edwardian manor, converted into a business centre. It once housed German prisoners of war and retains an institutional feel. There are twelve students and three lecturers, two of whom are American. They speak with a religious fervour. We are to be assessed on initiative, innovation, adaptability, decision-making and in our role as a team player. The format is similar to officer training, but with an evangelical flavour.

We are all holed up together in one dormitory. Just like school. So is the food. My fellow students are a really mixed bunch. Most are complaining about the facilities. I think they are OK. I quite like the spartan approach.

Sunday, July 20th
A bizarre week. Thank God it's all over. Lectures, presentations, IQ assessments, role playing and even

one day given over to outdoor endurance. (What a laugh that was!) In retrospect, I quite enjoyed the whole experience. It's good to know that the brain still functions.

I came second overall. The winner was a charming Jewish chap. So intelligent, but a bit of a rebel. I really liked him.

Mary seemed pleased to have me home. She has convinced herself that my star is in the ascendancy. She is obviously back in favour at the Hall. We have been invited to supper next Saturday.

Wednesday, July 23rd
Arthur has resigned. He intends emigrating to Australia. A land of true opportunity, he reckons. I shall miss him. I have itchy feet. In truth I would love to go, too. I raised the prospect with Mary. She was dismissive. A life listening to those ghastly accents – no thank you! It's at times like this that I want to scream. She is only interested in my buying a car. I think a house would be more sensible. Why pay rent to the Bruntons?

Saturday, July 26th
Supper with the Bruntons. We ate in the main dining room, dotted round a huge refectory table and served by uniformed staff. Timothy was there with his girlfriend, Melissa (the mouse).

Everything very civilised. Mary in a new dress – light green with a tight bodice and flared skirt. A present from her mother, she insists. I don't believe her, but she looks great. The Brunton men find it difficult to take their eyes off her. I try flirting with Melissa, by way of distraction. No joy. The fragrant

63

one looks on with a superior smile. I hate that expression. I had an urge to be outrageous, but gritting my teeth continued to make small talk. The men wore dinner jackets. The Bruntons are in a pretentious time warp.

The ladies retired, and we enjoyed some excellent port. I sensed real tension between father and son, as Stuart congratulated me on my appraisal from the management consultants. I am aware the old man is attempting to knock Timothy down a peg or two. Stuart underlined my potential in the company. He beams; Tim glowers.

Next week I am to go to Liverpool, whilst the manager is on holiday. Stuart assures me I will soon get the hang of things. Timothy looks very doubtful. I'm with Tim on this one.

Sunday, August 3rd
The Liverpool experience was OK. In fact, I enjoyed myself. The assistant manager, Audrey Reader, was really welcoming and generous in sharing her knowledge. My tenure included three apprehended shoplifters, a flasher in the dress department and peppermills that ground metal filings along with the pepper.

I met up with Alex Cunningham, who served with me for three years during the war. He has piled on some weight, but he remains an intimidating figure. He insists on calling me sir, which is so embarrassing. He appears to have fallen on hard times and is returning to Belfast. He was the most fearless man I ever met, yet diminished now. Like me, he seeks a new meaning to his life and hasn't found one. I felt a real sadness as we parted, magnified by the fact that as a proud man he accepted the couple of quid I offered him. He isn't just hard up like me. He's broke. As he disappeared across the hotel foyer, I noticed his shoes shone as if he had spent hours buffing them into a blinding sheen.

Sunday, October 5th
We are enjoying a fantastic Indian summer. The leaves are falling, but the sun beats down from a cloudless sky.

I have now worked at stores in Rochdale and Kidderminster. Next week I take over in Harrogate. I am likely to be up there until the New Year whilst the manager recovers from an operation. I have tried to get interested in stock control, display, space allocation and sale trends, but increasingly I find myself in the dispatch department or loading bay. This makes me very popular with the staff, who think I am prepared to muck in. Actually I prefer physical work. It has the effect of stopping me thinking. Good. Can I really stand a lifetime of this type of existence? I feel guilty because I know I am so much better off than most people. But Mary continues to be a worry to me. Just when I think we are at last building up an understanding, she changes tack. For some weeks now she has been remote. Everything I do or say irritates her. Snap!

Wednesday, October 18th
I love Harrogate. Unfortunately Harrogate doesn't love me. At least the staff at the store don't. They appear to think my style of management most unbecoming. I'm constantly being told that Mr Thomas (the manager off sick) wouldn't approve. I am in the process of reinventing myself. I scowl and bark, constantly finding fault. This is what they understand. What a sad lot. I

could turn into a tyrant. Anyway it suits my current mood. I am fed up, lonely and unfulfilled. It is now three days since I spoke to Mary. I ring each night. No reply. The operator assures me there is no fault on the line.

Monday, November 10th
I have now been stuck here for almost three weeks without a break. I was going back home on Saturday, but Mary insisted she has to visit her parents. She says Harold is unwell. Shame.

A new girl has started in the glove department. I know it's crazy, but I honestly believe she is the most beautiful woman I have ever met. In fact, that's untrue, because I haven't met her. I only spotted her last week as I went on my tour of the store. I now take surreptitious peeps at her. I caught her eye earlier this afternoon, as she was wrapping up a purchase for a customer. She coloured, peering at me from behind her fringe. I felt my stomach lurch. Stupid, I'm acting like a schoolboy. My reaction speaks volumes. This constantly being away from Mary is becoming damaging. We must talk. I don't want to go on living like this.

Back tonight to my small hotel and a group of commercial travellers trapped in a similar existence. The younger ones brag about work and women, whilst eking out their remaining dregs of beer, each one waiting to be offered a refill. No one does. I go to bed. It's hours before sleep comes.

Sunday, November 16th
Went to Scarborough for the day. Train just about to leave when the girl from the glove department came

and took the last seat in the compartment. She coloured up as she noticed me and had second thoughts about taking off her coat which she had unbuttoned. I smiled in acknowledgement and mouthed a silent hello. Just the slightest nod was her reply. She stared intently out into the corridor. Her name is Sally Clarke. I looked her up in staff records. She is nineteen. I tried not to stare, peeping at her from behind my paper.

She is tall and slender. Although stunning, she appears shy and unsure of herself. Her eyes are usually cast down. She views the world using her fringe as camouflage. On arrival at Scarborough, she slipped out whilst a stout lady sitting next to me asked me to help her down with a heavy case, stowed above her on the luggage rack. Out on the platform I broke into a trot in an attempt to catch the young girl up. I was right behind her when she reached the ticket barrier, where she was met by a hefty young man wearing a duffle coat and a college scarf. I felt a huge sense of disappointment as I saw them walk off into the rain.

Lunch in a busy café close to the seafront. Still raining when I left, but I walked for miles. The wind had whipped up the sea. I found the spray breaking over the deserted promenade quite invigorating. No sign of Sally Clarke on my return journey.

Tuesday, November 18th
Good news. Mary is coming up for the weekend. She sounded quite animated. I offered to meet her at the station. She was strangely evasive, saying she didn't know what time she would be arriving and that she would make her own way.

Monday, November 24th

Mary was waiting for me at my hotel when I finished work on Saturday. She declared the hotel to be a pit. Not a great start to our reunion. As the place was almost empty, I had managed to transfer to the master bedroom for the weekend. She sulked. Told me she had been driven up by Tim, who was on his way to visit friends in Knaresborough. I sulked.

Dinner that evening at the Old Swan. Rather grand food and clientele. Mary cheered up. I didn't. I sense something going on between Mary and Tim. Perhaps I am being ultra-sensitive. I'm sure she knew what I was thinking. Neither of us said anything. My mood gradually lifted helped by the wine and a couple of nightcaps. We swayed back to our hotel. Our lovemaking was energetic, but undertaken I'm sure by both of us out of a sense of duty. I woke later to discover Mary crying. She was very quiet, but her body was shaking with emotion. I tried to comfort her, but she pushed me away.

Yesterday we used the Old Swan as a base. Morning coffee, lunch, tea. Hours in the lounge spread in front of a log fire reading the papers. Mary's mood improved with the surroundings. She would make a great social hostess. She strikes up conversation with strangers if they look vaguely interesting. With me she only makes small talk. She has no interests, other than fashion or gossip. She did nag about my getting a car, but she was happy enough with her gin and mixed, her roast lamb and later tea served in fine china cups.

Now she has gone home again, and it's unlikely I shall see her until Christmas. Not before Timothy had made a tour of the store. I felt he went out of his way to be critical, but it was difficult for him. Sales have been running at record levels and the place was packed. I watched as he drove away with Mary sitting at his side. I felt an acute pang of jealousy.

Wednesday, December 3rd
I now have daily chats with Sally in her department. She must sense how much I am attracted to her. She tells me her boyfriend is studying history at York. I hate him. I'm sure she knows I'm married, but she flirts. At least I think she would like to, but pulls back almost as soon as she has started. I suppose it underlines my own unhappiness, but I think about her constantly. In fact, I fantasise about her, though in the romantic sense, rather than the sexual. Crazily, I imagine us hopelessly in love. Since my mother died, it is what I have lacked. Comradeship is a form of love, also painful when someone close to you is killed, but a woman's love is what I crave.

Why did I marry Mary? Convention. A middle-class set of values inculcated into me over the years. Anyway she was beautiful, and I expected to be killed before the war ended. I should have been.

Sunday, December 7th
I couldn't stand the prospect of another aimless day off, so after work yesterday I hitched a series of lifts arriving home in the early hours. The house was in darkness. The kitchen untidy, with unwashed breakfast pots. No sign of Mary. The bed unmade. I worried and fumed till daybreak, convincing myself that she was tucked up in bed with Tim. So I decided I would hammer on his door and confront them. As I marched

past the farm, a flustered Mrs Wilford ran after me. She has been trying to contact me in Harrogate. Mary had taken a bad fall whilst out hunting. She had broken her leg and is suffering from concussion. Feelings of relief and guilt. I went back home and then cycled down to the cottage hospital.

Mary looked pale and vulnerable, her leg hoisted and encased in a cage. She was still somewhat disoriented, but pleased enough to see me. Much of the day spent fetching nighties, bedjackets and makeup. She bucked up as the day wore on. The colour returned to her cheeks. Or was that the makeup? Anyway, she was soon looking very glamorous again and the centre of attention with an endless stream of visitors. I thought she would be furious that I had to return to work, but amazingly she understood. Her mother arrives tomorrow. As I cycled to the station to catch the 7.20, a familiar Alvis passed me heading towards the hospital.

Friday, December 12th
A real rumpus today. Our store detective saw the wife of our local MP slip a cardigan under her coat. Following her at a discreet distance, he watched as she continued to hide a whole range of goods, seemingly picked at random, in her shopping bag. He tried to contact me without success. Eventually she left the store, where he apprehended her. To his horror, she only had one item, which she had paid for. She went barmy, shouting abuse. He retreated under a hail of invective. Later he found a trail of goods that she had dropped in the store.

Her husband arrived within the hour. He would not be placated. It was only after he had spoken to Stuart

70

Brunton on the phone and fifty pounds had been donated to a charity of their choice that the problem was defused.

Monday, December 15th
She came back. She is in her late forties, dumpy but with a pretty face. This time she was quite brazen. The store detective alerted me, and I watched her stuffing children's clothes, Christmas cards and costume jewellery into a large plastic shopping bag. She knew she had been spotted. She smiled, as if challenging me. I made to shake hands, wishing her a happy Christmas. She hesitated for a moment and then handed me the bag. She made no noise, but tears smudged her mascara. Turning, she walked unsteadily towards the exit. The woman needs help. Don't we all?

Tuesday, December 16th
It's almost impossible to get to talk to Mary on the phone. Her mother protects her like a secretary. I am told she is either asleep, attempting to have a bath or testing her crutches in the garden. I was granted a few minutes today, although it was hardly worth the bother. Mary was strange, not antagonistic, just uninterested. She can't even decide what she wants for Christmas.

This constantly living apart is hardly a recipe for a happy marriage. Mary quite rightly points out we have always lived this way. I have never asked Mary outright if she has been unfaithful. Years ago there was a lanky guards officer, Oliver Hampton, who was always hanging around. He is just a friend, darling, she would always assure me. I chose to believe her. He was tall and good-looking. He was also wealthy. A vital attraction that I lack.

Mary has so much that I admire. Not only is she beautiful, but vivacious, witty and fun to be with. She is more lover than wife material though.

Monday, December 22nd
Office parties are notorious for indiscretion. I have made a fool of myself and I cringe with embarrassment thinking about it. Too much drink. Misreading signals. Result, humiliation and a swollen lip. The evening started well enough. A collection had been made for me and I was presented with a fine pigskin wallet, as I finally leave the store in a couple of days. The canteen had been cleared to make room for dancing. There was a three-piece band, sandwiches and plenty of booze. Sally looked fantastic, even when I was sober. A simple, homemade dress, hair corkscrewing to her shoulders. When I finally managed to get a dance with her, she stroked the back of my neck, squeezed my hand and said how much she would miss me. She stayed behind, when most had gone home, helping stack chairs and washing up. I waited for her outside. She seemed surprised to see me, looking round as if she was expecting someone. I offered to walk her home and she agreed.

She didn't object when I took her arm. Neither did she when I stopped in an unlit stretch of the street and pulled her towards me. At first she responded to my kiss, but suddenly she was pushing me off. I am still not sure if it was that she had changed her mind or had seen, or sensed, the approaching figure. She shouted for me to get off. I was confused. A figure in a duffle coat swung me round and sent me reeling with a hefty punch. Sally ran off up the road. The young man seemed in two minds whether to give me a few more digs, but confined himself to telling me what a disgusting bastard I was, before running after her. Now I feel mortified at my stupidity. I have behaved in a way that I have always despised in others. I wonder what Mary will make of my split lip?

Friday, December 26th
Happy Christmas. Forget it. Yesterday was a disaster. Tension in the camp from the moment we struggled from our beds. We went to church in the morning. Mary now expert on her crutches, the centre of attention. The Bruntons occupy the front pew. Mary and Tim exchange furtive glances. Am I imagining it, or is it my guilty conscience?

Lunch was an overcooked capon and watery sprouts. Mildred is a lousy cook but insists she needs no help. I managed to buy two bottles of red wine. They all prefer white with chicken. All the more for me. I tried to be cheerful, but I feel resentful at having to spend my precious holiday with the in-laws. Actually Mildred has really been a help this week, but she aggravates me so much. As I reach well down the bottle, I become quite belligerent. Mary, who has been increasingly distant towards me since I came home, tells me I am drinking too much. Mildred adds her two-pennyworth. I tell her what I think of her. Hysteria all round. The second bottle is confiscated. I storm out of the house.

Stopping at the telephone kiosk opposite the pub I ring Sally. A male voice answers. Her boyfriend. I tell him I want to apologise. 'Bugger off you creep,' he shouts and slams the phone down. I ring again. The phone is off the hook.

A wall of disapproving silence greets me on my return home. They are playing cards. Harold demands I apologise to Mildred. I do, with ill grace. Went to bed with a hangover already closing in. Woken later by Mary. There is drink on her breath (the second bottle), as she bets I've never done it with anyone wearing a plaster cast before. She's right. I took her with a frightening feeling of repressed anger. I was brutal. When we were done, she asked why I couldn't be like that more often? I felt a deep sense of shame.

Wednesday, December 31st
I feel uneasy about the past and apprehensive about the future. Without the war I would have gone to university. Then what? Become a lawyer or a teacher? I had no more ideas then about what I wanted from my life. Now I am flawed. I am obviously still ill prepared for life outside the forces. Perhaps I should have stayed in. How does being blown up in Palestine compare to working at Brunton's? I know I'm lucky. It's just that it doesn't feel like it. Another six months living out of a suitcase doesn't have much appeal. Nor does a home life that lurches between extremes. Perhaps a baby would bring us closer together? Mary has become vehement in her opposition to the idea. It's probably just as well we can't see into the future.

The Second Diary – January–June, 1948

Tuesday, January 6th
My father came to stay over the New Year. I haven't seen him for several months – quite a shock. I tend to think of him as he was when I was young. He appeared such a commanding figure then. Now he is diminished. He has been since Mother died, but his relative poverty eats away at him. He was surely destined to stride through life as a success. He finds his current role, living on his brother's largesse, difficult. His clothes are old. Jackets patched at the elbow, shirts frayed at the collar. For the last year he has endured diabetes. He injects himself with a cavalier indifference to the outcome. He had three blackouts during his stay with us. Mary showed little sympathy, particularly when he keeled over in the pub.

Mary was far from welcoming. She seemed to spend most of her time out of the house, on the pretext that I needed time alone with Dad. When she did appear, she was moody and taciturn. On first introduction all those years ago, she had given him the full Mary treatment. Gushing and full of compliments, as she had sought his approval. I knew that this had never quite been achieved. He remained slightly reserved. Now, though, he is of little importance to Mary. Far from being an asset, he is potentially a drain on our limited resources. I find her attitude towards him infuriating. He's no fool. He asked me several times if everything was all right between us. I lied. I know he has never approved of our marriage. He is right – it's a mess. I think he was pleased to be helped onto the train and heading back to his dingy, damp rooms in Hertfordshire.

Mary's mood hasn't improved with his departure.

She is distant and uncommunicative. She has started taking long walks on her own, in all weathers. I suggested we bought a dog to keep her company. No reply, just a theatrical sigh.

Saturday, January 10th
I am working at head office until the end of the month. The days pass so slowly. This is just not the life for me; boredom and frustration eat away at me. Seven years of my life in the forces, has left me with no qualifications. I'm tempted to apply to go to university as a mature student. Mary would love that!

Tuesday, January 13th
Mary is as miserable as sin. It occurred to me that Tim has been abroad since the end of December. Jokingly I asked if this was why she was being so bloody. She flew at me and stormed out of the house. Too close to the mark perhaps. Either that or she's ill. Still a terrible atmosphere tonight. She has gone to the spare room with a migraine (that old favourite). For much of last year our marriage was only sustained in the bedroom. That comfort is now being denied me. Mary reads poetry by way of compensation. I just fume inwardly and curse myself for having let my life degenerate so.

Tuesday, January 20th
Tim returned today. He has been to the States and the Far East. The suntan has been topped up, as has his enthusiasm for change and modernisation in the stores. A management seminar has been called for next week. More indoctrination no doubt.

Mary's mood has lifted. Tonight she was talkative,

flirtatious and ultimately outrageous. I am sore. She is a mystery.

Wednesday, January 28th
How can grown people get so excited about kitchen utensils and women's outfits labelled the 'New Look'? The seminar was conducted with a fervour that I found laughable. I was a minority of one. My colleagues clapped and cheered as a new company logo was launched. There are to be new ranges, new stock control systems, and Tim has been appointed group MD. The applause was deafening. Creeps!
    Mary went to the tennis club AGM. Back very late. Woken by a car driving away. She went to the spare room. She reckons she was being considerate in not waking me. I may be stupid, but please!

Friday, January 30th
Memo from Tim. I am to report to the Carlisle store, for a further spell of training.

Thursday, February 5th
I sense a new agenda. The store manager is outwardly antagonistic towards me. I am consigned to the most menial jobs. My accommodation has been downgraded to a miserable boarding house, twenty minutes' walk from the store. It is impossible to get home for the weekends, as the manager insists that I work on Saturdays. I have joined a local athletics club. It's the only thing keeping me sane.

Saturday, February 21st
Today I snapped. I've had enough. I phoned in saying

I was sick and then walked through a hailstorm to the station. It's time for a change of direction. I am not prepared to be sidelined in Carlisle any more. Mary never seems to be in when I ring, but we need to talk. The house was cold and empty on my return. It is now almost midnight and no sign of Mary. My mood shifts from resignation to fury. I could go and confront them at his house, but I decide to bide my time.

Sunday, February 22nd
Still no sign of Mary by midday, so I walked down to the farm. No one had seen her, but they were unable to hide their embarrassment. Why is the husband always the last to know?

She came rushing into the house at about four o'clock. I have to hand it to her. She feigned real pleasure at seeing me. Kisses, cuddles, fluttering (false) eyelashes. At first she was evasive as to where she had been. When that failed to deflect me, she became aggressive. It was obvious she had only popped into the house to collect something. She kept looking anxiously out of the window. With another abrupt change of mood she moved into seduction mode, urging me to come upstairs. Too late, the Alvis drew up outside. Tim blared on the horn. He obviously expected her to be ready. She seemed quite mesmerised. Uncertain what to do, how to react. For a fleeting moment I felt quite sorry for her. She insisted she could explain everything. As Tim clambered out of the car and sauntered over to the front door, he saw me peering out of the window. I would have had a degree of admiration for him if he had confronted me. Instead he turned, throwing himself into the driver's seat and with screeching tyres roared away.

Mary went through her entire repertoire. She denied everything. Of course she wasn't having an affair. He offered her a lift now and then, that's all. How was she to manage? Stuck miles from anywhere with no transport. She could be so convincing. If I didn't know her so well I might have believed her. She tried to act normally, asking me about Carlisle and preparing supper. I was having none of it. I think she realised. Then it all came rushing out. It wasn't an affair. It was love. Of course I wouldn't be able to understand that. I was cold, incapable of any real emotion. (She could be right.) She assailed me with a list of my shortcomings, before dissolving into floods of tears. Strangely she came to me for sympathy, resting her head on my chest, crying like a child. That's how I think of her. A spoilt, impulsive child. I don't know how long we clung to each other. I tried to calm her, kissing the top of her head, her smell so familiar to me. I felt empty and sad.

Later we ate the supper she had prepared. I even opened the only bottle of wine we had in the house. Her makeup had run and her face was blotchy. We didn't talk. After the meal I cleared the dishes away. When I returned from the kitchen, she had gone. The front door was open. I could hear her high heels clicking on the road. I didn't go after her. I felt an overwhelming sense of tiredness. I think it's my way of blanking out reality. I slept soundly for the first time in weeks.

Monday, April 5th
I have outstayed my welcome. Uncle Robert views me with mounting distaste. Like my father, he thinks I

should go back to Mary. For better or worse and all that nonsense! If only they knew what has happened. They would both disown me. Self-control is central to the family's beliefs. Strangely it is a trait I have previously prided myself on. I'm still not sure if my actions were just an aberration or if I have set a trend.

I knew what I was doing. I had gone through it in my mind repeatedly, on waking that morning. The calm of the night before had been replaced by anger. In truth, fury. Not with Mary. Somehow it was as if she was an innocent party. (Not true, of course, but I still feel a sense of protection towards her.) It was Tim Brunton who represented everything I hated in a man. His suave sense of superiority had rankled since we first met. I thought he was a coward. Not so much by his avoidance of service during the war, but by his tendency to bully those unable to stand up for themselves. I realise that jealousy could have been instrumental in my loathing, culminating in him helping to ruin my marriage.

No one would have sensed anything wrong as I walked through the typing pool, smiling and wishing them all good morning. Knocking politely, I entered Sandra Bevan's office. She had only recently joined the company and for a moment I don't think she realised who I was. I told her I had an appointment with Mr Timothy. She peered short-sightedly at her diary. I was past her before the penny dropped. As I flung open Tim's door, she let out a stifled cry.

Tim was brave. For a moment anyway. 'Get out,' he bawled. I strode across the thick carpet. He remained seated. The heavy-lidded eyes changed from disdain to fear. He reached for the telephone. I snatched it from his grasp and threw it across the desk. 'Security!' he shouted to his secretary. 'Get security!' I heard her scuttle from the room. He stood up, a sickly smile on his face. He could explain everything, we were men of the world. 'I only came to give you this,' I said, handing him an envelope. He visibly relaxed, his confidence flowing back. 'Ah, your resignation. Well done, Emms. I knew we could settle this like gentlemen.'

'Just one more thing.'

He looked up from my letter. 'Yes?'

'This is for fucking my wife.' I brought my knee up hard into his groin. His cry was like that of a choirboy. A soprano squeal. I picked him up by his tie and sent him reeling across the room with a right hook.

The security guard took one look at his crumpled boss and disappeared, presumably to find reinforcements. Sandra Bevan shrunk back from me as I walked into the outer office. The room was in total silence.

'What was all that about?' a young typist asked.

'I've just resigned,' I replied.

Saturday, April 17th

Repercussions continue to reverberate. Although I was formally warned by the police, I now understand no action is to be taken. The Bruntons have erected a wall of silence. Never apologise, never explain. They probably feel they have nothing to apologise for, and they are certainly not in the business of explaining. Our former home has been cleared. Mary rang me to say she has been set up with a flat in Edgbaston. She was quite friendly. I think being fought over rather appeals to her sense of romance. Hardly a fight though. I enquired after Tim's undercarriage and was assured there was no permanent damage done. 'Back in full working order,' she giggled. I'm sure she was trying to make me feel jealous. Trouble is, I am. She's going to the States with him in the autumn. She sounded really happy. I'm not sure if the old man and the 'fragrant one' know what's going on.

From my point of view prospects aren't so bright. Today I received my fifth job rejection. Worrying because this was set up through a friend of the family, a vacancy at a merchant bank in the City. Each interview follows a similar pattern. Real interest shown until I tell them about my time at Brunton's. Initially I never mentioned the Tim incident, but job offers were withdrawn when they received references. Now I am open about it, but with the same result. I have been so naive. What did I expect? I'm unemployable.

Tuesday, April 20th
Tortuous journey to London. Green Line bus, and an hour's wait. The train arrived late. Another failed interview. I must be desperate, having sworn I would never work in the retail trade again. As least the personnel manager at Peter Robinson was sympathetic. Same result though. I may be forced to go labouring. I suppose there is always the Foreign Legion!

Thursday, June 3rd
Uncle Robert says I must move out in the next couple of weeks. I only have one of the old servant's rooms at the top of the house. So much for family solidarity. Dad was rushed into hospital today. They are keeping him in for a couple of days in an attempt to stabilise him. I have a feeling that he now knows why I left

Brunton's. He appeared very upset about something, before he did his nose dive. I would love to talk to him about it, but I know he finds discussing personal problems impossible. He changes the subject whenever I try to talk about Mum. So strange, because he surrounds himself with her photos.

Friday, June 11th
Borrowed fifty pounds from Dad. Feel very guilty, but I have no option. Uncle Robert is adamant I should leave soon. Miserable old bugger. I have offered to mow the grass, which is overgrown, and do some weeding for a small wage, as his gardener is off sick. He thinks I should do it in return for my keep. Now at least I'm busy, but no money, hence the loan.

Monday, June 21st
What a day! Turned down for another job, this time at Harrods. (Hardly a surprise.) Feeling very sorry for myself, I strolled towards the Basil Hotel where I had arranged to meet Archie Tavistock. I had served for two years under Archie and was hoping he would have some contacts which could be useful to me. His family has wide interests in food importing. I have to explore every possibility, no matter how slim.

Head down deep in thought, I was vaguely aware that I was following a schoolgirl. It was her bobby socks and suntanned legs that caught my attention. It was only later I took in the blue gymslip and smart purple blazer. By then a black Humber had screeched to a halt. A man in a suit and wearing a trilby leapt out and grabbed the girl. She screamed. Passers-by just stood as she tried to fight off her assailant, who was now trying to push her into the back seat. The driver was tugging at her arm, his face red from exertion. She fought ferociously, lashing out with her feet. Running forward, I saw the guy with the trilby pull something from his jacket pocket. He gasped with pain as I applied a vicious arm lock, before throwing him yelping head-first into some newly painted railings. The driver let go of the girl's arm and drove off at speed. I tried to grab at the back door, which was open and flapping, but he evaded me by mounting the pavement and overtaking the stationary cars in front of him. Annoyingly the man who had been wearing the trilby darted through the gathering crowd holding his injured arm. No one attempted to stop him. His hat lay on the pavement. So did a small revolver.

The girl was crying. She seemed more angry than frightened. Someone in the crowd said they were going to phone the police. To my amazement the girl, who I reckoned was only about fourteen, picked up the gun and pushed it into her satchel. She hailed a passing taxi, and, addressing me, said, 'The hat, quick!'

I scooped up the trilby. 'What about the police?' I queried, as I climbed into the taxi next to her.

She didn't answer. She gave the cabbie an address in Kensington. She stopped crying. Turning, she told me her name was Claudia. She was pretty. On the cusp between puberty and maturity. Her shoulder-length hair was black and her eyes still flashed in anger. We solemnly shook hands. She didn't thank me or respond to my attempts at conversation. She appeared not to hear me. In any other youngster this would have seemed rude. She had an intensity that was reflected through the tension in her body. She sat bolt upright next to me.

We pulled up outside a block of luxury flats in High Street Kensington. A doorman helped her out of the cab. She invited me up to meet her parents. Although fascinated by what had happened, I was already late for my meeting with Archie. She shrugged. Handing me a pen and a slip of paper, she asked me to write my name and telephone number. 'My father will want to thank you,' she told me. I said that it wasn't necessary, but wrote down the details anyway.

She paid the cabbie and asked where I wanted to go. She wouldn't hear of me going by public transport. She gave the driver an extra ten-shilling note. The doorman carried her satchel. He would have been shocked by its contents. I watched them disappear into the carpeted entrance hall.

It was only as we pulled up outside the Basil Hotel that I realised that the trilby still lay on the seat next to me. It was too small for me, but I took it anyway. Archie had gone. He left no message. Another wasted opportunity.

Lying in bed tonight, I decided I really should have insisted on calling the police.

Tuesday, June 22nd
Uncle Robert told me he had taken a strange call from some foreign chappie. A Mr de Bono with a Kensington number. I'll ring him tomorrow.

Wednesday, June 23rd
Rang Mr de Bono. Very thankful for my help. Even more so that I hadn't contacted the police. Rather strange. Have arranged to have tea with the family next Tuesday when I'm in town for another interview. Uncle

Robert would die. I have applied to work for a private detective agency. I rang them and let them know about the Tim fiasco. I'm fed up wasting time, getting turned down at the last minute. They said come anyway. Probably a bum job, but I must start earning, even if it's only washing dishes.

Monday, June 28th
A strange letter from Mary. A mixture of apology, recrimination and nostalgia. Where did we go wrong? (You tell me, sweetheart.) She misses me and hopes I'm OK. For a moment I'm tempted to ring her. I won't, though, nor will I reply. Perhaps all is not going smoothly for her. I hope he chucks her out – it would serve her right.

Tuesday, June 29th
Offered a job at the detective agency. A really run-down outfit in Kilburn, run by an ex-CID sergeant who left under a cloud. They specialise in divorce cases. Hours spent outside flats waiting for the erring spouse. Lousy wages, but I can start next week. That's if I can find a room to rent that I can afford.

I was in two minds about going to High Street Kensington. Curiosity overcame my lethargy. Arrived on foot, hot and sweaty. Uniformed doorman obviously expecting me. Escorted to the penthouse suite on the top floor. Welcomed by Claudia. No school uniform today. Wearing an expensive 'New Look' dress. Very fetching. Mrs de Bono must have been good-looking, too, in her time. She is rather overweight, but still attractive. She is festooned with expensive jewellery. No sign of Mr de Bono. We took tea on the roof garden. The noise of the traffic just a murmur. There was a lovely breeze as we sheltered from the sun under huge parasols. Mrs de Bono fussed about me, pressing cake and éclairs as if I were a hungry schoolboy. Young Claudia didn't enter into the conversation, but she never took her eyes off me. Rather disconcerting.

I had eaten three large slices of delicious Fullers chocolate cake by the time Mr de Bono arrived. He is bald, overweight and beautifully tailored. I assume he is Italian. He has a thick accent and laughs seemingly without reason. His eyes are small, deep-set and wary. He gives the impression of being jovial – a smokescreen I fancy. His English is far from fluent but is sprinkled nonetheless with barrack-room language. Claudia doesn't blanch, but Mrs de Bono tuts in disapproval.

We went inside to talk. It was like walking into a foreign country. Strange smells. A whiff of food being prepared by a maid in the kitchen. A picture of Christ dominates the room. Mr de Bono's swearing accelerates. Christ, like Claudia, who had joined us, maintained a look of serenity. A fine grand piano is crowded with photographs, mostly of Mr de Bono in the company of the famous. Film stars, sportsman and politicians.

Our meeting is brief. He thanked me for rescuing his daughter, brushing aside my queries as to why anyone would attempt to abduct her. He was particularly impressed that I had apparently broken the arm of the attacker. The problem had now been resolved, he assured me. How, I didn't ask.

He seemed more interested in me and my background. I was honest, telling him about the break-up of my marriage and my spat with Tim. That made him chuckle. I was too ashamed to mention the lousy job at the detective agency. Instead I said that I was looking at a number of job opportunities. He saw through that façade, offering me a wad of notes as I prepared to leave. I refused. Middle-class pride I suppose. He was most pressing, insisting it was a small price to pay for his daughter's safety. I remained steadfast. I walked the couple of miles to the station to save the bus fare. Overwhelmed this evening by self-pity and depression.

Wednesday, June 30th
Phone call from Harry de Bono offering me a job. Reckons he needs someone with management experience and, as he puts it, a bit of class. Not sure that I qualify on either count. He was very vague about my duties and the nature of his business. When pressed, he told me it was 'a people's business'. That could cover a multitude of sins and probably does. All very suspect, but better than working as a private eye. I hope. Anyway if I don't like it, I can move on. I asked about salary and was told I would be well looked after. What clinched it for me was the offer of free accommodation. A room in Greek Street. I can move my things in on Sunday.

Mary rang tonight. Assures me she is so happy, but worried about me. Wants to know what to do with the contents of our house. Told her to keep the lot, as I'm making a new start. I thought she would be pleased, but she started sobbing. I think she was trying to gain sympathy. Why should I feel sorry for her? Silly bitch. If she rings again, I'll hang up.

A Visit to Mary, 1986

This is the last time the diary records direct contact between Mary and my father. There are brief references later to their divorce.

Mary split up from Timothy Brunton in the summer of 1949, with the announcement of his engagement to Lady Annabel Irving. Mary subsequently married the barrister George Muscat in 1951, following her divorce from my father earlier that year. The marriage was a relatively happy one, until Muscat's death in a boating accident whilst on holiday in Bermuda in 1955. Still only in her thirties, she was now a wealthy widow.

Her marriage to the financier Malcolm Bateson was a disaster. It was her inheritance that attracted him. She by his urbane manner, his seeming wealth and his circle of influential and famous friends. She never understood money. Only how to spend it. It didn't occur to her that she was at risk when he invested her inheritance. He promised her substantial income combined with a rapid growth of the capital sum. Some months later he was arrested on fraud charges involving major banks and hundreds of investors. His wife's name was added to a long list of unsecured creditors.

Her subsequent years were dominated by declining health and financial hardship. When we met in 1986 she was living on the ground floor of a semi-detached house on the Western Avenue, in Acton. The traffic noise was so great it was difficult to hold a conversation.

She had made an effort. Although the room was cold she wore a floral summer dress, with a toning cardigan draped over her shoulders. The false eyelashes still fluttered and the compliments flowed effortlessly.

89

(She had seen me on TV – 'You are so talented darling.')
She reminded me of an actress from a previous age
who had fallen on hard times. Her beauty had faded,
like a watercolour exposed to too much light. The fine
bone structure remained, but her eyes had paled and
the bouffant hair thinned.

Although talkative, it took a deal of persuasion to
get her to discuss my father. Time plays tricks. She
didn't remember the tempestuous relationship my father
described. Physically he was attractive to her. 'Scrummy'
was how she described him, but emotionally cold and
socially dull. She had been astonished by the course
his life had taken. Frightened too, never admitting to
anyone that she had been married to him except George
Muscat. He was such a gentleman though; he never
raised the matter with her even during my father's
trial.

She was a disappointing source of information. Her
memory was selective. She preferred polite social
conversation, focusing on the good times. Hardship,
disasters, even the traffic thundering past her window
relegated to the back of her mind. A rather shallow
person, she sat surrounded by the few pieces of antique
furniture she had kept from her former homes.

A photograph of Mary taken at about the time my
father must have met her stood on the mantelpiece. I
could see the attraction. She was beautiful, almost
flawless, but as she prattled on, for the third time
during our short meeting, about a date she once had
with David Niven, I could see why she used to irritate
him.

Within a year of my visit Mary died of lung cancer.
She was 61.

PART 3
IN AT THE DEEP END

There were still many people at the end of the seventies who remembered my father's arrival in Soho. Esther, his landlady, although well into her eighties, had vivid memories. Barmen, petty crooks and ageing prostitutes were all able to recall this seeming misfit. Everything about the man set him apart from the colourful but shady background in which he found himself. 'Gentleman' was the word that came up most frequently. His accent, clipped and precise. 'Dead posh' was the overall verdict. Then there were the clothes. Tailored suits, chunky sweaters with cavalry twill trousers, screamed of a type who only entered the area for entertainment, not employment. The cravat he wore at weekends only confirmed his status as an outsider.

Under the façade of an English gentleman, many soon became aware of a genuine toughness. He was quiet but not shy. Approachable yet wary. To some he appeared old for his years. Although he had a good sense of humour, the underlying impression was of a young man who came with a deal of unwanted emotional baggage. It was difficult to get close to him. He was outwardly friendly, but the barriers he erected were never lowered.

It was a really difficult period for him. He obviously suspected he was entering a rather dubious world, but felt he had little option.

So it was, at the age of twenty-six, that Derek entered the last area of London that could still be genuinely described as a village. Welcome to Soho!

The Third Diary – July–December, 1948

Saturday, July 3rd
Spent the afternoon preparing for my move. Everything I possess fits into one battered suitcase. Apart from clothes, I am reduced to a few photographs, an address book and passport. A sad reflection on my impact on the world to date.

Dad is delighted I have found a job. Uncle Robert's pleasure is prompted by relicf that I am leaving. I am vague but enthusiastic about my new role. In truth I have no idea what I am letting myself in for. I went to the local library yesterday, looking for information on Soho. The Royal Commission of 1906 referred to Greek Street as being one of the worst in London. It was supposedly frequented by the 'vilest reptiles to be found in the capital'. I doubt if it has changed that much.

I have only been in Soho a couple of times, as a schoolboy. Our school carol concert was held each year at St Martin-in-the-Fields. As young teenagers, having sung like angels, we would plunge into the temptations offered by Soho's bustling streets as darkness fell. My memories were of prostitutes in doorways. Stuffing our school caps under our coats, we would dare each other to ask one of the shadowy figures, how much? The smells from the cafés and the bustle of Berwick Street market added to the heady atmosphere. As did the film posters, displayed in the windows of buildings occupied by the major studios in Wardour Street. The area seemed quite intoxicating. Now, I'm not so sure. I'm nervous, even apprehensive, but I have little to lose.

Sunday, July 4th

Well I'm here. I don't know what I expected, but at least my room is comfortable enough. It's on the first floor and I look down on a bustling Greek Street. Opposite is a French pâtisserie and a rather squalid-looking Italian café. People hang around in clusters. They talk and puff at cigarettes, watchful as if expecting something out of the ordinary to happen. It doesn't. The night is humid and the clustered groups break off and join the crowds of pedestrians. They walk slowly. Vague snippets of conversation rise from the street. Foreign accents, different languages. The warmth of the night adds to the feeling that I am not in London at all. Close my eyes and it could be Milan. Open them and I'm in Paris.

Below my window is a shop that sells catering equipment. Being Sunday, it was closed when I arrived. I was ushered through a side door by my landlady who was obviously expecting me. Esther is possibly Italian, but her accent has more than a hint of cockney. She is a large woman, probably in her late fifties. Her dark hair is speckled with grey, held off her face by an army of pins. Wisps constantly break loose, creating a rather untidy impression. Inside the house the opposite is true, everything sparkles. She was extremely welcoming. Very deferential. Slightly embarrassing.

My room is well furnished and fully carpeted. There is a lingering smell of sweet perfume which hangs heavily, even with the windows open. Esther treats me like an honoured guest. Within an hour of my arrival, she prepared a huge plate of pasta for me. She seemed quite taken aback when I asked her about the rent. There is to be no charge, on the instructions of Mr de Bono. She tells me that he owns the property. She refers to him in hushed tones. She assures me it's a real pleasure to welcome a proper gentleman for a change. She infers the other tenants don't quite fall into that category. I haven't met them yet.

I sauntered over to the Three Greyhounds earlier this evening. Started chatting to the barman. On my mentioning Harry de Bono he became quite wary. Thought I was from the police. I told him I was working for Mr de Bono and he appeared even more nervous. I noticed a number of men at the other end of the bar turning to stare as I left.

Monday, July 5th
I went to sleep against a babble of street noise. Up early, having slept soundly. Esther already in the kitchen. A superb breakfast. This is better than staying in a hotel. No sign of the other tenants, but I did hear someone moving around in the room above mine.

I arrived to meet Harry on time, at the address he had given me in Dean Street. The premises locked up and run down. Hung about for twenty minutes. Still no show. Went for a coffee. Doors open on my return, but no one at the reception desk. Voices upstairs, so I went to investigate. Three unshaven characters were draped over easy chairs, with feet up on a coffee table. They all wore loose-fitting suits, with trilbies pushed to the back of their heads. The smallest of the group peered at me through a cloud of smoke. I noticed his fingers were stained yellow with nicotine. He asked me if I was from the law. If not, I must be flogging something. I tell him I have an appointment with Mr de Bono. They look me up and down, grinning stupidly.

The small one with the ferret face leans forward whispering. The other two break into convulsions of laughter. I felt uncomfortable and out of place, in my formal off-the-peg Brunton's suit and old boy's tie. A smell of cigar smoke and heavy footsteps stops the banter. They stand up. I am introduced. They nod, grudgingly. I can see they are appalled. Harry tells them to 'piss off'. They slouch away mumbling and resentful. I ask Harry who they are. He tells me they help him out sometimes, but work mainly for his brother. I didn't know he had a brother. I have a feeling there is a great deal I don't know about my new employer.

My first task is to sort out his office. Where do you start? I have never seen such a mess. Papers, invoices and magazines clutter his desk and lay strewn on the floor. Cartons of wine are stacked high against the walls. He declares the place to be a shit house. Agreed. Amidst the jumble on his desk are several photographs of his daughter. Mrs de Bono doesn't feature. Throwing more envelopes onto the floor, he eased himself behind the desk. He tells me he is still worried about Claudia. He has received more threats. He thought he had sorted the problem. What about the police? I suggested. Silly question. He insists that they are all corrupt. I asked him why he was being targeted. Jealousy, he assures me. His empire is too successful. He has interests in catering, property and entertainment (he is very vague), and these tearaways are demanding protection money. Until he is honest with me I can't really add anything.

I did suggest that sending Claudia away to school in the country might help. A boarding school I prompted. Out of sight, out of mind. The idea appealed to him.

'Fix it,' he tells me. I explain it may not be that easy. She would probably have to take an entrance exam. He's not interested in detail. He wants the best, money no object. I think he now has an image of his daughter being educated with the cream of English society.

There is a safe behind his desk. He took out a wad of notes and peeled off four white fivers. Expenses, he explains. He also handed me a key for my office, which is downstairs. 'Sort it, Captain,' he instructs waving a hand at the mountain of littered paperwork. 'And the school,' he adds as an afterthought.

Monday, July 19th
Two weeks down the track and I'm still here. A fortnight in which I have learnt a great deal about myself and the de Bonos.

My office is stark and grubby. Just a rickety desk, swivel chair, telephone and layers of grime. I spent hours with a sponge and soapy water. I was just finishing the cleaning on my first afternoon when an attractive redhead barged in. She was looking for Fred, who from her description turned out to be the ferret face I had met earlier. She was very agitated. I told her I was working for Mr de Bono. She looked very doubtful but handed me a small wad of notes that she wanted passed on to Fred. I told her I wasn't happy handling cash. She became quite hysterical, insisting she was already late with the payment. She was convinced they were going to 'do her' this time. I hadn't a clue what she was talking about.

Enter Fred of the ferret face, who snatched the money and informed the girl she was pushing her fucking luck. Not my favourite type, Fred. Uncouth, mean and ignorant. She scurried off. He counted the money slowly, silently mouthing the amount. Satisfied on the third count, he looked round my newly cleaned office. My hands were still wet from the soapy water and I wore an apron I had borrowed from a neighbouring café. 'Wanker!' he sneered before turning and wandering out into the afternoon sunlight.

That night after supper, I went for a drink at the Nelly Dean. As I emerged into another balmy evening, I saw the redhead who had come into my office earlier. She was standing against a shopfront, smoking. She had found a punter. He walked at discreet distance behind her, before following her into a darkened doorway. No prizes now for guessing what business Harry de Bono is really in.

Tuesday, July 27th

I feel more at ease now, but there is no doubt that my first few days here have been extremely difficult. Fred and his two pals have set out to annoy and intimidate me. Finally it ended in blows. Little more than a skirmish really. They arrived each morning and hung around trying to goad me. For several days I ignored them. They tended to get bored easily and left once the pubs opened. By the Friday I was really fed up with them. It was difficult enough, without their juvenile interruptions. I was about to carry a huge pile of files downstairs. I sensed something was up from the silly look on their faces. As I reached the staircase Fred snaked out his foot, in an attempt to trip me. I kicked his foot away sending him sprawling. A look of utter astonishment crossed his ugly face. Charlie, the larger of his companions, launched himself at me. I threw the files at him. He was caught off guard. Kicking out I whipped his feet from under him. He fell with a resounding crash and hurt pride. Barry, the third man, is older. He threw a punch in my general direction, more out of duty than conviction. A push in the chest was all that was required to get him to join his spreadeagled companions. He scrambled to his feet and made for the stairs. Halfway down he stopped and asked rather pathetically if he could have his hat. I threw it to him and he disappeared. Taking the other two by the collar, I frogmarched them out onto the street. They struggled without much belief. I told them to stick to threatening women. They honestly think they are tough. What a joke! They retreated muttering threats. The street was quite crowded. My stock will have risen with my neighbours, but I have made enemies.

News travels fast. Harry called in later. He reckoned I was shaping up well. They were useless bastards. Time they were taken off the payroll, he reckoned. We are in agreement there, Harry!

Stinking hot tonight. Another heatwave forecast.

Sunday, August 1st
Having survived a month, what are my overriding impressions?

1) I am sex-starved. I can't remember the last time I made love. Now, of course, I am surrounded by sex. I'm in the business. Harry is no longer coy about it. Help yourself he tells me, you are part of the family now. He does, I know. Frequently. Something in my background precludes or at least delays it. A Calvinistic streak. Anyway, my friends always

scoffed about chaps who had to pay for it. Stupid thing is, I wouldn't have to pay. Perks of the trade, but still it's no. Although some of Harry's girls are really attractive. Watch this space.

2) Money, or lack of it. Payment is made on whim. Sometimes generous, then weeks with nothing. (I must talk with Harry about a regular salary or wage.)

3) Fitness or again lack of it. Esther continues to feed me mountainous meals and I am taking no exercise. I called in at the gym in Windmill Street, but they only cater for boxers. I should start running in Hyde Park.

4) Harry's office is still a mess. I have cleared massive piles of paperwork and I reckon I am only halfway through it. Much of the correspondence dates back years and remains unopened. I've found warrants for Enrique and Franco de Bono, for failing to report for military service. There are deeds to properties, details of deposit boxes and bank accounts. His filing system involves just adding to existing piles. There are pornographic magazines from pre-war Germany and current batches from France. He has told me to take anything I don't know what to do with to his lawyer in Berwick Street

I am taking Claudia for interview on Thursday to my mother's old school in Norfolk. I tried dozens of leading schools, but they are all full. Some were extremely sniffy. I think it was only the family connection, although remote, that prompted success at St Helen's.

Another milestone next week. Harry's brother returns from a trip abroad. I have yet to meet him. He sounds pretty odious. Harry with a much tougher streak and without the humour. I know Harry will be relieved to see him. I understand problems with the 'tearaways' have been increasing. Harry hasn't brought me into his confidence yet, but there was a fire at one of his clubs last week. No accident is the consensus. Will I still be here in a month's time? I honestly don't know. I am beginning to have a real problem with my conscience. The more I learn, the more I realise I have entered a thoroughly sordid world.

For the moment though, I can see Esther returning from Mass and I am due to take her out for lunch. It's the least I can do. She has been a brick!

Monday, August 2nd
Spent the last of my money yesterday taking Esther to Wheelers. Very good. Two bottles of wine. She was quite tipsy, but still very reluctant to talk much about the de Bonos. She is rather prim and proper, but I have the feeling she used to be 'on the game'.

She is far more forthcoming about my fellow tenants, who fascinate me. The eldest must be about fifty. She insists on being called Madam Beatrix. She has dyed-blonde hair, but a sallow complexion that rests uncomfortably with peroxide. When we first met a couple of weeks ago, she was very friendly. She refers to herself as a 'corrective therapist'. Latterly she has become more wary of me. The de Bono connection no doubt. She's obviously one of his girls! Some girl. She told me her consulting rooms were in the basement and they seem to attract a constant stream of rather nervous, well-heeled customers. Her assistant, Gaynor, looks hardly old enough to have left school. She is

Welsh. She has a lovely singing voice. I listen to an endless repertoire which includes hymns coming from the room above mine. She sings like a bird, but getting her to talk is like drawing teeth. Off duty she tends to wear simple gingham frocks, making her seem like a complete innocent. She obviously isn't. Presumably that's the attraction.

Esther grumbles darkly about what they get up to. She declares their activities to be unnatural. Beatrix, however, insists they fulfil a social need, and besides they meet such a nice class of gentleman!

Thursday, August 5th
My trip to Norfolk with Claudia is a success. I collected her from Kensington. Gleaming Jaguar parked outside waiting for us. Good news, Harry came up trumps with 'petrol money', although the tank was already full. Enough to keep me in funds for weeks. Harry looked pained when I suggested a meeting to discuss a regular salary. The payments may be haphazard, but overall I am being well paid for what I do. Claudia looked very demure for her interview, wearing the same uniform she had worn on the day of the kidnap attempt. She is amazingly self-possessed for her age. She displayed no nerves. She told me she was looking forward to boarding. She was finding her home life claustrophobic.

St Helen's is situated right on the coast, north of Felixstowe. From a security point of view it appears ideal. Approached through a manned gatehouse, it is surrounded by a high flint and stone wall. A locked door leads straight onto the beach, where the girls are expected to swim each day, whatever the weather.

Whilst Claudia underwent written tests, I wandered

around the grounds with its extensive playing fields. It was strange to think of my mother being there some thirty-five years before. For a moment I was overcome with a deep sense of sadness. Not wholly at my ongoing sense of loss but also, because of my current circumstances. I knew my mother would have been deeply upset by my new lifestyle and not for the first time I resolved to break away. I am in the process of becoming a sad and deeply flawed individual. Guilt presses in on me whenever I reflect, and not only for my present activities. My answer, as always, is to deny or ignore the facts. Retrospection will be my undoing. Live for the day, I try to convince myself.

The headmistress was quite glowing about Claudia. She starts next term at the end of September. Claudia was very chatty as we drove back to London. The only awkward spot in her interview was when she was asked for her father's occupation. 'Well, I could hardly say brothel keeper,' she told me, laughing. Financier was how she described him. Well, he certainly makes plenty of money. I did learn a little about the de Bono empire. They do have a catering supply business, and Frank runs several amusement arcades and clubs.

Claudia shows no embarrassment about the prostitution side. She tells me her grandparents ran brothels in Cairo and Morocco, before coming to this country in the twenties. Now the two brothers control Soho. At least they did until the Murphy boys tried to get in on the act. They apparently make their money on the southern racecourses and are trying to expand their activities. 'Uncle Frank will sort them out,' she told me confidently. I get the impression he's the strongman in the outfit He is the younger of the brothers and runs the family business south of Shaftesbury Avenue, whilst her father's interests are confined to the north with an outpost in Paddington. I can't help reflecting on my return tonight, how bizarre my life has become. Talking of which, I have just seen a leading member of the shadow cabinet dart down the steps into the basement below my window.

Friday, August 27th
I've been living here for almost two months and still I have hardly ventured outside Harry's territory. I am being pathetic. I am surrounded by theatreland and cinemas showing the latest films and yet I spend my evenings skulking in my room or propping up a bar. I am not a prisoner. There are huge changes taking place and yet I do little more than glance at the newspapers. I'm lethargic. All my good intentions about keeping fit have been postponed.

No wonder I am sleeping so badly. Today I woke shaking. The same ghastly image. His face so clear. The look changing from fear to resignation and then the blood pumping from his nose and seeping from his eyes.

Wednesday, September 8th
Frank de Bono makes regular visits to Harry's office. Presumably Harry has explained who I am. His brother ignores me, even if we pass on the stairs. I sense trouble. They are preoccupied.

Whilst Harry is fat, Frank is solid and powerful. He has a brooding presence. He runs his business ruthlessly. I'm told his girls are beaten regularly and yet they remain loyal. He rules by fear. In contrast, Harry's regime appears benign. He smiles, laughs. Charm is interspersed with anger. Sometimes he lurches into uncontrollable rages. He is unpredictable. The methods are different, but the results similar. Until recently, very few people have been prepared to challenge them. Whilst Frank has absolute control of prostitution in his area, Harry has allowed a number of freelance girls to operate. The rumour is that Murphy senses weakness and is targeting Harry.

Tuesday, September 14th
I made two major decisions today. The first, I hope, will get me away from here and back into the real world. The second I now regret and has left me feeling cheapened and ashamed of myself.

Having finally brought order to Harry's office, I decided it is time to move on. I am little more than a clerk. Anyway, I have applied for three jobs advertised in the *Daily Telegraph*.

I had sex today for the first time for months. Despite Harry's offer, I have continued to deny myself. It has occurred to me that he thinks I'm queer. The girl was a freelance. That was half the attraction. Most of Harry's girls know me by sight. I feel the need to keep aloof from them. Tonight I acted on impulse. I darted in front of the woman, into the darkly lit doorway. She guided me up the stairs. Her room was overbearingly hot. I remember the constant hiss of the gas fire. Half light can be deceptive. She was much older than I had imagined when I saw her in the street. Fatter too. I should have just paid her and left. I didn't. Embarrassingly it was all over in seconds. She seemed quite proud of herself, for being so irresistible to me. Feeling dirty and sullied, I ran down the stairs as if being pursued. Leaning on a wall opposite as I stepped out into a rainy evening was Charlie, Fred's sidekick. He grinned stupidly. 'Lovely girl!' he shouted after me. I don't know why I care that he shares my guilty little secret, but I do.

Tuesday, September 21st
Took Claudia to Norfolk to start her new school. I was hoping Harry would give me the generous allowance that I had on our first visit. No such luck. He handed me a fiver. Told him I hadn't been paid for weeks. He said to remind him when I get back. An emotional send-off for Claudia. Tears trickled down Harry's face. Mrs de Bono was inconsolable. Claudia was composed and stylish in her smart new uniform. On our journey I asked her what she wanted to do when she was grown up. 'I am grown up,' she replied. 'When you leave school then?' I expected her to say law or medicine. 'Take over from my father,' she said. I must have looked stunned. 'Why not?' she queried. 'You meet all sorts of people, and the money is good.' She wanted to know what I would like to do. I was honest and told her I didn't really know. She suggested that perhaps we could go into business together. She flirts with me. She *is* growing up fast. I find her increasingly attractive. Don't even think about it!

She wandered off to find her housemistress on our arrival, leaving me to negotiate her trunk up two flights of stairs to her dormitory. Surrounded by giggling girls from the Shires, I again felt a profound sense of loss. These kids come from a background I know and understand. I have been sidetracked into another world which is foreign to me still, but one from which I must break out of soon or ... or what?

Thursday, September 23rd
I delivered batches of papers to Leo Joseph, Harry's lawyer. They cover a wide variety of seemingly pressing problems. Threats to sue for non-payment of numerous outstanding invoices. Correspondence to do with properties in Paris and Valletta and some begging letters from ex-employees who have fallen on hard times.

Leo is at odds with his surroundings in Berwick Street. He's suave, confident and urbane. His office is small, untidy and grimy. Better than Harry's before I got to work on it – but not much! He tossed the files onto an untidy heap already lining his desk. Obviously he shares the same filing system. Although not much older than me, his outward confidence confers a maturity I cannot match. He expresses surprise that I have got tied up with such an outfit. Not to be outdone I suggest he would be more at home in a leading City practice. He smiled and reminded me that we all have to start somewhere. I don't believe him. He is here by choice.

Sunday, September 26th
'Gang Warfare Breaks Out in London'! screams today's headlines. Hardly. It appears the Irish boys have been demanding five pounds a week protection money from each girl on our patch. Frank sent over a couple of his heavies to confront the 'micks'. Razors and knuckledusters wielded along the length of Old Compton Street. Lots of shouting and posturing, but hardly any damage done. Great spectator entertainment.

'Organised Crime Grips Soho' propounds the *News*

of the World. Organised? They must be kidding, it's totally disorganised! I have a feeling that you are safer in Soho than most parts of London.

Friday, October 1st
I have been turned down for all my job applications. I had two encouraging interviews, but the Brunton legacy persists. I am really depressed. I have no money. I haven't been paid for weeks. I've no work to do either. The three cavaliers have started hanging around again. Bloody annoying. They must sense my star is on the wane. Harry spends most of his time with his brother. I understand they are having trouble with the police. The papers continue to carry on about crime in Soho.

I have found a gym near the side entrance to Foyles. It's used mainly by wrestlers. They spend hours practising their holds. Huge men, with huger guts, throwing each other around. They all deserve Oscars. The place smells of decades of sweat. I love it. Better to spend time here than sitting at an empty desk with nothing to do. Everyone is very welcoming. I'm known as 'Captain'. Harry's nickname for me is spreading.

Saturday, October 2nd
Spent the last of my money going to see Dinah Shore at the Palladium. A great family show. I must ring Dad.

Monday, October 4th
Harry left ten pounds for me in the top drawer of my desk. This afternoon Beatrix showed me round her consulting rooms. Amazing. Why do men want to be

tied up and beaten – the place is like a torture chamber. I think they must be warped, but I shouldn't sit in judgement.

The girls are convinced they are undertaking an important service for society. Maybe they are. It appears that the British generally have a guilt complex about sex, and some require punishment to satisfy them. I have a feeling that sex, however outlandish, never satisfies. Not without love anyway – whatever that is.

Sunday, October 10th
Soho on a Sunday morning is deserted except for a few souls on their way to church. The debris from Saturday night's excesses litter the streets. An amazing selection of bottles and fag packets congregate in the gutters. For almost a couple of hours there is an eerie silence. A pause to catch breath, then the cafés roll up their shutters. Smart restaurants open for business, as do the girls who line the streets. Soho launches itself into another hectic, confusing week.

Friday, October 15th
I've had enough. I'm bored, broke and disillusioned. I rang Father to say I would be visiting him for a few days. He sounds in good spirits. Probably because Uncle Robert is away, visiting friends in Devon.

Left a note on Harry's desk telling him I'm quitting. I was saying goodbye to a tearful Esther, when the phone rang. Harry. He wants me to meet him on Monday at his brother's office. He has big plans for me. I'm offered a regular wage of twenty pounds a week. I told him I would think about it over the weekend.

110

Sunday, October 17th
Having promised myself I would come clean with Dad, I again failed the honesty test. Instead, I boasted I had been promoted and would be earning a thousand a year. As far as he is concerned I am the personnel manager for a financial group with business interests worldwide.

We enjoyed a pleasant weekend. So much better with Uncle Robert not being around. We walked his dog, drank his whisky and lazed in front of a log fire in his comfortable living room. We lunched each day at the village pub.

Back in London a letter was waiting for me from Arthur. He has settled in Sydney and is working in insurance. He sent some photographs. He looks fantastic. Slimmer and without the handlebar moustache. Quite a transformation. He insists Australia is a land of opportunity and urges me to join him. I had hardly enough money to get me back to London, let alone Sydney. Had supper with Esther and the correction girls. What a strange bunch we are, and yet I do feel quite at home here. I haven't unpacked. It will depend on what Harry has to offer. It's my birthday tomorrow. I hope it's a good one.

Monday, October 18th
Frank's office in Newport Place is no smarter than his brother's. At least it's tidy. They presumably lavish money on their homes, rather than office accommodation. No sign of Frank. No idea why we were not meeting in Dean Street. Anyway Harry is all smiles and charm.

I told him I have an opportunity to go to Australia and that I am fed up with acting as a glorified clerk cum chauffeur. My talents are being wasted and I have my long-term career to think of. He suggested, not unreasonably, that I have been serving a period of apprenticeship. I told him that he surrounds himself with deadbeats and that much of his organisation is a shambles. He continued smiling but I could sense his annoyance. He asked me how much money I had in my wallet? I knew what he is getting at. 'Well?' he queried. I played the game. I laid a single ten-bob note on the table. He reached into his back pocket and threw a thick wad of notes secured by an elastic band onto my lap. Checkmate. Game, set and match. He made his point. He's obviously doing something right. The proposal he makes is intriguing. Twenty pounds a week is just a start. I will be on an agreed percentage of any increased turnover I am able to bring him. Big money, huge dangers. I will become as culpable as him if I accept. Any illusions I have about acting only marginally outside the law will be dashed. I will be involved in serious crime. I need time to think. A few days, perhaps a week. He nodded his agreement. I handed back his money. He waved it aside. 'An acceptance fee,' he said. I didn't want to feel under any obligation, but I pocketed it anyway.

As I was leaving an adjoining door opened. It was brother Frank. I'm sure he had been listening. Harry introduced us formally. We shook hands. Previously he has cut me dead. He smiled as if the very act was painful to him. His voice is strangely high-pitched. He thanked me for saving Claudia. A bit late in the day, Frankie! That's not his real message. My trouble radar kicked in. He pulled a revolver from his pocket. I recognised it. He pointed it at me. I didn't flinch, he

112

was playing games. He pulled the trigger. Nothing. I didn't react. He laughed. Did I know the gun wasn't loaded when the Irish bastard tried to snatch Claudia? No I didn't. So what?

'They will regret it,' he boasted. 'Nobody messes with us and gets away with it. Remember that, Captain. Now you work for us.' I could tell he was quite agitated. He had a facial tick. It was as if he was winking at me. I ignored him. In a show of independence, I told Harry I would think about his offer. He smiled benignly. He knows the answer.

Back in my room I slowly counted the money. Two hundred and sixteen pounds. I have booked a table at L'Escargot tonight for four. The school of correction will be closing early today.

Thursday, October 21st
Dreadful dream. Woke to find my bed surrounded by the three ladies of the house. I had woken them with my screaming. They were alarmed. So was I. Sitting round the kitchen table at three o'clock in the morning, they looked pretty frightening too. Beatrix had her hair in curlers and wore men's pyjamas. Esther's face was caked with what appeared to be mud. It was so thick she could hardly smile. Gaynor wore a short-sleeved nightie. The tops of her arms were covered in bruises. As she poured the coffee I could make out what appeared to be weals across the backs of her legs. Beatrix seemed to read my mind. She puts a finger to her lips and I didn't say anything. 'I'll explain later,' she whispered. Gaynor handed out the coffee and lowered herself very gently onto her chair. Something terrible has happened. I must find out.

113

Monday, October 25th

Decision day and I was still undecided. I had a headache
and was generally out of sorts. In the afternoon I
wandered aimlessly up Greek Street past the Gay Hussar,
where the last of the lunchtime diners were spilling
onto the street. It was a foggy, depressing day. I needed
a couple of shirts, so I headed for Marks and Spencer's
in Oxford Street. I don't know why I veered right into
St Patrick's Church in Soho Square. Until I was inside,
I wasn't even aware that it was St Patrick's. Certainly
it hadn't occurred to me that it was a Catholic church.
My initial reaction was to turn and leave immediately,
but I was struck by the tranquillity of the place. I made
my way past two lifesize marble statues of angels each
holding holy water.

The church was seemingly empty except for an old
tramp huddled and asleep in the back pew. Then I
spotted a group of nuns at the altar praying in Latin.
The church was an oasis. Not a sound penetrated from
the street. Some of the day's fog had managed to find
its way in and it hung in a ghostlike band, some feet
from the ground. It didn't obscure the huge painting
of the crucifixion above the altar, or the white marble
pulpit. I knelt as if in prayer. Yesterday I had taken
Gaynor to the accident department at Middlesex hospital.
The client, a regular, had persuaded the young girl to
manacle herself to the wall, their normal positions
reversed. Apparently Beatrix had popped out for some
cigarettes and had stopped on the way back for a quick
drink. Half an hour later she found Gaynor bruised
and bleeding. The punter had disappeared. I thought
I might be accused, but neither doctor nor nurses
showed much interest. It was almost as if young girls

being thrashed and beaten was commonplace. 'It's not that,' Gaynor assured me. 'It's just they know from my record that I'm on the game. You see we don't count in their eyes.' How sad.

Gradually I felt the calm atmosphere of the church begin to influence my mood. Perhaps it was not chance that I had come in off the street. Was this a sign that I should walk away from the tawdry life that beckoned me. As these thoughts formed, I suddenly had the feeling I was being watched. I noticed that one of the windows to the gothic-styled wooden confessionals had been opened. I sensed a figure peering out at me. I felt uncomfortable. Stumbling to my feet I hurried out onto the street. The fog had thickened. It was difficult to be sure that I was heading in the right direction. The irony was not lost on me.

This evening I rang Harry at his home. I told him I was accepting his offer.

Friday, November 5th
The past couple of weeks have been taken up with detailed negotiations with Harry. He is very difficult to deal with, constantly changing his mind. He always claims his lack of English leads to any confusion. His English is fine. His accent may be thick, but his understanding is perfect.

Certain interesting facts have emerged. He is not well. During the last year he has suffered two heart attacks. His blood pressure is dangerously high. Interestingly he has not told his brother. I think he senses a takeover of his interests, that's why I have been brought into the equation. Once I know what I'm doing, he intends spending more time down in

Brighton. He has bought a flat overlooking the promenade near the Metropole Hotel.

It has been agreed that I will be taking over the catering business. It will act as a perfect cover for me. A genuine business. Run down, losing money, but bona fide. Leo Joseph is arranging the transfer. The existing company has been put into liquidation. I inherit no debts, but one sad ineffectual manager. Perfect. Today I went to Austin Reed and bought myself a new suit. Very conservative. I look the epitome of a legitimate businessman.

Monday, November 8th
Beatrix complains bitterly to me that her rent has been increased. I didn't dare tell her it was a quid pro quo for me taking on the catering business rent free. The Lord giveth, the Lord taketh away!

I have set up my new office at the back of the shop. My manager is Donald Watson. Donald is ginger. His hair, moustache and stained overall are all an identical shade and the colour is maintained when he struggles into his sports coat on leaving at night. The only relief is usually the brown brogues he wears, but today he sports a suede pair. I have never seen ginger shoes on sale, but Donald has found them. He is pleased by my arrival. He senses his job is secure. He enthuses over the new stock arriving.

I am to act as Harry's cashier. Donald may be less impressed by the human stock that will be visiting the shop regularly to pay their dues. I will have to start viewing the girls as commodities alongside the fish-kettles and pans. The only difference being, the kitchen equipment can only be sold once.

116

Tuesday, November 16th

Princess Elizabeth has given birth to a son. The country rejoices. So do I. I'm a confirmed royalist.

In further discussions with Harry, I have learnt that his earnings from the girls are less than half that of his brother's. However, thankfully, he doesn't resort to beating them with electric light flex to retain their loyalty. Frank has a total monopoly of his area, whereas Harry's gentler approach has allowed competition to grow. To complicate matters, the French and Belgian girls have been married off to British men to enable them to stay in the country. The husbands received a small payment for their trouble. A couple of these characters started acting as pimps, drawing off their cut before paying Harry's 'rent money'. Now Mr Murphy is trying to get in on the act. It's my job to try and find a way of reversing the decline. Harry is not receiving the money he feels he is entitled to. He sounds like a benefactor as he explains the trouble and expense he goes to for his girls. Then they try to rob him, he complains. I explain it's hardly the type of business where we can call in time-and-motion experts. Do I detect an undercurrent of threat? He tells me that my very future could depend on the results I achieve for him.

Thursday, November 18th

This morning I found myself drawn back to St Patrick's. Why? Perhaps because I feel the silence and the vague smell of incense helps to clear my mind. I hope for God's forgiveness, as I ponder problems not normally associated with His house. I am developing a radical plan, which will not be very popular with a certain group of people.

My brooding was interrupted as I sensed someone

117

standing beside me. A priest. A young priest, with dark good looks. He asked me if I was new to the area. I told him not exactly. Caught unawares, I looked guilty. It was as if I imagined, he could somehow read my mind. He welcomes me, without smiling.

I love the atmosphere of the church, but I prefer it empty. People somehow detract from its power to influence me.

Making my excuses, I hurried out into the street.

Wednesday, December 1st

Harry approves of my plan. Four girls are to receive huge rent increases. Four 'husbands' are going to be furious. The deal is, they will be rehoused in downmarket Paddington. Harry has some property interests there, and they will be allowed to act as freelances. I expect trouble, but he is confident he can sort it. My task is to be recruitment. English girls this time from the provinces.

Takings down this week. No money for me. Harry is now denying that he agreed to pay me a wage. That was before he set me up in the catering business, he insists. He was quite angry, blood pressure rising. I'm not too pleased. I reckon I've been conned.

Thursday, December 9th

Although I still see Harry most days, he insists I deliver the money over to his flat. Takings very poor again. I'm told this is seasonal. The great British male is out buying Christmas presents rather than whoring. No money for me, but he stuffs notes into two envelopes. These are to be collected from Greek Street. He gives descriptions of the men who are to pick them up. I don't ask who they are. I think it's better I don't know. Harry is off to Brighton until the New Year. I'm in charge. On my own. I sense trouble brewing. If there is an emergency, he tells me to contact Frank. No thanks, I think he could be the source of any trouble.

Monday, December 13th
I really don't approve of violence, but I think some of the girls believe I'm a soft touch. They are either late with their payments or try to short change me. I think I have found the solution. I have employed Karl Cripps. I've got to know him at the gym. He is possibly the ugliest man I have ever met. He must be twenty stone, wears an eyepatch and wrestles under the name of the Terrible Teuton! In fact he's from Cardiff but promoters need a bad guy to get the crowds going. He gives Nazi salutes and constantly repeats the few words of German he knows. He happens to be one of the gentlest men I've met. He has agreed to pay a courtesy call on a few of the girls. Wrestlers are great actors. I anticipate an improvement in takings.

Wednesday, December 15th
Pay day. I've warned the girls about Kurt. No shouting, nice and calm. I think they have the message.

Thursday, December 16th
Summoned to Kensington. Mr and Mrs de Bono returned en route to the carol concert being held at Claudia's school. They wanted approval for their outfits. They are so nervous. Worried they will embarrass their beloved daughter. They are uneasy at being exposed to middle-class scrutiny. Mrs de Bono has lost weight.

119

Her attractiveness may have been hibernating somewhat, but it's fighting back. She looked great. Harry is swathed in yards of expensive cloth. I congratulate them both. Their relief is almost childlike. Mrs de Bono sends me off clutching a box containing my favourite Fullers chocolate cake.

Friday, December 24th
The catering business is beginning to build up. Ginger Donald take a bow! I paid him a small bonus. He was very grateful. He tells me he will be spending Christmas alone. Apart that is from his mother and three Persian cats. I feel a twinge of sadness for him.

My adverts have already appeared in the regional press. I anticipate a huge response. A life of glamour in the big city! Well that's what the adverts promise.

Esther asked me to go to midnight Mass with her. Standing room only. I recognise a number of our girls. The collection plate is stuffed with notes. Conscience money. At the end of the service I noticed the young priest standing at the entrance, shaking hands with many of the congregation. Esther introduced me, rather proudly I thought, as Captain Emms. Father Boldini, he murmurs, holding my hand for a fraction longer than necessary. He has a London accent. I think he knows who or rather what I am. I am annoyed with myself for feeling uncomfortable. Conscience obviously extends beyond the collection plate.

Wednesday, December 29th
Spent a rather sombre Christmas in Hertfordshire. Uncle Robert relatively welcoming by his own austere standards.

I feel very guilty on my return. My room was festooned with brightly wrapped gifts from Esther and the girls. I didn't even send anyone a Christmas card.

Friday, December 31st
I have been invited to a party at the French pub. Outside the street is full of revellers. I sit alone, stolidly drinking my way through thirty-three shillings' worth of whisky. I long for agreeable company. I crave intimacy and friendship, but I suspect I might have forfeited these.

The Fourth Diary – January–June, 1949

Monday, January 3rd

The New Year started with a bang! A bang on the head that is and a couple of razor slashes. I was listening to the wireless yesterday afternoon when the phone rang. It was Frank, who said he needed to see me urgently at one of his clubs in Rupert Court. In retrospect I should have had my suspicions, but I was drowsy after a huge lunch. Certainly Frank had never contacted me direct before and he was so abrupt, my immediate reaction was anger, rather than doubt.

Rupert Court is little more than an alley which runs off St Martin's Lane. Punctual as ever, I arrived on time. I sensed something wrong as soon as I turned off the main road. It being a Sunday evening, the alley was dark and deserted. Turning, I noticed a number of men loitering at the entrance to St Martin's Lane. They were seemingly innocent, yet forming a barrier for anyone wanting to follow me. Three figures appeared from the gloom. The cosh caught me only a glancing blow, but it was sufficient to send me into the path of my second assailant. I recognised the features of a small hunched figure as he slashed out at me with a razor. I raised my hand in self-defence. The blade sliced through my jacket sleeve. There was a jolt of pain, followed by a warmth that spread down my arm. I roared in anger. A second swish of the blade caught my eyebrow, as I instinctively jerked my head back. The third figure launched himself at me. As I ducked, the knuckleduster ripped at my ear lobe. Pain was sent screeching to my brain. Blood splattered onto my shirt front.

They formed a semicircle around me, peering, trying to assess the damage they had inflicted. They paused as someone above us opened a window and asked what the hell was going on. I could hear a radio playing. 'You,' I bellowed. Ferret-face backed off. The other two blocked my path. A light in the shop behind me was turned on. I could see them now. Knuckleduster man was my old friend Charlie. Certain things you never forget. My training at Inverailort Castle was not wasted. Stiff-fingered I jabbed deep into his eye socket. Bull's-eye! He danced a jig of agony and alarm, his initial howls subsiding to the wimperings of a child. 'Go!' I bawled. The man with the cosh was in two minds. 'Now!' Again my army training was helping. It was a command. Perhaps he had served in the forces. He pocketed his cosh and almost stood to attention. 'All right,' he said, 'keep your hair on,' and went off in search of Charlie.

Fred made a dash for it. I sprinted after him. He was obstructed by a line of dustbins that had been left out for collection. He slashed out at me but with little conviction now. I wrenched the razor from him. It clattered to the ground. I could smell his fear. He insisted he had nothing against me and that he had been paid to 'do me'. The cosh man joined us, now no longer a threat. 'You should see what you've done to Charlie. I reckon you have blinded the fucker.'

'I told you to go,' I barked. My head was aching and my blood was dripping onto the pavement. 'OK,' he said petulantly. 'But there was no need to be so bloody violent. We were only going to give you a working over for Christ's sake.'

'Then don't try it again,' I snapped. 'You, drop your trousers.'

123

'Please,' Ferret-face cried.

'Drop them!' I was in a cold fury. 'And your pants.' The cosh man sniggered, now just an interested bystander. With shaking hands, Fred lowered his grey underpants. 'Now kneel,' I commanded.

'Kneel!' I bawled. I shoved his head roughly between his knees. He was crying like a child. Savagely I rammed the handle of the razor up his hairy arse. He collapsed snivelling, feverishly clutching to extricate the razor. 'Jesus,' said the cosher, before he legged it towards the main road, turning round to make sure he was not being pursued.

A group of neighbours stood huddled in a doorway. A couple were trying to comfort Charlie, who was still bleating. I heard a police siren in the distance. It was time to leave. I kept to darkened backstreets, as I made my way home. I was feeling quite faint. Reeling rather than walking, I staggered into the hall to be welcomed by Esther. I was covered in blood. I remember her laying me on the sofa in the living room, whilst she went for help. I was aware of Gaynor tending my wounds, before the doctor arrived. Doctor Bird was well known locally. He had been struck off years before for supplying illegal drugs on prescription. He viewed me with evident distaste. His manner was grand and in no way sympathetic. He did a good job though. Neat stitches and an injection that brought a sense of well-being. I do remember being undressed and tucked up in bed by Beatrix and Gaynor. I apparently even made some extremely disgusting suggestions. Esther was quite shocked. She was also appalled that the doctor helped himself to ten pounds from my wallet, which she felt was outrageous.

Tuesday, January 4th
Much hilarity today. Beatrix and Gaynor had come to
my aid immediately on hearing of my condition from
Esther. An increasingly distressed punter was left
manacled and forgotten whilst they tended to me.
Returning a couple of hours later, they found an elderly
gibbering wreck, who had convinced himself that he
was in the early stages of a kidnap attempt.

The doctor came again this morning. I am to rest
for a couple of days. I had a constant stream of callers.
Welcome initially, but tiresome by the afternoon. Harry
rang. He was very agitated. He denies his brother had
anything to do with me being set up. I don't believe
him. He is coming back from Brighton tomorrow. He
urged me not to confront Frank, without him being
there. For the moment I am content being looked after
by my nurses of mercy. I think Esther is rather overdoing
it, with my invalid diet consisting of a thin soup and
steamed fish. There is something really comforting lying
in bed being looked after. I'm reminded of childhood
illnesses, surrounded by familiar household noises and
the hum of the traffic.

Wednesday, January 5th
Crisis meeting at Frank's office. I still look a real sight
and am feeling weak. Frank plays the innocent. He
would, wouldn't he! He doesn't have a club in Rupert
Court. It was not him on the phone. I should have
checked. What happened to my bloody army training?
Fred and Charlie had a go at me because they had
been exiled to Paddington with their slags and they
resented it. Frank was working himself up into a fury,
but was it genuine? Harry looked uncomfortable, but

insisted my assailants were finished in London. Banished for good, he added. His use of English is faultless when it suits him. I doubt if I will ever be able to prove anything one way or the other. Our relationship has changed though. They are more wary of me. Charlie is still in hospital. Local gossip says he may lose his eye.

I have a mangled ear and a scar of honour on my eyebrow. I have earned my stripes. I'm just furious my suit jacket has been ruined.

Friday, January 7th
Still feeling groggy. Light supper at Luigi's. Conversation in the restaurant stopped when I entered. Service more attentive than usual. When I called for the bill, I was told there was no charge. News travels fast, I am now someone to be feared. I left the waitress a tip that was probably more than the bill. I hope she's allowed to keep it; Luigi is a fat, obsequious slob.

Had a visit from the police yesterday enquiring about my 'punch-up'. The same guy who regularly gets a pay packet from Harry. I told him to bugger off. He appeared quite offended, insisting he had a job to do. Going through the motions more like. I've obviously been cast as a mean tough guy, so I shall act the part.

Thursday, January 13th
I took Esther to the Prince of Wales Theatre to see *Harvey*, which opened last week. My way of making up for completely ignoring Christmas presents. Sid Field and Athene Seyler were wonderful in the lead roles. I wore a new suit I've had made. It's black and loose-fitting. Esther prefers me as I was. Am I consciously

trying to look tough? Black does convey a certain menace. The current state of my face only adds to that impression I suppose. Quite funny really.

Saturday, February 8th

I have fired Karl Cripps. Far from frightening the girls, the Terrible Teuton merely sampled their wares, and takings have continued to fall. Harry has become increasingly agitated. It must be tough living on the thousands he has coming in each week. He insists his expenses are massive and escalating. Would you like to swap, Harry? I'm still as broke as ever.

I have persuaded Harry to spend some more money. Each girl's flat is to have a window hatch. New maids are to be hired and they will be responsible for collecting the money after each punter leaves. The maids are to get a better wage than available on the open market and are to be threatened with dire consequences if they are tempted to cheat. To help offset the girl's annoyance at the new arrangements, we are introducing a dress exchange scheme. Fashionable clothes will be purchased on a regular basis and changed every month. The outfits will then be cleaned and passed on to another girl of the same dress size. More work for me, but most of the girls welcome the idea. Are they all stupid or just amazingly vain? The maids will now pay the money into Greek Street, rather than the girls. Will it work? Maybe for a while, but everyone will soon start milking the system. Perhaps I should start putting my hand in the till, I'm sure Harry wouldn't know.

I've noticed Frank hanging around here more recently. I think he's still tempted to stage a coup. Illness or not, Harry is certainly losing touch. Maybe he's contemplating retirement. He could certainly afford to. There is no way I would work for Frank. My life remains a mess.

Friday, February 14th
My interviewing of the girls who answered the adverts was a farce. I know I have sunk pretty low, but there's no way I can hoodwink a star-struck kid from Chichester to walk the streets. A couple of girls were accompanied by their mothers. So embarrassing. I felt really guilty, pretending to be a talent spotter. Some insisted on doing their act for me. I did sign on a couple of girls from Manchester. They were already on the game up there and understood the coded message in the advert.

Felt thoroughly depressed. Went on a bender at the Colony with some other deadbeats. Out-of-work actors, artists who haven't picked up a brush for months and professional alcoholics. We all have one thing in common, we talk rubbish. Loudly.

Thursday, February 20th
Harry back from a holiday in Palma. Slimmer, suntanned and angry in that order. Turnover is still only slightly up despite all our new plans. There is also much more police activity. He is convinced they are targeting the girls. I think he's bluffing me. They are just going through the motions. Two-pound fines are hardly draconian. Harry appears to find it impossible to be honest with anyone on a consistent basis. There is still a great deal going on of which I know nothing. I'm still only a clerk, and yet if things do go wrong, I have an increasing impression I will be 'the fall guy'. I do

get the odd free meal and discounts on most things I buy, because I now have something of a reputation. In truth I'm really pathetic, trudging around in satanic black pretending to be something or someone I'm not. I must make a complete break, before it's too late.

Saturday, February 22nd
I'm still making regular visits to St Patrick's. Am I a hypocrite? I think it's calmness I seek rather than enlightenment, or even forgiveness. The place seems to encourage me to think more clearly. It creates an atmosphere where I am able to place my existence in some sort of perspective. Once again I have decided to transform my life. It is only a question of whether to apply to go to live in Australia or South Africa.

He was waiting for me in the vestibule. Father Boldini. He wanted to know why I didn't attend Mass. I told him I wasn't a Catholic. He was unfazed. 'Did I need to talk?' 'What, confession?' I queried. 'No, just talk. Would I fancy a coffee?' I felt awkward. I told him I had an appointment and left rather abruptly. I must have appeared extremely rude. I want to talk to someone. Why not him? I need help.

Tuesday, March 8th
I now have sex twice a week with the girls I recruited from Manchester. Tuesday afternoon with Doreen who is dark and bubbly. I think she has a touch of the tar brush. Skin like milk chocolate. She originates from Liverpool. She never stops talking – I mean, *never!*

Viv is bigger and older. She's not even attractive or amusing like Doreen. I think she's quite frightened of me. I don't know what she's heard.

Wednesday, March 9th
We have completed the appointment of all the new maids. Harry is smiling in anticipation of increased earnings. The catering side seems to be picking up. I have opened a deposit account. I can't remember ever having spare cash. I feel happy for once today.

Friday, March 11th
Had a mug of tea with Father Boldini (Tony, we are now on Christian-name terms). He insisted on buying. Perhaps he feels mine is the devil's money. We sat, a strange pair, in a steamy workmen's café. He's really rather impressive, intelligent, amusing and far too good-looking to be a priest.

Our discussion is wide-ranging, yet avoids any mention of my involvement with the seamy side of Soho. He's clever, though. Almost without being aware of it, I have told him about my upbringing and my split from Mary. Nothing about the war though.

He was very open about the difficulties of growing up in London during the war with an Italian name and parents who were interned. He's smart, but I sense he feels he has an obligation to save me from a life of sin. He suggests we meet again next week. I'm not really sure I want to, but I agree. He has an air of innocence about him, underlined by a guileless smile. I imagine he gets his own way most of the time.

Monday, March 28th
Stunning news. Madam Beatrix is to retire. She has bought a bungalow in Peacehaven. I can't believe it, but I suppose we all have to hang up our boots sometime

(in her case, it's her whip). I am arranging a farewell party. Harry says he will pay. Amazing!

Monday, April 11th
What a party! We took over Quo Vadis in Dean Street, the building where Karl Marx lived when he was in London. What a motley crew. Street girls, favourite punters, shop-owners, pub barmen and a couple of gatecrashers. Beatrix was soberly dressed, as becomes her new persona. A casual onlooker would have imagined a valued manager or secretary was retiring. Harry made a moving speech, about a lady who had dedicated her life to the service of others. Beatrix beamed. We all applauded. Gaynor cried. Although the drink flowed, there was no ribaldry and decorum was maintained until she was presented with her farewell gift – a multi-thonged whip with a gold-plated handle. For a moment it seemed that the evening would degenerate, when one of her regulars prostrated himself across the top table, but luckily he was playing it for laughs. We all sang 'For she's a jolly good fellow'. There was scarcely a dry eye to be seen. What a crazy world I inhabit and yet, at times like this, a really warm one. Beatrix has achieved what all the girls seek – a certain financial security and respectability. Harry beamed his way through proceedings, at his avuncular best. He was happy to pick up the tab. Beatrix has become a role model. I will miss her.

Monday, April 18th
Tearful farewells to Beatrix last Wednesday. We waved her goodbye at Victoria Station. Soberly dressed except for a hat more suited to Royal Ascot, she leant out of

the carriage window waving until she was out of sight. Heading south to reinvent herself, in the mould of middle-class respectability.

Gaynor has already recruited Beatrix's replacement. Her choice has not gone down well with Esther. Winnie is stunning. She towers above me, even when she isn't wearing high heels. She is statuesque and curvaceous. She is also black. Esther took a deal of convincing and not a little bullying for her to agree to let the girl from Antigua lodge with us. Her prejudice is born of ignorance rather than malice.

Winnie is the perfect foil for the childlike Gaynor. She also sings. Soulful blues now compete with Welsh hymns. It's a madhouse, and for the moment I love it. Within days, it's as if Beatrix never existed. Winnie fills the house. Not so much with her size, but by sheer force of personality. She chuckles, giggles, jokes, sings. She is a joy to have around the place. Esther is visibly melting. She thought all darkies were dirty and lazy, but Winnie helps Esther with the cleaning and is a sublime cook. They compete to make me amazing meals. Who needs restaurants when you're treated to such a stream of Italian and Caribbean delicacies?

Gaynor and Winnie appear to be the hottest act in town. Queues form in the street. Their takings have doubled. I bet it will only be a few years before they are heading for the South Coast too.

Wednesday, April 27th
I have become quite friendly with Father Boldini over the past few weeks. I still visit St Patrick's regularly, and usually the good priest appears as if by magic. We have now graduated from the workmen's café to a

132

coffee bar on Wardour Street. For our first few meetings we skirted round my activities, but I knew this was central to his interest. We must make a strange sight to casual onlookers, as, clasping cups of coffee that have gone cold, we lean towards each other in earnest conversation.

Today the defences came down. He urged me to quit my sordid world. I tell him I am merely fulfilling a need just like him. I can tell he is annoyed, but he is very self-contained, calmly explaining his point of view.

I went on the offensive and asked if he had ever had sex with a woman. He nodded. 'Is that a yes?' He doesn't avoid my gaze. 'Yes.' 'Since you took orders?' What a cheek I have!

'No!' He shouts his reply. People at the adjoining tables stare at us.

'Do you still think about it?' He doesn't reply. 'Sex,' I prompt.

'Sometimes,' he mumbles. He looks downcast.

I shove the knife in by insisting that at least I am being honest with myself, and, instantly, I feel guilty. He is a good man, but he has demons to fight like the rest of us. Women obviously adore him. Waitresses, whores and matrons all look at him with a far-away look in their eyes. We are sometimes taken as brothers. I am flattered, but our fleeting likeness only underpinned by our both wearing black.

I'm afraid his urgings for me to change my lifestyle are increasingly falling on deaf ears. I am going to apply myself to making some real money, which I hope will allow me to walk away. I realise that I am quoting a familiar mantra, no different from the average girl who walks the streets.

Thursday, May 5th
The world passes me by. I scarcely glance at the papers. The country continues in the grip of austerity, whilst the Chinese are causing trouble in the Far East. None of this impacts on my world.

Harry continues to spend much of the time in Brighton. I pay huge sums into a variety of deposit boxes sprinkled across the West End. Meanwhile I have had to withdraw my limited savings to pay outstanding invoices. I'm not happy.

Friday, May 13th
Unlucky for some! The shop was raided today. The vice squad, represented by an inspector and two constables. I protested, but they went through our books and the safe, which, luckily, was empty except for a few cheques and petty cash. I was questioned by the inspector about a succession of women associated with prostitution visiting our premises. I played the innocent. Aggrieved, hurt and ultimately angry. I demanded to know the name of the inspector's superior officer in my poshest accent. They found nothing. I banked Harry's takings yesterday. The raid was poorly timed. The police withdrew with ill grace. It occurs to me that I'm being set up.

Have I outstayed my welcome with the de Bonos? I know they have 'close ties' with the police. I rang Harry and arranged to see him in Brighton tomorrow.

Saturday, May 14th
Took the train to Brighton. Harry's apartment is almost a replica of Kensington, even down to a painting of

Christ which dominates the living room. Claudia was home on an exeat. God she's attractive and she knows it. She's too old to have a crush on me, but that's how it seems. Compliments me on my new image. The suit, hairstyle, all meet with her approval. Rather embarrassing really. I have fleeting, rather irrational thoughts of marrying the boss's daughter.

Mrs de Bono also seems genuinely pleased to see me. She clucks away, whilst we are served lunch by a chef in full regalia. Tender steak, cooked in a cream sauce. The meal cried out for a good wine, but Harry is on the wagon.

After lunch I joined Harry for a stroll along the promenade. He was unfazed by the police raid. He advised me to arrange a number of different collection points until further notice, with no set pattern or collection times. Mr Wilson was new, he would sort him. How? Surely there must be some straight coppers in London? Harry just sniggered. He's inscrutable. I don't trust him.

Back in the apartment we had afternoon tea. Fantastic apple strudel, but Mrs de Bono insists I have my favourite chocolate cake. I was groaning by the time the taxi came to take me to the station. Harry came down to see me off. He pressed a wad of notes into my hand. 'Expenses,' he explained beaming, pressing my arm. He told me I was doing a great job. He can be charming, but he's as slippery as an eel.

Wednesday, May 18th
I have bought myself a bike. It's only second-hand, but it's a smart James racer with a confusion of gears. I now get up early each morning and pedal up to Hyde

Park, before the traffic builds up. I then run about three miles, before returning red-faced to a huge cooked breakfast.

Friday, May 20th
Dad made one of his infrequent sorties up to town. He has had a small insurance policy mature. He was very chipper. He took me to lunch at Simpson's. I wore a shirt and tie in his honour, but he declared I looked like an undertaker. We had excellent rare beef and a nutty claret. He reckons Uncle Robert has taken a shine to a widow, who has just moved into the village.

The old man asked me to point out my office as we took the taxi to the restaurant. I waved airily in the direction of a building on Regent Street. Perhaps I should let him know about my catering interests. At least they are above board and I could prime Donald before a visit.

Wednesday, June 1st
Winnie my West Indian flatmate informed me at breakfast that she is still a virgin. Spluttering, I showered her with cornflakes. She thumped my back, as I threatened to choke courtesy of the Kellogg's Corporation. Gaynor confirmed her partner's claim, as she drew on her first fag of the day.

I think they are having me on. Winnie insists it's all look and no touch. She's happy to give the punters a real beating, but she assures me it's Gaynor who gets 'the sticky end of the wicket'. They both fall about laughing. Winnie's full of cricketing analogies. Esther tuts disapprovingly in the background.

Thursday, June 2nd
A sleepless night. The same old nightmare.

Friday, June 3rd
Frank called on me today. He has had a visit from Inspector Wilson. He wants me to persuade Harry to come back from Brighton. He reckons his brother isn't taking Wilson seriously enough. Frank may be good at the rough stuff, but Harry has his uses. I tend to agree with Frank. I had a feeling today that I was being followed.

I rang Harry later. He was very relaxed. Too relaxed. He told me everything was under control. He's a cunning devil. I think he gets a kick out of his brother's discomfort. Not all business has to be conducted in London, he told me before hanging up.

Saturday, June 11th
I had a date today. With a normal girl. In other words, she's not 'on the game'. It wasn't a success. Perhaps I have lost the capacity to mix with people outside my own grubby circle. Janice works at Marks and Spencer's in Oxford Street. She's rather pretty, in an elfin-like way and intelligent too; or so I thought.

I took her to see the Arthur Miller play *Death of a Salesman*. Janice didn't like it or me. Lee Cobb overacted in the key role, and I gave a terrible performance in trying to behave as I would have done before coming to Soho. I felt awkward and tongue-tied. I realise my social conversation has all but dried up. Except that is, when I'm talking to hookers, fighters or drunks. There was no mention of us meeting again, when she departed hurriedly after the performance, clasping the large box of chocolates I had bought her.

Disconsolately, I walked towards Greek Street, pausing to hover outside Doreen's flat. She appeared briefly, but there were several men waiting in the shadows. Sad men like me needing to disgorge their frustration. I felt a sense of self-loathing. Lying here on my bed, I have made a vow to enter a period of celibacy.

Sunday, June 12th
The papers are full of a swoop by the vice squad in Soho. Scores of prostitutes have been arrested and illegal clubs raided. The operation was headed by the newly appointed Inspector Brian Wilson. I am aware only a handful of our girls have been pulled in. The freelances and their girls have taken a terrific hit. Harry has obviously worked his magic again.

Thursday, June 16th
Joe the manager at the gym told me some bloke had been asking questions about me. He wasn't sure if he was from the law.

Harry called in. Turnover was still below expectations. More disturbingly for me, we have suffered two bad debts on goods delivered to a small chain of cafés based in Hoxton. I have an appointment with the bank to try and arrange an overdraft.

Wednesday, June 22nd
Told Father Tony that I am a week into a vow of self-imposed celibacy. He shakes his head in disbelief. We now have something in common.

Thursday, June 30th
Went with Father Tony to visit his parents in Kentish

Town. They run Alfredo's, a café specialising in bacon sandwiches – greasy rashers protruding from monstrous doorsteps of bread. Every other delicacy is served with mountains of chips. The chip pan sizzles and tea is served from a massive urn that makes noises like an impatient locomotive. Steam and huddled bodies form condensation on the windows obliterating all signs of life outside.

The place went quiet when we entered. A dog collar has a strange effect on the British public. Tony's mother is tiny, but expansive and welcoming. Both of us were enveloped. His father is lean, balding and more wary. His mood lightens somewhat when he realises I am a friend and not a priest. Mr Boldini is an Italian rarity – an atheist. It's mama who encouraged Tony towards the priesthood. He tells me that his parents find it impossible to agree on anything. They even support different football teams.

The three of them chatted away in Italian whilst we ate a plateful of ham, egg and chips washed down with sweet tea (not a sign of any pasta). Two Italian ladies interrupted our meal. Politely Father Tony rose to talk to them. On leaving they both bent to kiss his ringed finger. Other diners looked on with interest. Mrs Boldini glowed with pride.

We were both very quiet on the bus taking us to Shaftesbury Avenue. I had enjoyed just a glimpse of his family life and of another world. As we walked towards Greek Street several girls stifled their normal 'Looking for a good time?' to say 'Good evening, Father.' He stopped to have a word with each of them. We shook hands as we bade each other goodnight. I don't know why but when he said, 'God bless you my son,' I felt my eyes fill with tears. I was pleased that no one saw me as I climbed the stairs to my bedroom.

139

A visit to Beatrix, 1981

It was some time after my first meeting with Esther that she finally agreed to give me Beatrix's address. She was convinced that my arrival would be unwelcome and embarrassing. I promised I would be most discreet.

Beatrix had moved up the coast, to a small development of expensive houses just outside Worthing. The gentrification of the former dominatrix was complete. She was a social member of the local golf club and a leading light in the Women's Institute. Her whip had been replaced by a trug basket. Her garden, which sloped down to the eighth fairway, was her passion now.

Arriving unannounced, I explained who I was. She welcomed me into the house without a moment's hesitation. She must have been appalled by my arrival, but she gave no hint of it. She settled me in her comfortable chintz-dominated sitting room, before going off to make tea. She told me she had spent the last thirty years half expecting someone from her former life to turn up. The nearest escape she had was when she had been seated next to a Grand Master at a Masonic dinner who had been a regular client at Greek Street. She giggled like a schoolgirl, as she poured my tea, explaining she didn't know who had been the most embarrassed. In the event they both acted as if they had never met, although the Grand Master, a man of pale complexion, coloured each time he spoke to her. As he made his speech of welcome, she had recurring images of him being led round by Gaynor on all fours with a spiked collar round his neck. He was into 'props', she reckoned, suggesting it was probably why he joined the Masons. All that lovely regalia!

Beatrix had married a retired builder shortly after her arrival in Sussex. Conveniently he had keeled over within three years, leaving her financially secure and his daughter bitter and resentful. The builder, a widower, had been fifteen years older than Beatrix. 'No fool like an old fool,' she beamed. He had gone to his grave a happy man. His heart may have weakened, but she insisted other parts of him had staged a bit of a comeback.

Far from being reticent about her past, Beatrix seemed to revel in the opportunity of looking back. It was strange talking to this frail old lady, with her grey hair pulled back in a bun, about her colourful life in London. She spoke fondly of my father. She described him as being far happier than he suggested in his diaries, during those early years in London. He was, she assured me, charming, amusing and kind. Generous, too. She remembered special occasions celebrated at local restaurants. It was domestic scenes that she recalled with most affection. He would always help Esther with the chores. Washing up, hoovering and generally making himself useful. After Sunday lunch the four of them would play cards or Monopoly. It seems bizarre that they made time for such mundane pleasures. She felt that they were a real family. A strange one perhaps, because of their circumstances, but a close one certainly. It was Sundays that Beatrix remembered with real nostalgia. In the morning Esther would go to Mass, whilst the girls prepared lunch. Then after cards a formal tea, which they lingered over. A conventional unit, for a few hours at least, before the girls resumed their normal duties.

The change in my father started after his beating

in Rupert Court. Suddenly he was a feared figure. To Beatrix he seemed less happy, brooding, preoccupied. Not that she witnessed this change for long. She wanted out. She was too old. A new life beckoned. She cut herself from her past, only contacting Esther by sending a card each Christmas.

The next she heard of my father was when he came up for trial. She felt guilty for not attempting to contact him. She said silent prayers for him each night in bed and cried the day of his execution, but it was time to forget the past. To move on and enjoy the rest of her life, albeit latterly with the help of a walking stick.

Travelling back to London, I was pleased I had made the effort to track Beatrix down. My compulsion to uncover the real Derek Emms was still incomplete, but thanks to Beatrix I felt some of the shadows were beginning to clear.

The Fifth Diary – July–December, 1949

Sunday, July 3rd
After lunch we learnt to play canasta. I think we might become addicts. The girls were late 'on parade' because we were having such fun. They lingered over tea, when we polished off the cakes I had bought yesterday from Maison Berteaux. Delicious!

Tuesday, July 12th
Two of Frank's girls were involved in a fight in Gerrard Street. Serious stuff. This has brought some very unwelcoming publicity, both from the police and the press. Frank is seething. The women have been committed for trial. I sense trouble. Harry is impervious. He's just bought himself a Rolls Royce. I took Donald for a drink tonight. He has been working very hard and I wanted to show my appreciation. I was astonished how quickly he became tipsy, suggesting in a roundabout way that he thinks he may be queer.

Poor Donald. He left me and his half-finished drink in a haze of embarrassment. Some of us have darker secrets, Donald!

Monday, July 18th
Harry informed me he had sold a number of freehold properties. I can't understand why he prefers to rent. He is awash with cash and property values are certain to rise. If I ever manage to get hold of any money I will invest it in bricks and mortar.

Wednesday, July 18th
I heard on the grapevine today that Harry is now

selling all his remaining freehold properties. Surely he is not thinking of pulling out? He did tell me that the police are getting greedy.

Now is the time I should break away. I have a couple of hundred saved. I've learnt a little about catering supplies. The problem is the de Bonos would never allow me to set up in competition. Even in a legitimate concern, no matter how small. I'm living in a comfort zone. My job is undemanding. I'm lazy. Father Tony is getting on my nerves, urging me to change my ways. I've told him in future my life is not up for discussion. Fat chance of that.

Saturday, July 23rd
Some idiot decided to pick a fight with me tonight as I left the Nelly Dean. I had never set eyes on him before. I was drinking alone, when he came over and started swearing and abusing me. A group of his friends watched from the other end of the bar. Ignoring him, I finished my drink and made my way to the door. This seemed to infuriate him. He was about my age. Bigger, fleshier and drunk. He hit me whilst my back was turned. A solid blow, behind my ear. The bar went quiet. People edged away. One of his mates smashed a glass against the bar and came towards me. Smiling I extended a handshake in welcome. For a moment he looked confused, until my knee crunched into his groin. He collapsed onto the grubby carpet squealing.

The guy who had originally thrown a punch at me, stared angrily through drunken eyes. He swung at me again, a real haymaker whom even Harry could have avoided. Applying a half nelson I marched him outside. He continued to struggle, so I rammed his head against

144

the pub wall. He went quite limp, so I gently laid him out on the pavement.

For effect I went back in and offered the rest of his pals a drink. They were suddenly very subdued and declined. I think they were just a group of lads out for a drink, but I suppose this latest bust up will underline my reputation as a tough guy, which is crazy.

Sunday, July 24th
I bumped into the bloke who had a go at me in the pub this afternoon at the pâtisserie. He apologised. He's a professional boxer for God's sake! I fear for the state of British boxing.

Thursday, July 28th
Give me strength! Donald has been arrested for exposing himself to a woman on the Tube. This after telling me he's queer. The man is obviously very mixed up.

Tuesday, August 2nd
Donald was fined for flashing. He was very upset by his court appearance. He is desperate that it shouldn't be reported in the papers. He dreads his mother finding out. He has no idea what made him do it. Worryingly, the lady on the train was in her seventies. He cried for ages on his return to Greek Street. I really don't know how to help him.

Wednesday, August 10th
I have been invited to the opening of a new restaurant next week. Jimmy's is a strange choice of name for an area awash with good restaurants. Still there is a certain

logic, I suppose, in having a Greek restaurant in Greek Street.

Friday, August 12th
Went on my own to see Mary Martin in *South Pacific*. A fantastic show, but an occasion that needed to be shared. I was surrounded by couples and family groups. I felt awkward and out of place.

Back home I drowned Gaynor's hymns out with my version of 'There Ain't Nothing Like a Dame'.

Tuesday, August 16th
Had a visit from Bert Hodges, a bookie's runner and small-time crook, who informed me that some 'geezer' from the *Sunday Record* is snooping around asking questions. His interest is not confined to the de Bonos. He's trying to get the low-down on me as well. I gave Bert a couple of quid and asked him to keep his ears open.

Saturday, August 20th
Jimmy's is great. It's run by Jimmy Christodolous and his family. The restaurant is stark. It has whitewashed walls and wooden tables, some of which are covered with seersucker cloths. Moussaka, salad and chips are served piled on huge platters. Fiery wine is slurped from kitchen tumblers.

The place was as crowded as a Tube train. There was the usual cross-section of Soho life, together with old Greek men and large ladies smoking and drinking strong, sweet coffee from tiny cups. Through the smoke haze I could see well-known actors, young artists, writers and the usual smattering of crooks. Some were seated, others stood balancing drinks alongside dollops of steaming moussaka. Loud Greek music added to the general mayhem.

I had a long conversation with a young artist called Lucien Freud. His girlfriend has amazing green eyes, but only for Lucien unfortunately. I enjoyed myself so much I was one of the last to leave. Earlier in the evening I had spoken to a charming journalist called Jeffrey Bernard. He told me a bloke called Desmond Bailey is the crime writer for the *Sunday Record*. It's probably him who's making the unwelcome enquiries. By midnight the charming Jeffrey had turned into a roaring, offensive bigot. I staggered off to my bed.

Wednesday, August 24th
Mr Bailey of the *Sunday Record* is still sniffing around. Doreen tells me she had this strange punter who paid up front but didn't want any action; just information. She assumed he was from the police, but they don't pay good money to sit and talk. This bloke wanted the low-down, not only on the Brothers Grimm, but me as well. In fact, particularly me. Doreen played dumb and pocketed the money. She tells me some of the other girls have had similar visits. I shall have to check out Mr Bailey.

Friday, August 26th
I mentioned our friend from the *Sunday Record* to Harry. He obviously has his mind on other matters. He thinks the tax authorities may be on to him. Money is his overriding obsession. The thought of paying a penny in tax appals him. He is trying to find out who

is handling his case. Faceless bureaucrats are difficult to bribe. It looks like change-of-name time.

Harry tells me to 'sort' the reporter. He doesn't make any suggestions on how this might be done.

Thursday, September 1st
I've seen him. Our ace crime reporter continues to trawl the area. He's now asking questions in local shops and pubs. I followed him today. He even carries a notebook, seemingly taking down conversations verbatim. He's a conventional chap. Slightly down at heel, in the classic mould of journalists portrayed at the cinema. He comes complete with belted gabardine raincoat and trilby. He adopts a crusading zeal. He apparently lectures the girls on their vile way of life. He's been offered all manner of sexual inducements, but affects disgust, hands over his money and leaves. Something about Mr Bailey doesn't quite add up.

Thursday, September 15th
Obsessed with our resident crime reporter. I had a meeting with Frank, but he showed only a passing interest. He suggests getting the bugger 'worked over'. I strongly advise against this stupid idea. I don't think the de Bonos understand that an exposé in the *Sunday Record* could ruin them. Their answer to all problems is either bribery or violence.

Feeling very poorly tonight – so early to bed.

Sunday, September 18th
I have spent the last few days in bed with gastric flu. Once again the girls looked after me wonderfully. I

148

look a dreadful sight this morning. Weight has fallen off me and I am as weak as a kitten. At least I have had a chance to think through my current situation. As well as obvious dangers, I sense the possibility of exciting opportunities.

I ate a little soup for lunch. Feeling somewhat better I managed to keep down some scrambled egg for supper.

We played canasta this afternoon. I lost eight shillings

Tuesday, September 20th
Our ace reporter continues to burrow away. Harry and Frank are only interested in an investigation into their non-payment of tax. I won't warn them again. I will make my own enquiries into Desmond Bailey.

Monday, October 3rd
I followed Mr Bailey back to his home in Colindale tonight. All the way on the Northern Line, strap-hanging. He disappeared into a mock-Tudor semi-detached. Doing my own spot of detective work, I discovered he is not married. He lives with his widowed mother. Hello, Donald! I wonder if there are any other similarities.

Friday, October 7th
We have had a spate of bouncing cheques. I struggled to find enough cash to pay Donald. To add insult to injury Harry has announced that my rent-free arrangement is to end. He intends charging a market rent for both the shop and my room. I'm furious. He insists he has no option. The police have increased their rates, and he is facing a huge tax bill. Bastard!

Saturday, October 15th
It would be a dangerous game, double-crossing the Brothers Grimm. I can dream, though; except the thought keeps me from sleeping.

Thursday, October 20th
The net is closing, but I'm not telling Harry. I shall have to act quickly before the balloon goes up.

Winnie and Gaynor had a visit from Desmond Bailey today. Luckily I had warned them about him. He wanted to know how long they had worked for the de Bonos? How much were they paid? Were they ever physically threatened? They played dim. He became quite angry. Why were they lying? Others had confided in him. He wanted information on me. They confirmed I was their flatmate and that I was in the catering trade. He was now becoming really agitated. In his view I was almost worse than the de Bonos. A product of a privileged upbringing, a former army officer who had become mixed up in a filthy trade. What has being an officer to do with anything. In my experience a commission didn't attach any additional morality to an individual.

To avoid a scene they beckoned him off the street into their 'consulting rooms'. He was scandalised. He scribbled pages of shorthand into his notebook. Scandalised, but fascinated. Winnie thought he was about to become a client. She ran through a menu of temptation. With beads of perspiration breaking out on his brow, he thrust a fiver at her and ran up the stairs as if pursued by the devil.

My enquiries in Colindale haven't helped much. He is a devoted son, church warden and member of the choir. In his spare time he ferries old people to hospital

150

for out-patient appointments in his battered Standard
Eight. He appears almost too good to be true.

Monday, October 24th
Is my luck changing at last? Today I discovered that Esther
has a sister, whose youngest son has recently joined the
Sunday Record. He's really no more than a tea boy, but
I'm meeting him tonight at a pub off Fleet Street.

Tuesday, October 25th
Esther's nephew Terry is a spotty, cocky, Jack-the-lad
know-it-all. He asked the questions; I bought the drinks.
His conversation is full of smutty innuendo. He reminds
me of a boy I was at school with, 'Wanker' Wright.
He's full of testosterone with nowhere to aim it –
except at the lavatory pan that is! I stopped his chatter
in full flow, by slapping a fiver in his hand and promising
plenty more to come, if he could get the information
I require. I gave no explanation, just my telephone
number and a second pint for him to slurp. I emphasised
discretion was essential. Being discreet won't feature
very high on Terry's list of talents, I fancy. I think
be's a greedy little sod, so he may be useful.

Saturday, October 29th
A riotous evening at Jimmy's with a group of aspiring
artists and poets. They seem to think I bring colour
to their lives. I am seen by them as a sort of refined
mobster. Normally I would find this acutely embarrassing,
but I was drunk, so I played the part.

Tuesday, November 1st
A phone call from spotty Terry. Perhaps I have mis-

judged him? Do I see an ace investigative reporter of the future? No matter, but he has been able to confirm that Bailey is on a massive assignment from his editor into the vice trade in London. His research is almost complete. The project is so secret that the files are not being kept in the office. Bad. The series of reports are scheduled to begin at the end of January. Good, it gives me time. I told Terry I was sending him another fiver in the post. Hc's warming to his task. He says he will come back to me in a few days.

Wednesday, November 2nd
Terry rang. Ace reporter has a meeting with a key informant at the Leather Bottle, a pub in Edgware tomorrow.

Friday, November 4th
Terry's information was correct. The snake in the grass is Charlie, complete with eyepatch. A worrying development. Charlie knows a great deal about the de Bonos' set-up. He will also have it in for me.

Thursday, November 10th
Had coffee with Father Tony. He can tell I'm worried, but I don't let on about the *Sunday Record*. I'm amazed Frank, or Harry, hasn't taken on board the danger Bailey poses. Anyway I'm sure it's too late for the rough stuff now. I feel quite impotent. I shall be finished. Donald told me we have had two more bouncing cheques. No wonder I am sleeping so badly. When I do drift off, I wake in a panic, convinced I'm back on that bloody beach again.

Friday, November 11th
An excited Terry rang. Our intrepid tea boy has pinched an envelope from a drawer in Desmond's desk. He was almost caught. Bailey had been called to the editor's office. Usually he is paranoid about keeping his desk locked. Remembering, he returned even before he had left the general office. Just giving Spotty time to lift one envelope from a bulging pile. He assures me I will be astonished at its contents. I'm meeting him at Holborn Station.

Saturday, November 12th
A breakthrough, but not what I was expecting. I thought the envelope might contain some of Bailey's research, but instead it dealt me a potential ace card. I'm not totally surprised. Always be suspicious of those who adopt a holier-than-thou attitude.

Sunday, November 13th
I have contacted Ted Saunders who served with me for a few months. Unlike Alex Cunningham, who is huge and forbidding, Ted is small, wiry and ruthless. He, too, has found it difficult to settle back into civvy street. He works for a photographer in Ilford, taking wedding and passport photos. He jumped at the opportunity of a little excitement. The twenty pounds forwarded helped. My overdraft is creeping towards its limit. I remember a phrase Tim Brunton was fond of using, 'Risk management'. Well, I am taking that to the limit as well.

Friday, November 18th
The trap is set. I went to church this morning. I prayed

153

for the first time in years. My prayers are sacrilegious, but nonetheless heartfelt. I am basing my future on a hunch, admittedly an informed hunch, but a hunch nonetheless. If I'm right, will Desmond Bailey act as I presume? Will he agree to my plans to compromise? What of the Brothers Grimm? How will they behave? There are too many imponderables, but there is no going back now.

Monday, November 21st
I am a bystander. An onlooker. Ted has chosen well. My nerves are on edge. I have been rude to Esther. I should be able to control my emotions better.

Wednesday, November 23rd
The first meeting is planned for Sunday. We are banking on Desmond Bailey being a true creature of habit. Last night I lay awake for hours. Why did Desmond keep his vice files away from the office and yet store all those magazines in his desk? Worried about his mother finding them perhaps.

Sunday, November 27th
The wait at home for the telephone call was intolerable. Obviously I couldn't risk being seen by Desmond. Instead Ted took up his position in good time. Desmond arrived at Dino's at exactly one o'clock, having earlier taken his mother to church. Each week he takes a stack of Sunday papers which he wades through whilst eating a plate of spaghetti, followed by endless cups of coffee.

The seemingly chance meeting worked. The Sunday papers were forgotten. They chatted openly. Telephone numbers were exchanged. Now we must await developments.

Monday, November 28th
Disappointing news. Bailey made no attempt to set up another meeting. He was even wary of giving his telephone number. I may have misjudged the man.

Tuesday, November 29th
Today I'm convinced I've made a terrible and very expensive mistake. Bailey continues to question people about the de Bonos. He appears to be checking out ownership and lease details on some of their properties. It now seems possible that the envelope that Terry took from the reporter's drawer was part of his wider investigation. He's presumably not just targeting the de Bonos. I appear to have dug myself into the deepest hole.

Saturday, December 3rd
Just as I had given up all hope, our friends are meeting tonight. Fingers crossed.

Sunday, December 4th
It didn't happen. Just a trip to the pictures. The flat in Wigmore Street remains empty, unused. It's an attractive apartment on the first floor a few doors down from the Wigmore Hall. It's comfortable without being luxurious. The type of place businessmen who are averse to hotel living use. It has a smallish living room, bathroom and kitchenette. The bedroom is impressive, though spacious and with a dressing room. The bed is huge, but will it be used? Another sleepless night.

My mood is foul. I am in danger of alienating Esther and the girls. I can't help myself.

Thursday, December 8th
How on earth did Ted manage to get such shots without being discovered? The man is a genius. They are enough to make your eyes water.

Ted tells me Desmond hung around the flat for hours this afternoon. Poor chap. The bird has flown, Desmond. Some bird!

Friday, December 9th
Terry rang. The date for the articles has been put back to the end of January. Good. Later I rang Bailey to set up a meeting. He refused. Bad and unexpected. He insisted he had no intention of meeting me. I persisted. Telling him I had something of a personal nature to give him. He was contemptuous. He doesn't have an inkling. He lectured me on my shortcomings and assured me I was finished. Don't bank on it, Desmond.

Sunday, December 11th
The same Italian diner next to Edgware Tube Station. The spread-eagled newspapers. He was startled by my arrival. No doubt he was hoping for the same dining companion as a couple of weeks ago. He made to leave, only sitting down again when I promised I was there to cooperate with him. Well, sort of! I told him I had some vital information for him. He relaxed. I ordered ravioli. He emphasised that however useful I might be, he would still be listing my involvement with the de Bonos in his exposé. I listened to him attentively

as I chomped on my pasta. He enjoys having power over people. I had conclusive evidence of that. 'Well,' he said showing signs of impatience. 'What have you got for me?'

I ordered coffee and passed over the buff envelope. His face showed no emotion. I was impressed. He was a cool customer. So far. 'You stole these? I did miss them. Am I supposed to thank you for returning them?' he said. I didn't respond but just smiled at him. He showed the first sign of discomfort. 'They form part of my investigation,' he was blustering now. I handed him a second envelope. Did the penny drop then? I don't know, but the colour drained from his face. Gingerly this time, he drew out the contents. He was unable to stifle a cry of anguish. People turned, alarmed by his reaction. Panicked, he thrust the photos under the table, feverishly seeking to return them to the safety of the envelope.

I suggested that the shots had produced a good likeness. Rising from the table, I instructed him to meet me tomorrow morning at St Patrick's in Soho Square at ten. He stood hunched, pleading with me to come back. I walked out, leaving him to pay the bill.

Monday, December 12th
I arrived early for our meeting and seated myself in the shadows of a side aisle. It was a perfect venue. Father Tony is away on a few days' deserved holiday. We could talk unseen and uninterrupted. Desmond was late. A full ten minutes. I was beginning to worry that he had found an inner strength and contacted the police. He arrived alone and flustered. I watched him

157

for a few moments, before attracting his attention. We moved further into the shadows.

He was desperate, distraught at the thought of exposure. I suggested that trust should be our mutual friend. His dark secrets were safe with me, provided he co-operated. Neither of us wanted our names flaunted over the national papers.

My plan shocked him. To gain his confidence I brought some additional information, backed up with documentation. I had further details which would guarantee his scoop, once we had established our trust in one another. He tried to demand the incriminating negatives. All in good time, Mr Bailey, you have to dance to my tune for a little longer yet. He understood the score.

I told him that I wanted the publication date for his articles brought forward. I'm still worried that the Brothers Grimm will wake up to the dangers facing them. He promises me he will speak to his editor. We agree to meet again on Wednesday. I went to another church this afternoon. This time to St Martin-in-the-Fields, to witness my old school's carol concert. I sat at the back behind the rows of parents. Years ago I sang the solo of 'Once in Royal David's City'. My mother had been proud of me then. Today I joined in the chorus, but my thoughts were a world away. A murky world.

Wednesday, December 14th
We meet again. The same pew. The deal is done. He gets the negatives, once his articles are completed. I shall keep some prints. A form of insurance. That's show business, Desmond! Not that I expect him to

cause any trouble. Poor chap, kept on asking about John. Actually John is Julian. Julian Templeton, a high-class male whore. Well perhaps not high-class, but certainly bloody expensive. He is normally consort to various well-known celebrities. Very discreet is our Julian. More used to a suite in the Savoy than a flat in Wigmore Street and to well-groomed stars rather than grubby hacks with BO. Forget it, Desmond, you're history.

He tells me the articles will start on January 8th. I gave Bailey ten minutes to get clear. Father Tony was waiting in the vestibule. I thought he wasn't due back until the weekend. Thrown off-guard, I mumbled a greeting whilst struggling with the heavy door onto the street. He didn't reply. I have a crazy idea that he can sometimes read my mind. This makes me feel really uncomfortable.

Friday, December 23rd
Harry invited me for drinks this evening. Frank was there with his wife, Zoe, who I haven't met before. I'm told she used to walk the streets for him. You would never guess. She is haughty and aloof. I am an underling and accordingly ignored by her.

Claudia and her mother made a huge fuss of me. Claudia has blossomed. She is quite lovely.

Harry called me into his study. At last the de Bonos are taking notice of the *Sunday Record* threat. Dangerous ground for me. I played dumb. Changing the subject I told them that I had been to my old school's carol concert. Their eyes glazed over. They are thrown off the scent. I am becoming a convincing liar.

159

Tuesday, December 27th

Christmas almost a rerun of last year. Went to midnight Mass with Esther. This year I have bought Christmas presents, so I'm back in the girls' good books. Christmas Day with Dad and Uncle Robert, who is a changed man. Enter the glamorous widow. Maisie Jenks is amazingly well preserved and good company. I sense wedding bells. Dad more subdued than usual. Jealousy perhaps?

I introduced them to canasta. Fierccly competitive games. I lost twenty-two shillings. Uncle Robert pocketed the money with a satisfied smirk.

Saturday, December 31st

Went to a party given at Jimmy's. The usual eclectic mix, to which was added a band led by Chris Barber. Vocals by an outrageous young man called George Melly.

I was already tipsy when Winnie arrived, looking sensational in a clinging velvet dress. Dancing with her, I had the most enormous erection. 'Well, and I thought you didn't like me,' she said thrusting her groin against mine. She has a wicked laugh. I thought I was about to explode. I did later, several times in her bedroom. She has the most original methods for exciting me to the point of delirium. Well, she should be good for God's sake, she's a professional. She still insists that she is a virgin. Based on my experience, technically she may be right. What a way to see in the New Year!

PART 4
EXPOSURE

Amongst the diaries and notebooks was one newspaper cutting from the *Sunday Record*, dated January 8th, 1950. Photographs of Harry and Frank de Bono are prominent on the front page. The article was headed:

ARREST THESE TWO MEN
THEY ARE THE KINGS OF VICE IN THE HEART OF LONDON

THE DE BONO GANG EXPOSED

by DESMOND BAILEY

Today I offer Scotland Yard a dossier I have compiled which uncovers the activities of a monstrous vice gang that is operating in the West End of London. This is an unsavoury story which will appal every decent citizen. It is, however, one which this paper feels bound to reveal, so that immediate action can be taken.

I intend, over the coming weeks, to expose in detail the way these sordid men operate and profit from their shameful trade. The two men I am accusing are brothers:

Harry de Bono, who is sometimes known as Henry Marshall, lives at Dorchester House, Kensington High Street.

Frank de Bono, whose many aliases include George Harper and Cedric Dempsey, recently moved into a luxury apartment in Bruton Mews, Mayfair.

Although born in Cairo they came to London in 1936 from Malta and hold British passports.

At first glance, it appears these men are engaged

in legal activities as merchants and dealers. More detailed investigations have proved that they control a chain of properties which are used for immoral purposes. There are dozens of women of the streets who are completely in their power. Many of these women have come from the Continent to ply their disgusting trade. Frank de Bono's wife still openly takes part in this life of shame. This is a state of affairs which would disgrace the most licentious ports of the Middle East. This paper considers it a public duty to uncover the de Bonos' operations.

Although the de Bonos have been talked about in high places for years, nothing has been done to close down their operations, which defame the good name of our capital.

Let me put on record some of the facts which I have discovered about these ghastly men and their cohorts. I estimate the de Bonos control well over half the prostitutes operating in Soho. It seems they are able to flout the law because they operate on such a grand scale. I have records, observed over long periods at flats, or other residential properties owned or leased by the de Bonos. They have attempted to cover their tracks by using bogus names and companies to act as a smokescreen for the activities that take place in their properties. Over the coming weeks I will be listing these and the names of the women who use them. Today by way of example let us consider 28 Newport Place. For rating purposes the property is registered in the name of Franco de Bono, whilst next door, number 30, has as its leaseholder George Harper, a name de Bono commonly employs. This flat is constantly used for immoral purposes. The woman operating there is Maxine Brewer, a French national who married a British citizen four years ago. This woman has 132 convictions for soliciting. Between them, the women controlled by the brothers have many thousands of such convictions.

Joan Foster is also a prostitute, working from a flat in Meard Street. Hers is a remarkable story. I have a sworn affidavit from her husband, William Norman Foster, a merchant seaman. He married his bride in Gibraltar on July 12th, 1938. When he met Joan she was constantly in the company of a man he knew as Arthur Sanderson. He appeared to be a man of considerable wealth. He extended lavish hospitality to William Foster, promising him a job in his London estate agency if he agreed to marry Joan. The wedding was fixed, and Sanderson paid all the expenses. Within days of the wedding Joan disappeared, and Sanderson told him she had gone to England. A week later Foster received a telegraph, telling him to collect a cheque for £50 from a local travel agency. It was only then that he realised he had been duped into the marriage, thus enabling Joan to ply her trade in London. The man, Sanderson, was in fact Harry de Bono, for whom Joan Foster stills works today.

Many such women have been imported by the de Bonos, often working in tandem with 'buying' organisations engaged in bringing foreign women to walk the streets of London. Women are taken to Gibraltar or Malta to go through marriages with British citizens. These are often sailors who are picked up in port, plied with liquor and paid up to £100 in cash for their compliance.

Why do these women submit themselves to such a tawdry life? A comfortable flat is provided, together with first-class meals served in their own room. They have no need to worry about clothes, as these are all taken care of. The de Bonos even run their own clothing-exchange scheme. In addition to generous holidays, the women are all offered protection by the de Bonos and their henchmen. They are guaranteed the most profitable pitches. Any freelance who dares encroach on their territory is soon warned off. In exchange for their generosity the brothers expect a frightening level of productivity. My survey logs the average time spent with a client as $8^{1/2}$ minutes. It is not unusual for them to entertain five clients in an hour.

I have made it my duty to check on the prices charged. I found that £2 was the absolute minimum. Later investigations revealed that certain women indulged in the most ghastly perversions. These practices encouraged clients to pay up to £20, for a half-hour session. Not that the women reap the rewards. Each flat is operated by a trusted maid, or madam. In some apartments, glass panels have been installed, so that observation of the amounts of money changing hands can be witnessed. In the following weeks I will report on the savage beatings inflicted on women suspected of cheating. Vast amounts of money are retained by the de Bonos each week. These vile men live in great style. They each drive a Rolls Royce.

I have already given conclusive proof of the guilt

of these two debauched men, who run an empire of vice that is a disgrace to London. Over the coming weeks I will be disclosing massive new evidence of their foul trade. My full dossier is available to Scotland Yard. I hope they will act upon it by arresting these two brothers, who are exploiting women in this appalling manner.

Let me assert I can provide absolute proof of the facts I have recorded. This should ensure that this disgusting traffic in vice is not tolerated for a single day longer.

There was no diary for 1950, or for the first couple of months for the following year. This period was covered by two notebooks written by Derek Emms in prison whilst he awaited trial.

The First Notebook – HMP Pentonville

Cécile continues to visit me in spite of everything. She is amazingly loyal. I had asked her to bring my diaries. They had to be vetted by security and the governor's agreement sought. Reading them has helped to fill the vacuum of boredom which each day presents.

I can't now remember clearly why I suddenly stopped writing my diaries, which had been such a cause of comfort to me over the years. Whilst the imminent exposure of the de Bonos' activities was obviously dominating my mind, I think it was more to do with my indiscretion with Winnie. Our exertions had left us exhausted and we were discovered, still asleep, in the morning by Esther. Horror, disbelief! Her tears were a gentle prelude to hysterics. Her screams brought her an ally. Gaynor was outraged and upset. Winnie tried to laugh the whole thing off whilst I just stumbled around looking for the Alka Seltzer. I really couldn't understand what all the fuss was about.

Esther withdrew all services. She refused to clean my room or cook for me. The atmosphere in the house was poisonous. We both apologised. We promised it would never happen again. (Shame!) I realised that the delicate balance that made us such a happy unit had been disrupted. It was many weeks before the household returned to its former harmony. Weeks that were going to change my life.

During those first days of 1950, I tried to keep a low profile. This was made easier by my disgrace at home. I avoided Father Tony and Harry whenever possible. I ate most of my meals in cafés. I closeted myself in cinemas, even resorting to watching endless cartoons. I was waiting for the balloon to go up. I was in contact with Desmond Bailey by telephone. I think he was as nervous as me. He confirmed the first article was to be published on January 8th. I was convinced that the de Bonos' position was going to become untenable. I reckoned the exposure would lead to their arrest, despite their police contacts. The other possibility was that they would be forced to go abroad. Either way, I was sure that I was about to get the opportunity to instigate the plans I had worked on so meticulously.

The immediate period following publication was the most dangerous for me. Although it was guaranteed that I would not be mentioned in the *Sunday Record*, it was possible that new police officers would be assigned to the case and take an interest in me. Amazingly they made no contact. I was also concerned that Murphy or some other gang might try and fill the temporary vacuum left by the de Bonos' absence. I had already recruited Alex Cunningham, who had arrived the previous week from Belfast. He was staying at the flat in Wigmore Street. I had a meeting there with the big man and Ted Saunders. We had all worked together on some really hairy missions. What I was suggesting was child's play and offered them a lifeline. I knew that both of them had criminal records before the war. They had no scruples about what I was proposing, nor did they express surprise, which I found strange. It is corny to suggest that in the past they were used to accepting my orders without question, but they never once queried my descent into organised crime. I was offering them a fresh start. It was enough. I explained my short-term plans. Fully briefed, we now awaited the waves about to be created by the *Sunday Record* exposé.

169

That Sunday I was up early to collect my copy from the newsagent in Old Compton Street. I sat at the kitchen table poring over the article. Before I had finished, the phone rang and I had Frank screaming at me. I pretended I was still in bed. I feigned shock, stuttering and stammering. True to type, he was threatening to kill Desmond Bailey and carve up anyone who had given information. As his fury subsided, he demanded to know where Harry was. I had no idea. It was evening before Harry rang. His day had been well spent emptying numerous cash deposit boxes. He sounded quite pleased with himself. Mrs de Bono was already on a flight to Paris, and he was holed up at a secret address. Clever old Harry had obviously made contingency plans. It was almost as if he had been expecting trouble. He told me he would contact me when everything quietened down. It never did.

The article caused a sensation. During the next month, twenty per cent was added to the *Sunday Record*'s circulation. Questions were asked in Parliament. Scores of prostitutes were arrested. Winnie and Gaynor took a holiday, both going off to Neath for a few weeks. The basement doors were locked. I attended to my catering business. Alex and Ted waited. Soho was awash with police. Harry kept in touch by phone. I didn't hear anything from Frank.

Each subsequent article produced more damning evidence against the de Bonos. After publication of the third exposure on January 22nd, Harry slipped out of the country, driving his two-toned Rolls Royce. Neither the police nor customs officials made any attempt to stop him. The old fox had woven his magic again.

170

Frank didn't believe in magic. He waved a razor rather than a wand. Seven girls named by Bailey were slashed and taken to hospital. It transpired that only one of them had spoken to the journalist. No matter, Frank dealt in rough justice. I met him in Paris at the beginning of the new year. I have no idea how he left the country. Once more the brothers had used their opposing skills to achieve a like result.

Frightened that I might be followed, I took the most circuitous route to Paris, via Dublin and Brussels. The brothers had taken adjoining apartments on the boulevard Sébastapol, in the heart of the mercery area. Surrounded by needlework and tapestry wholesalers, they were already establishing themselves in a business more familiar to them. Mrs de Bono was delighted to see me. It seemed only the location had changed. The same furniture, the piano and the picture of Christ all spirited from Kensington. There was even chocolate cake. The de Bonos were, it seemed, indestructible. Grudgingly, I couldn't help admiring them.

After the social niceties, we settled down to business. I really believe in their own minds that they had almost written London off. Frank dismissed my initial suggestion. Harry as usual was more astute. I had rightly assumed they were going to attempt to continue their London trade with the help of hired hands. I don't think they had seriously considered that I was either suitable or even capable. For my part, I realised that to set up on my own would have been impossible without their support. To do so would have invited serious injury or worse. We bartered and haggled, each of us trying to extract the best deal. The discussions went into a second day. Their demands were unrealistic.

At times it seemed agreement would be impossible. Harry piled on false charm. It was unthinkable that I could carry on without their support. Slowly they realised that I could be a source of ongoing revenue, albeit at a reduced level. The negotiations were gruelling. Eventually we agreed on a figure, which I knew represented just over half what their average haul had been. In addition, I was taking on all the expenses. Even so, I calculated I should be able to make a reasonable profit, which would allow me to branch out into other areas. Nothing was put in writing. We shook hands solemnly to secure the deal. Frank couldn't resist telling me the consequences of my failing to honour my payments. Harry beamed and opened a bottle of champagne. Arrangements for safe delivery of the money was discussed. It was noticeable that Frank didn't raise his glass to the toast proposed by his brother. At one stage in our negotiations, he had suggested that I was in league with the *Sunday Record*. I exploded in anger, creating a passable impression of being mortally offended. I wasn't sure if he was just sounding off or had real suspicions. Harry came to my rescue. As always, his main interest was money, and I was about to contribute from a source that I believe he thought had closed on him.

They insisted all bets were off when they finally returned to England. I was happy to agree. I was going to make it my job to see that they didn't come back; at least not until I had branched out sufficiently for me not to worry. Worry though, was still uppermost in my mind as I travelled back to London. It was Frank who escorted me down to my waiting taxi. Taking me by the arm, he pushed his face close up to mine. He had foul breath. He told me he couldn't understand why my name had not featured in any of the articles. 'Funny that!' he suggested, gripping my arm tighter. I broke away. 'Not very,' I replied. He assured me that if he ever found I had been implicated in any way he, personally, would kill me. 'Slowly,' he said with emphasis. Smiling, I suggested this was not the way to speak to a partner.

As the commissionaire opened the huge wooden doors onto the street, Frank mouthed off another warning. My old failing. A short fuse. The tension of the past few weeks erupted inside me. I slammed him against the wall. His look of anger slipped seamlessly into one of alarm. Discreetly, the doorman shuffled outside. I had Frank pinioned. His eyes changed gear again. Genuine fear now. He yelped with pain. His foul breath enveloped me. I told him never to threaten me again. Probably a mistake on my part. The eyes had reverted to position one; slits of black anger and resentment. Harry appeared. Smiling, he ushered me to the door, like a referee coming between two boxers.

'Don't worry,' he kept repeating. 'Everything is going to be fine.' And it was, for a few weeks anyway.

On my return from France every petty crook was trying to get in on our act. Most visible and voluble was Mick Murphy and his boys, taking time off from the racetracks. They had come looking for me. Unfortunately they had trashed the shop, smashing the stock and putting the fear of God into Donald. Worse, they then tried to force their way into the house. Luckily, Esther kept a chain on the door and was able to slam it shut. Fuelled by alcohol, the Murphys had then conducted a disorganised tour, threatening our girls and claiming to be their new boss. Think again, Mick! I was not about to be intimidated by these deadbeats.

Alex and Ted were waiting patiently in the Wigmore Street flat. It was time to let them off the leash. Alex was from the Shankhill in Belfast. He was a self-confessed bigot, with a hatred of everything Catholic and Republican. He couldn't wait to get to the Murphys. Our plan had been made as a contingency before I left for France. Now it was confirmed; Murphy had to be taught a lesson. Four new recruits had been selected by Alex. I never knew who they were. They were all ex-colleagues of the Ulsterman. It was a job. They were paid and then disappeared. The less I knew of them the better.

Ted had done the surveillance job. Murphy hung out in a prefabricated building, posing as a café, on a bomb site just off the Essex Road in Islington. It was his territory. The local police had never risked a raid. There was a stand-off, an understanding. Murphy confined his activities away from his home patch. In return, the police kept a low profile. A sensible agreement which suited both sides.

Ted had learnt that an important meeting had been arranged at the café. Murphy's gang members were constantly changing, but it was reckoned that, on average, there were about fifteen of them. Presumably the get-together was to discuss their plans for expansion into Soho.

A black Ford van had been hired for our journey to north London. Black was the predominant colour that night. Everyone except Ted, who was driving, was

174

blacked up. Clothes, balaclavas, faces. Memories came flooding back. The familiar tightness in the pit of my stomach. Parking the van, we slipped into the shadows. Ted had now blackened his face.

The café was perched on an island of rubble, set back from the road. Inside, lights blazed. We could make out quite a crowd standing around drinking and smoking. We eased our way up to the building. I could see Mick Murphy lounging back in an armchair beside a serving hatch that looked through to the kitchen. I noticed that the gathering appeared to be some sort of celebration. Voices were raised, punctuated by raucous laughter. It wasn't coffee they were drinking.

There was a small yard behind the kitchen, littered with rotting vegetables which hadn't made it into the overflowing dustbin. A foul smell hung heavy in the night air. I was to take the back door, with Ted and one of the recruits. Alex and his team were to take the front route. We waited whilst Ted slipped off. Nervous now. Excited. It seemed an age, then the lights went off. We crashed in throwing fireworks. Just bangers. We shrieked blood-curdling cries. The element of surprise. There was confusion. Grunts, shouting, swearing. Bodies were sent crashing to the floor. They were easy meat. Mainly large and out of condition, their reactions slowed by drink. Our torches went on. Blinding light, more confusion. Murphy and a man in a loud check suit slashed out with razors. Alex caught the suit man a mighty karate chop. He fell to the ground without uttering a sound. Murphy was looking for the exit, but Alex moved quickly for such a large man. Murphy dropped his arms, shrugging in a gesture of surrender.

I was fascinated, Alex was almost gentle with him. He accepted the razor Murphy was offering in defeat. Alex carefully folded it and pushed it into his trouser pocket. Murphy didn't speak. He had a stupid grin on his face. The sort of expression a young boy tries on his mother when he's been caught doing something terrible. It never worked with my mother. Murphy must have realised charm was not about to win the day. Alex was still quite gentle as he pressed his hands on pressure points either side of Mick's neck. For a moment there was a convulsion, before he, too, sank to the floor. Rolling him onto his back, Alex then stamped on his groin. The cry was frightening. It silenced the room.

We counted fourteen including Murphy. His disciples left standing were lined up, arms extended, fingers pressing against the wall. We bound each of them round the ankles, using electrical wire, which cut into them as they tried to keep their balance. Murphy was coming round groaning, his hands clutching at his crutch. Sweeping glasses and plates from a dirty table, four of us hoisted up the whimpering figure. We forced him into a kneeling position, holding onto him so that he didn't fall. We tied his wrists and ankles with wire. One of his friends made a lunge for us but fell helpless in a blaspheming heap. It was humiliation time. I had to leave a trademark sign. Savage violence now I reckoned would guarantee less trouble in the future. I yanked his trousers and pants down. Alex rammed Murphy's head between his knees and handed me the razor. 'Stop in the name of God,' an Irish voice cried out. Ted toppled the dissenting voice. Murphy's huge white belly was quivering like a giant blancmange. He cried for his mother and Jesus in that order. Alex

176

parted his cheeks. I was becoming quite an expert. Roughly I thrust the handle of the razor as far as it would go. He made only a small whimpering noise. Nobody spoke. Alex held onto Murphy so that he didn't fall. We left him wavering, trussed like a turkey. Several of his men had chosen to slide to the floor, to relieve the pain of the wire biting at their ankles.

Alex wiped the blackboard that had listed the limited café menu. He wrote in large capitals 'STICK TO THE RACE TRACKS, PADDY'.

I honestly hate violence and yet my whole adult life has been tainted by it. I was conscious that by degrees I was being drawn into its web. I tried to convince myself that war had dehumanised me. Yet many men had settled back into a contented civilian life. My sense of being quite apart from the mainstream increased. I was convinced that my ability to even mix with ordinary people had been eroded. I had become some sort of a freak, incapable of sensitive feelings. I was confined to the perimeters of life. My friends were either crooks or drop-outs. My love life – well, I didn't have one. Sex I had, but it was furtive, guilt-ridden. My reputation in Soho had never been higher, but I was full of self-loathing.

News travels fast. Our trip to Islington established our control. Humiliation is hard to throw off. Mick Murphy was damaged goods. His authority on the race tracks was challenged. Within weeks he was back in Dublin. Wild rumours swirled around. We were feared. Both Alex and Ted played the part. I had a visit from Inspector Brian Wilson accompanied by a very smooth sergeant. They went through the motions of questioning me about Islington. Of course I had an alibi. I told them I was outraged by their enquiries. It was a game. I knew Wilson was on Harry's payroll. The sergeant was, too. You didn't get the kind of suit he was wearing from the fifty-bob tailors. They were fishing, worried about a change in terms. I wanted nothing to do with the police on a direct basis. I suggested a chat with the smooth Leo Joseph in Berwick Street. I've never trusted lawyers, least of all him, but it was about time he earnt his massive fees.

Within weeks the fallout from Desmond Bailey's articles had declined. Questions had been asked in Parliament. Police had crawled over the area. Fines had been issued to almost every girl, or woman, working the area. Public reaction was of short-term outrage. More to do with the de Bonos being foreign, despite their British passports. Letters to the press emphasised the jingoistic nature of British public opinion. All foreigners were suspect, lacking in morality. Prostitution, they declared, was a filthy business, never controlled by the honourable British. Sorry, folks! And what about the punters? As a country, we are the world champions of moral indignation.

I thought I had struck a good deal with the de Bonos, but within weeks I was having serious doubts. Harry had been truthful for once. The outgoings were frightening. I was staggered at how many people had to be kept sweet. My income was way down on the de Bonos', whilst my expenses were greatly increased, not least because I had offered Ted and Alex such a good deal. Despite their looming presence turnover stubbornly refused to rise. I was seriously worried.

My plan had been to invest any spare money into property. I was genuinely anxious to expand my legitimate

178

business interests. Takings continued to be disappointing. I tried to obtain an overdraft from a number of banks but without success. I was a novice. My catering business was not inspiring confidence. Bankers wanted carefully kept accounts and well-researched business plans. I had neither. Donald reported difficult trading conditions. I was convinced the girls were continuing to short-change me, despite the reputation of Ted and Alex. I suspected they were straying as the wrestler had before them. Men and sex, the temptations are just too great. By the late summer, I actively sought Harry's advice. He suggested another trip to Paris.

Apart from money worries, life was not too bad. Winnie and Gaynor were back in business. Esther had forgiven me and was cooking me wonderful meals again. I had discovered another favourite restaurant, the Moulin d'Or in Romilly Street, where I took the girls occasionally as a treat. My only domestic worry concerned my father's health. I felt guilty about neglecting him, and when I finally made time for a trip to Hertfordshire, I was shocked by his decline. He now walked with the help of a stick and was constantly short of breath. The glamorous widow no longer visited. Much to Uncle Robert's distress she had taken up with their local doctor, whose wife had only died a few months previously. Tongues wagged, and Robert reverted to type – the original miserable old sod.

During that summer, I started going to watch cricket at Lord's. Compton and Edrich ruled supreme. Sitting in the packed stand, I was conscious that this was my attempt to make some sort of connection with the real world.

The Second Notebook – HMP Pentonville

I was frustrated at my inability to secure a loan from any of the leading banks. It was denying me the opportunity of breaking into legitimate business areas. I was anxious to regain a measure of respectability, which at the time seemed so important to me. I was convinced that there was going to be a property boom and I needed to get my foot on the ladder. My long-term plans were designed to lead me far away from my present environment. Perhaps, stupidly, I imagined a comfortable country home, with a wife and children. I craved a conventional life, instead of my sordid, violent world. My immediate problem was a lack of collateral. Meetings with bank managers in panelled offices, clutching unconvincing ledgers, had been disappointing. I decided new tactics were required. Mr Perkins from Harvey's Bank had accepted my invitation for lunch at Wheelers. The plan was then to take him back to look around the shop. Donald had been briefed, the stock carefully displayed. I was hopeful.

I was on my second gin and tonic, by the time the head waiter gave me the news. Mr Perkins had telephoned his apologies. He had been called to a meeting at head office at short notice. Furious, I was about to leave when the waiter asked if I minded sharing my table. A bulky figure slipped into the seat opposite. My companion introduced himself as Harold Jacobson. I mumbled my name in response. Smiling, he said he knew of me by reputation. He insisted on sharing his excellent Alsace wine. He was a convivial companion. We had a wide-ranging conversation, encouraged by a glass of port taken with our cheese course. He had the unusual ability of drawing information from me that I would normally withhold from a total stranger. At least there was no need for embarrassment, as he knew what business I was involved in. So I regaled him with some of my ideas for altering perceptions about what I coyly called the glamour industry. I was convinced attitudes were changing as more liberal voices were beginning to be heard. I could see a future for magazines, films and even discreet live shows in clubs. An industry not confined to a furtive existence. He appeared fascinated.

We met several times for lunch over the coming weeks. He reckoned it would be years before my ideas would become acceptable in Britain. It would require money to be spent on lobbying those with influence, particularly politicians. At one point we did discuss the possibility of forming a joint venture, but nothing came of it. Jacobson had informed me at our first meeting, that he was a property developer. He became an influential figure in my life at that time. I explained I was anxious to get involved in the property market. He was generous with his advice, explaining some of the complexities that existed. He had become enormously wealthy through his dealings, and I was hopeful that, once I had a basic knowledge, I could mirror some of his success.

Current legislation played right into the hands of the developer. The Rent Restrictions Act controlled rents in unfurnished lettings at pre-war levels, whilst giving security of tenure. Huge tracts of London property are owned by aristocratic landlords. Many families had bought the properties at the turn of the century and sold 99-year leases, relying on this investment as a source of income. However, most of the original tenants had now moved out, and after the war many of the properties were being sublet as flats, or even single rooms, for returning servicemen. Now, to their dismay, many of the descendants of the original owners found themselves in charge of buildings crammed with all manner of undesirables. In many cases the landlord only received the original rent. Well, what did they expect from a socialist government? Many of the families were deciding they wanted no dealings with 'the great unwashed'. The trend was set to sell the properties with sitting tenants. Enter Harold Jacobson and others. The trick was to empty the houses and then to sell them free of tenants on the open market for huge profits. How? Easy, as I was to prove later. As for capital, well, who needed Mr Perkins when there were unregulated building societies willing to issue mortgages.

It was just the first tranche of money I needed to get me going. I 'borrowed' five hundred pounds from the de Bonos in November and purchased my first house in Paddington. It was a rather splendid porticoed building. It had five storeys, counting the basement, five floors of peeling paint, rotting floors and penetrating damp. Five separate units, purchased for £3,400. Now all I needed was for the tenants to leave. As I was due to go to Paris in December, I decided to let them enjoy their Christmas. Then I would send in 'the persuaders' – Ted and Alex. Nice man, nasty man. I was confident the house would be on the market by the spring

I cancelled my visit to Paris in a show of independence. Within days Donald took a call, insisting I was needed urgently. I was busy with the Paddington house. I rang Harry's apartment. No reply. Reluctantly I took a taxi to the airport. I felt uneasy about the trip. How right I was.

Change. From the moment I was ushered into the apartment by a uniformed maid, I could sense it. Taste it almost. A lighter less traditional hand had transformed the room. White predominated. The carpet, its pile so deep that my shoes were almost submerged. Linen curtains stark but for seemingly random slashes of black abstract print. The furniture ultra-modern. Only the grand piano retained its former position, unencumbered now by family photographs. No carved sideboard, no patterned rugs, no picture of Christ, and no Harry or Mrs de Bono. Change. Enter instead Zoe, Frank's wife, followed by her scowling husband. He escorted her politely to an uncomfortable sofa. She sat demurely. I registered her modest black dress.

Then the bombshell! The first that is. Harry was dead. How? When? An accident on New Year's Eve. A heart attack whilst driving on icy roads. Frank's face somersaults from menacing stare to that of a bereaved brother. Zoe dabs at her eyes with a handkerchief. The eyes are cool and aloof as they stare out at me from behind the lace. Change and not for the better. My mind races.

The couple sit close together. They hold hands. Family solidarity in a time of trauma? I wasn't buying that. Seismic change, which I realised, spelt danger.

I only knew of Zoe by reputation. One of a rare breed; a woman who is feared. She formed a harsh, unforgiving partnership with Frank. He dispensed rough justice, but it was normally Zoe who first passed sentence. The fear factor had served them well and brought them huge success.

I enquired about Mrs de Bono and was told she was in Palma with Claudia. I wanted to know more. Blank stares were my reply. End of discussion. I got the message. I kept my own counsel.

Frank smiled at me, his face had not been designed for smiling. He had no laughter lines, just deep furrows etched into his forehead. Only half his face responded, creating a lopsided leer. He delivered his second bombshell. Why, he wanted to know, had I stolen £500 from Harry's takings? How the hell did he find out? My explanation that it was only a loan hung limply in the air, unanswered except for a sigh of exasperation from Zoe. There was more. They knew about my house purchase in Paddington. I have a spy in my camp. I remember the old maxim – 'never apologise, never explain'. I stared at them defiantly. Zoe lit a cigarette, deliberately blowing the smoke in my face. Both my pride and my eyes were smarting. 'You think you are so clever and tough, don't you?' she said. Again I didn't give her the satisfaction of a reply. Instead I treated her to one of my superior smiles, which I know is guaranteed to irritate. The colour rushed to her cheeks, and her false eyelashes danced in annoyance.

'Fucking AMATEUR!' she shrieked, as if 'amateur' was the most profane word in her entire vocabulary.

I returned to London bemused and flabbergasted by events. Harry's death was a shock. It was also suspect. They had obviously contacted Desmond Bailey. What was he playing at? Astonishingly, it was neither of these developments that was obsessing me.

That afternoon in the apartment on boulevard

Sébastapol there had been no discussion. Frank dictated the terms. They were crazy. Totally unacceptable. I protested, I refused to be neutered. A folder was thrust across the glass-topped table. Why was I shocked? Threats were made. Suddenly my position was frighteningly weak. I found it difficult to think clearly. I needed time. I didn't respond, attempting to create an air of confidence that I didn't feel. He expanded on their plans. The victorious look on Zoe's face was hard to stomach. My life was lurching out of control.

A taxi took us to the restaurant. It was empty except for a couple of waiters. No Parisian eats willingly at six o'clock in the evening. Frank and Zoe chatted. I downed a large whisky. I needed it. A waiter escorted a slim, dark figure to our table. She was obviously nervous. So was I. She was wearing a simple but expensive black dress. Mourning or just a fashion statement? I couldn't tell. I guessed she was about my age. Attractive in a frail, rather haunted way. Her hair was dark and shoulder length. She had good bone structure and eyes that changed colour in the candlelight. A classy face, except for the makeup.

Standing, Frank made a passable imitation of his late brother. With a smirk, he introduced me to Cécile. Solemnly we shook hands.

'I hope you will both be very happy,' he said. I sensed her wince. Her eyes, deep-set and camouflaged by mascara, threatened tears. Behind her, a thick-set man stood holding the hand of a beautiful three- or four-year-old.

'OK, Xavier,' Frank's gesture was dismissive. I recognised the look. Xavier was angry, but not afraid. For a moment I thought he was going to stand his ground.

Instead he exchanged a glance with Cécile, before turning. We watched him leave. Instinctively I crouched on my haunches and took the child's hands in mine. 'And what's your name?' I asked in my faltering French. For a moment her face stayed wary and solemn, before breaking into a cheeky grin.

'Nadine,' she replied.

PART 5
CONTROL

The Sixth Diary – January–December, 1951

Wednesday, February 28th
What a bloody mess! I swither from impotent rage to irrational amusement at the ridiculous predicament I find myself in. I try to obliterate my worries by a punishing run round Hyde Park. I then sprinted home on my bike like a demented Reg Harris. After a shower and breakfast, it's off to the gym. I work out with a dedication that even impresses the professional wrestlers. Fingertip press-ups, squats and a medicine ball hurled at my stomach by a middleweight who fights under the name of Pansy Potter. He is outrageously camp, but a fine fighter. A brave one too, enduring a torrent of abuse wherever he performs. I like him; he makes me laugh. Although I am aware arranged marriages are often successful on the Subcontinent, my proposed one hardly falls into that category. Forced, not arranged, is what I am to be subjected to. I must contact Desmond Bailey. How much did he tell Frank?

This afternoon, with physical therapy not working, I went out and got blotto. Staggeringly drunk, mindlessly pissed! Tonight I feel ghastly. I have vague memories of Esther putting me to bed. More depressingly, it was Father Tony who found me throwing up in the gutter on Wardour Street. He guided and cajoled me home. Apparently I was extremely unruly. My dignity has flown out of the window. I once thought I could absorb pressure; that's another illusion gone.

Thursday, March 1st
Plenty of black coffee this morning, with looks to match from Esther. Head splitting, I rang Desmond Bailey.

He was very evasive. I had to get angry before he agreed to meet me tomorrow.

I lay in bed for most of the morning feeling sorry for myself. I had the king of all hangovers. Esther decided it was the time for spring-cleaning. She has a cruel streak. The Hoover shrieked all around me. There was a conspiracy. As the house finally fell silent, Gaynor moved into singing mode and Winnie turned her wireless up. Opposite builders had started erecting scaffolding. Assailed by noise, I made a vow to give up the booze. The monastery calls!

Friday, March 2nd
I met Desmond at the delicatessen in Old Compton Street. They have a couple of tables marooned amidst the hanging hams and sausages. The place never looks too clean, but the coffee is good. Desmond was nervous, constantly looking at each new customer as they entered. He is deathly pale and has lost weight. He blames me for all his troubles in a whining voice, which I find intensely irritating.

I think I already knew what had happened; I just needed verification. He had received a visit from a couple of Frank's heavies. They slapped him about a bit. Poor Desmond, he obviously only enjoys that treatment in different circumstances. Within minutes he handed over his carefully documented file on me. He had convinced them that this was to be the basis for a second exposure. Well done, Desmond! Unfortunately Frank is now using this file to bend me to his will. Presumably he feels I am more use helping to earn him money than having me locked in one of His Majesty's jails.

Ironically both Desmond and I are now held hostage. He by the photographs I have retained, and me by the damning evidence Frank now holds against me. I would be a convenient scapegoat; an easily dispensable one. Desmond scuttled off, insisting he never wants to see me again. That will depend, Desmond.

Tuesday, March 6th
Writing my diary again is a great comfort. Words are permanent. You can refer back to them. Thoughts are just transitory, floating away, most soon to be forgotten. My problem is that the words covering my current situation don't make comfortable reading. For the moment I can't see how I can get out of this mess.

In just over a month's time I am to marry a woman whom I have only met once. What's more she has a child! The whole scenario is crazy. Somehow Frank expects this woman to transform his London business. Because she is a French national, she has to marry a Briton to enable her to work legally in England. Enter me, the fall guy! I have to dance to his tune or I will be exposed via the *Sunday Record*. Perhaps I should call his bluff and take my punishment. At least I would be able to start afresh on my release. Sorry, I don't fancy five years' slopping out. I'm a chancer. I always think I can slide away untouched. Who am I kidding? My gradual decline has turned into a gallop.

What the hell has Frank got over poor Cécile? I'm sure she is horrified at the prospect of marrying me. I understand that Frank and Harry bought their way into the Paris trade. Just like any other company takeover, worried no doubt that London appeared a lost cause.

Cécile, who had been the grand madam of the Paris organisation, has been placed on the 'transfer list' to enable Zoe to take over. How is this rather sad, little French woman going to transform Frank's Soho revenue? I'm quite unable to understand what the hell is going on.

Why don't I call Frank's bluff? Laziness and the thought that I can still extricate myself. Whilst ostensibly I remain in charge of the London operation I am in fact being sidelined. I am reduced to ensuring that no newcomers are allowed to set up in the area. My wages (Frank's description) will be paid to me weekly by my wife. She will have control of all money matters. I am to be neutered. On the plus side he has agreed I can develop some limited business interests, providing it doesn't conflict with his. Amazingly, he has suggested our first nuptial home should be Harry's old flat in Kensington, which still has three years of its lease to run. Only one snag: nobody seems to realise that my divorce from Mary hasn't even gone through yet. I'm keeping quiet.

Monday, March 19th
I knew it was too good to be true. Until now Mary has shown no inclination to rush our divorce through. Enter Leo Joseph. He tells me the decree absolute is due to be finalised next week. Once again I have underestimated Frank.

I have been trying to avoid Father Tony. He keeps telephoning. Today he called and there was no evading him. We are to lunch together tomorrow. What on earth can I tell him? I know I'm in for a long lecture. I deserve it.

Tuesday, March 20th

Lunch at Jimmy's in Frith Street. The dog collar has the usual effect. Everyone on their best behaviour. The noise level is way down, and there is no swearing. The waitress treats him like royalty. Other tables are ignored. Jimmy insists on giving us a carafe of wine on the house. Perhaps he thinks God will reward him for the gesture. Father Tony was rather embarrassed by the preferential treatment. I must try and find a Greek Orthodox priest to take. Free meals for life then, I reckon!

Tony didn't take long to say he is seriously worried about me. Snap! The confessional is probably the biggest plus offered by the Catholic Church. I only have my diary. I can't open up to a priest even though he is a friend. We used to talk about important things, football, music, gossip. Now he can't wait to lecture me. He wants to save me from myself. I wish he could. Instead I have an urge to shock and hurt him. I succeeded. I told him of my intended marriage to someone I have only met once.

I think he genuinely cares about me. After initial anger, he became quite watery-eyed. I can't bring myself to explain the truth of my situation. Poor Father Tony, surrounded by sin and corruption. I really believe he thought he could release me from my shitty lifestyle. We are the last to leave. Jimmy had contributed a second free carafe. This time it was me that guided the tipsy priest back to his presbytery.

Monday, March 26th

Good news at last. The house in Paddington has sold. I have money. The most I've ever had. I paid the cheque in with a flourish. The Alex-and-Ted combination

193

worked brilliantly. I must reinvest in another property. It's a lousy business, evicting people from their homes, but easy money. I have to banish any remaining moral qualms. I am still finding it hard not to hate myself. My old middle-class values do consistently try to assert themselves. I really don't have the thought processes of a crook, but that's what I am. It's time I faced up to reality. My latest imaginary escape route is based on a few more property deals and then an honest, conventional life. No chance. I'm hamstrung. Imprisoned by my own weakness.

Frank rang this afternoon. His earnings have taken a tumble. Usual threats and insults. No mention of the future Mrs Emms. Can I hope he has dropped his madcap scheme?

Wednesday, March 28th
Leo Joseph rang. I am a single man again. I celebrated with a vigorous session with Doreen, trying to imagine she was Winnie. No joy!

Sunday, April 1st
The dreaded phone call. Cécile is to arrive with her child on April 19th. I told Winnie and Gaynor I was going to be married. They thought it was an April Fool's joke. The girls were all very glum at the thought of me leaving.

Monday, April 2nd
Leo Joseph forwarded the keys for the Kensington flat and his bill for concluding my divorce. He doesn't need to break the law – he's a legalised crook. I'm in the wrong business!

Tuesday, April 3rd
It felt strange walking round Harry's empty apartment.
Only the carpets remain and piles of unopened mail,
which I took home. I have ordered the bare essentials,
a settee, chairs, dining furniture and three beds. One
double and two single. Well, you never know! Anyway
I can't have my bride and child coming over to an
empty flat.
    Why is she coming? What does Frank hold over her?
My mood swings are extreme. Walking round the flat,
I almost convinced myself that I could be happy in
my new situation. I conjure Cécile up in my head. For
a moment I project her as a sexy temptress. In reality,
I think she is a mousy, tight-lipped whore who will be
minding the purse strings. I hate her. I also loathe
myself for getting into this impossible situation.

Wednesday, April 4th
Most of Harry's post is outstanding bills. His tailor,
garage and Harrods are all obviously unaware of his
death. A couple of letters did intrigue me. One from
a law firm in the City, with a copy to Leo Joseph,
confirmed the sale of a freehold property in Lisle Street
to Redruth Property Ltd. A list of directors included
Harold Jacobson. Intriguing!
    Another letter was addressed to Claudia. It had been
forwarded on by her school in Norfolk. It was postmarked
Paris. Feeling rather guilty, I slit the envelope. It was
written in French. With the help of a dictionary, I was
able to gather the gist. The writer spoke of a violent
family row. It suggested her father was in real danger.
Just that. No suggestion for action, just a warning.
    The letter was signed *X*. A kiss or a name?

Tuesday, April 10th
The plot thickens. Esther received a letter today. We have new landlords, Redruth Property Ltd. I tried contacting Harold Jacobson by phone. The number is no longer obtainable. Strange!

Thursday, April 12th
A phone call from the odious Zoe. She issues orders like a disgruntled sergeant-major with dyspepsia. I am to meet the future Mrs Emms and child at Heathrow and take them to the flat in Kensington. Cécile will have the relevant instructions. Zoe cajoles and threatens me. I feel like telling her to bugger off; instead I tell her how attractive and sexy I find her. I'm not convinced she understands irony. She hung up on me anyway.

Saturday, April 14th
Tonight I'm back in my own bedroom. Cécile sent me packing. She arrived with a nanny as well as the child. Trouble is Alex is due to move in here next week.

The good news is Cécile's English is rather better than my fifth-form French. Close up she is neither the sexy temptress nor the tight-lipped harridan. She is very petite and attractive. The accent helps. She was obviously very nervous and yet self-composed. Her little girl, Nadine, is too young to understand what's going on. (She's not alone there.) The kid is stunning. She's very dark, with piercing blue eyes. She clung to her mother, whilst I played the fool. This was my way of trying to find favour with her. She viewed me from behind the longest eyelashes, as if I were mad. The maid, or nanny, is fat, sullen and smells of garlic.

I had assumed I would be staying the night, but

196

Cécile said she needed a couple of days to settle in. Our initial relationship is strange or more accurately strained. We are like two fighters shadow-boxing, neither of us quite sure where we are in the pecking order. God knows what they have told her about me. She has a certain presence on the surface. We have agreed to meet in my office on Tuesday morning. Bidding me goodbye, she smiled and suggested we were going to have to make the best of our crazy situation. I have a feeling we will not be enemies.

Later. Woken up by Winnie speaking in a hushed voice. My hopes and prick rose in tandem. No such luck. Winnie had broken the key to a gigantic padlock which was chaining a Lancashire industrialist to the wall downstairs. Winnie and Gaynor went off to bed, leaving me with the punter and a rusty hacksaw. I insisted on helping him into his underpants before setting to work. A sense of unreality, as I sawed away, whilst he explained the continuing problems in the cotton trade. He showed absolutely no embarrassment at his predicament. He tipped me five shillings, when he was eventually freed.

It was three o'clock before I was back in bed. This time it wasn't wartime horrors that kept me awake, rather the thought of Winnie in the next bedroom. I must cut all these thoughts from my mind; after all I'm to be a married man shortly.

Tuesday, April 19th
So many questions. Cécile was selective in her answers, as we sat huddled in my office for most of the day. She shuts up like a clam when I try and find out what

leverage Frank has over her. She is frightened. She insists that they have threatened to kill her child. Specifically Nadine will be targeted if Cécile doesn't dance to their tune. I really find that hard to believe. Exposure through the press seems quite tame by comparison.

She kept referring to the de Bonos in the plural, even though Harry is dead. Nasty shock! It appears there is another brother, Carlo, who operates from Milan. She assures me that he makes Frank seem benign. Their aim is to extend their influence throughout Europe.

I asked Cécile about Harry's death. Was it really an accident? This is another no-go area. The woman appears genuinely petrified. How this slip of a thing is going to get total control in London, where we have failed, beats me. She has arranged to meet Alex and Ted tomorrow.

Over a lunch of sandwiches and gateau, we finally discussed our marriage. I'm left in no doubt that it is purely a means to an end. She asked me to arrange a date, as if setting up a business meeting. I want to ask her about Nadine. Was Cécile married? Who is the father? I sense these questions must remain unanswered for the moment. Who knows, we may have a lifetime together.

Of more pressing importance to me is where I am to live. I had assumed in Kensington. Cécile told me she will think about it. I feel miffed. Instead of thanking me for furnishing the place, she criticises the fact that I didn't supply any kitchen equipment. This was soon rectified. She has ordered a sizeable chunk of our stock, with no offer of payment. I think I've drawn the short straw!

Much of the day was devoted to business. She sighed and tutted, as she went through each girl's individual takings, writing copious notes in a childish hand.

Saturday, April 21st
What a woman! Why did I think she was a timid mouse? Alex and Ted came to me licking their wounds. No sex with the girls, unless they pay. Disobey a single order and they will be looking for a new job. They are to get a generous weekly wage, but any fiddling and they are out. They are hurt by her tongue-lashing but accept the new order. They seem to think she is acting on my behalf; I didn't disillusion them. I've obviously been too lax.

Later Cécile asked me to show her round our territory. She dressed discreetly in a smart black suit. The two of us must have looked as though we were on our way to a funeral. I chatted to a number of girls as they stood on street corners. Cécile stayed silent, assessing each woman like a general inspecting his troops. Unusually there was no backchat from the girls. Either they have got wind of the change, or they understand Cécile's type. I sensed some sort of unspoken communication being transmitted.

We trawled every street and alleyway, starting in Newport Place and gradually working northwards. Finally in Soho Square, I gave a mock salute. 'Tour of inspection completed, madame.' She didn't smile. Hailing a taxi, she invited me to lunch tomorrow. Before I could answer, the cab had driven off.

Sunday, April 22nd
I arrived at one o'clock. The table had been set for

199

three (cutlery and glassware courtesy of yours truly, delivered with the kitchen equipment by Donald yesterday). The flat had been transformed. Attractive curtains, side tables, lamps and a huge radiogram had been added to the purchases. Tapestries and prints lined the walls. The place had a homely feel. I congratulated her on the changes. Shrugging, she gave me a kir, glancing at a gift-wrapped box I had brought. 'For Nadine,' I said. Her face relaxed, and she called for the child to join us. Nadine stood at the door, staring suspiciously at me from under her fringe.

The doll was a success. I bought it at Hamleys yesterday. It is an unconvincing brown colour and yet the cheeks are rosy. More importantly, the eyes open and shut. Cécile scolded me for spoiling the child, but was obviously delighted by my gesture. Nadine nursed it on her lap, still not sure about this strange man who had come into her life. I went through my repertoire of tricks and made paper aeroplanes, which I flew out of the window onto the traffic below. Still only the glimmer of a smile. She's her mother's daughter, that's for sure.

Lunch was a nightmare. A running battle between Cécile and the nanny, who was accused of ruining every course. Eventually the poor woman stormed off to her room crying. I enjoyed the meal. Cécile is a hard taskmaster.

I left about four, having still not raised the question as to when I can move in. It's difficult with Nanny taking what I thought would be my room. No headway there, but at least the child is gradually warming to me. As I was leaving she called out, '*Au revoir*, Captain,' before giggling and, clutching her doll, disappeared into her bedroom.

Wednesday, May 2nd
Cécile has been too busy to get married. However, the wedding has only been delayed not abandoned. Friday is the appointed day. My stag night is due to start in a couple of hours, allowing me twenty-four hours to recover.

Strangely, my thoughts have turned to Mary. I wonder where she is tonight? Is she happy? In spite of myself, I hope so. She was so convinced I was going to be successful, part of the Establishment.

Thursday, May 3rd
The idea was to drink our way through every pub and bar in Soho. I finally collapsed in the Coach and Horses. Alex put me to bed. Whilst Esther was out shopping, Winnie paid me a quick visit, considerably raising my spirits, amongst other things. I couldn't think of a better wedding present.

Saturday, May 5th
Well, it's done. Strangely, I enjoyed it. Not the service, that was soulless, but the day. I tried to do the decent thing. I bought the engagement ring with three goodish diamonds from a contact in Hatton Garden. 'Knocked off', I'm sure, but I bought the platinum wedding ring from a proper jeweller. Perhaps I'm superstitious, but I reckon a stolen wedding ring would be unlucky. I think Cécile was embarrassed, not just by the rings but by the support of my friends. Gaynor insisted on singing a hymn at the registry office, and Winnie covered us in pounds of rice. Esther had bought a new outfit, whilst Alex and Ted wore matching Prince of Wales check suits. A dozen or so of our girls attended,

as did Jimmy from the Greek restaurant and a few drinking chums. Speeches were made, toasts proposed, magnifying my sense of unreality.

On the surface, the whole occasion was rather conventional. Unfortunately my wedding night was not. Cécile refused to entertain a honeymoon, not even a weekend away. I spent the night on the sofa. Cécile did peck me on the cheek as I settled down under my blanket, but I noticed she locked her bedroom door.

Sunday, May 13th
I am still running in Hyde Park most mornings, before cycling back in time for breakfast. Outright war has been declared between Cécile and Nanny. Cécile is very hard on her. I'm beginning to feel quite sorry for the woman. I have started taking Nadine to a little playschool just round the corner from the flat. It's run by a splendid titled woman named Lady Slater. She insists on speaking to Nadine in French, which is worse than mine. I am finding it easier to get on with the child than my wife. There is something deeply humiliating about being handed a wage packet by her each week.

Cécile leaves the flat each morning after breakfast, returning in time to read Nadine a story before putting her to bed. She then goes back to Soho, sometimes not getting home until the early hours. She is amazing. She has managed to greatly increase the takings. Each girl is set targets and coached on how to increase the turnover. She is a great motivator using the carrot-and-stick approach. Alex and Ted are in awe of her. Even Frank is purring. She works as if she is haunted by the thought of failure. My duties have been relegated to the routine.

I have identified another property I want to buy in Maida Vale. As usual I am short of funds, my previous profits having been largely spent on furniture and the engagement ring.

Nadine is now sleeping with her mother, so at least I have a bed.

Friday, May 25th

A ghastly day. I went on my weekly visit to Doreen. She was crying and refusing to let me in. After much coaxing, she opened the door. She was nursing a bruised lip and was minus a tooth. She appeared petrified of me, sobbing and not making much sense. Eventually she told me it had been Ted and Alex who had been responsible. They had accused her of cheating. I am beside myself with fury. I know I have sunk pretty low, but I could never condone the beating of a defenceless woman.

Saturday, May 26th

Had a massive row with Cécile last night. She insisted that Doreen had been ferreting money away and I was only concerned because the woman was my whore. What about the others, she asked? There had been a series of beatings since Cécile arrived, which had all been blamed on violent punters. I have been duped.

My shouting woke up Nadine, who was frightened by my out-of-character behaviour. I stormed out and went to the pub. Cécile stayed up for me, and we had a calmer conversation. I insisted that in future there is to be no violence in getting the girls' cooperation. Cécile is convinced her child is in danger if she doesn't reach Frank's targets. I think that is nonsense. We talked into the early hours. Neither of us are prepared to be locked into this life for ever. For the moment though we can't see how to break out. At four o'clock we went to our separate beds.

Monday, May 28th
I read the riot act to Alex and Ted. Are they so stupid that they will follow any order? Probably. The British Army has a lot to answer for.

Thursday, June 7th
I hope I haven't overstepped myself. I have bought two adjoining properties in Maida Vale on a huge mortgage. They are not as grand as Paddington, but hopefully will show me a good profit.

Tuesday, June 12th
Had a call from Leo Joseph. He wants me to contact an Inspector Sweet. I have a feeling he is the expensive suit, who presumably has been promoted. Trouble?

Friday, June 15th
Lunch at the Savoy Grill with Inspector Bob Sweet. He booked. I paid. Inspector Wilson has been transferred to CID, and Sweet is now working under a nameless chief superintendent. The under-secretary at the Home Office has set them the task of tackling prostitution in the West End. Neatly dissecting his Dover sole, he suggested that arrangements could be made to suit all parties. He talked. I listened. He told me a gang of Corsicans were about to challenge our position. Initially they were working to bring all the freelance girls under

their control. 'Then...' He left the word hanging, smiling annoyingly.

The police he maintained were just seeking containment. They could never stamp out prostitution, but they wanted a degree of control. To work with someone they could trust. Another sickly grin. I waited for the punch line. They required a massive single down payment, plus a regular sum paid monthly. No other money was to be paid to any other police officer whatever the circumstances. In return, all our competition would be cleared from the streets, the Corsicans and remaining pimps jailed.

I told him his figures were crazy, but that I would report back. I also insisted we meet up with his new boss. He was evasive. I'm not sure his superior is even involved. I've agreed to meet him again next week.

I can sense an opportunity here. Can I trust Cécile or will she get all hysterical about the danger to Nadine?

Saturday, June 16th
I am still trying to come to terms with the figures. The down payment is far too high, but only having to pay one monthly sum is interesting. Currently, we are forking out money to seemingly every copper who enters our patch.

Sunday, June 17th
I have told Cécile about the Sweet copper and outlined my plan. She is shocked and appalled. Perhaps she will tell Frank, in which case I've had it. I don't care. I'm demob happy. This little scheme could secure my future. Cécile's, too.

Saturday, June 23rd

I rang Sweet and postponed our meeting until the first week in July. Cécile still hasn't spoken to me about the proposal. I'm pretty sure she hasn't ratted on me to Frank.

I now own the Maida Vale properties. Initial indications are that the tenants are going to be more of a problem this time. Three or four families are refusing to budge. I've told Alex and Ted to threaten only. I don't want any rough stuff.

I took Nadine to the cartoon cinema this afternoon. She's nagging me to take her to see *Bambi*. Cécile continues to work all hours, and when she is home just finds fault with Nanny.

Tuesday, June 26th

Cécile arrived back this evening for the ritual bedtime story, before putting Nadine to bed. To my surprise she suggested I might like to take her out for dinner. We went to an Indian restaurant in Beauchamp Place, not so much for the quality of the food, but because the tables are set back in alcoves and it is possible to talk freely without being overheard.

She told me that Donald was a spy reporting regularly to Paris. It had been him who had let them know about the £500 I had borrowed from the takings. This and the threat to Nadine are her overwhelming worries. She understands that a new arrangement with the police could enable us to bank serious money each month, but annoyingly she says she can't risk it. She is also worried about Leo Joseph. So the answer is a big 'no'.

Even so, I enjoyed the evening. She is very intense, but probably because she feels so vulnerable. At least she is delighted that I have become so attached to Nadine. We have agreed to take the child to see *Bambi*. Back at the flat we had a brandy together. Sadly, I made a clumsy pass at her. She slipped away to her bedroom locking the door, leaving me feeling pretty abject.

Saturday, June 30th
What a lovely day. I actually felt like a member of the human race for once. Nadine was one of the few children who didn't cry when Bambi's mother was killed. Her bottom lip quivered, but no tears. I enjoyed watching her, as much as I did the film. Afterwards, we had tea at Lyons Corner House in The Strand. Nadine thought it was very grand. Even Cécile approved. Crowded tables, brightly dressed waiters carrying huge trays with cakes and pots of tea. Pure theatre for a child. It was impossible to find a taxi when we left. We walked for miles, Nadine asleep on my shoulder. Cécile can see how fond I have grown of the child. For the first time since we were thrown together Cécile is at ease with me. Her body language is more relaxed. She smiles more, jokes sometimes and teases me. She has toned down her makeup. Tonight I told her how attractive she looked. She seemed embarrassed. Later as she prepared to go to bed, she kissed me goodnight. On the lips - a real kiss! I'm so sex-starved I now think of her in much the same way as I used to when I lusted after Winnie.

Monday, July 2nd
Inspector Sweet was anything but - sweet that is. He was visibly angered by my refusal to go along with his

plans. There were veiled threats. This has the potential for turning nasty.

Wednesday, July 4th
Against Cécile's advice I have put the fear of God into Donald. Like Desmond he had been contacted by Frank and threatened with extreme violence. He was tearful and full of regret. I insisted he owed me loyalty (what's that?). He agreed. I offered him protection. He was grateful, grovellingly so. I promised if he let me down in any way, his mother would learn about the incident on the Tube. He was appalled. Anything but that. Even being beaten up. In future, his reports to Frank will be vetted by me.

Thursday, July 12th
Three Maida Vale tenants are refusing to budge despite us turning off their electricity. Enter a group of young West Indians I met last week. They called into the office looking for work or accommodation. I have let Maida Vale to them rent free for three months, providing they hold regular noisy parties. They can't believe their luck.

Sunday, July 29th
Real movement on the romantic front. Tonight Cécile and I had what could be described as a heavy petting session on the sofa. I think she had been drinking earlier in the evening. Never mind, it's real progress. I thought for a moment that we were going to consummate our marriage at last, but it was not to be. We are engaged in a rather coy and protracted courtship. She's mighty attractive. Not beautiful, but

incredibly sexy. Fabulous legs. She's playing me like a fish on a line. I just wish she would hurry up and catch me. Tonight I feel happier than I have done for ages.

Saturday, August 11th
I sense a new agenda. Four of our girls were arrested last night. Three were beaten up, presumably by the Corsicans. Alex wants to smash them straight away. I've told him to lay off whilst I make enquiries.

Monday, August 13th
Sweet rang. He says Saturday is just a beginning. There is nothing he can do to help prevent massive problems developing for us. Devious sod. I've arranged to meet him on Thursday. I've explained the situation to Cécile. No hard façade now. Floods of tears. She is petrified. We are caught between corrupt police and the unstable de Bonos.

This evening Cécile had a terrible row with Nanny, who was obviously fed up with the constant criticism. She packed her bags and walked out on us. More problems.

Thursday, August 16th
The inspector's demands are quite specific. Either we play ball or we are finished. I played for time. I told him his demands were outside our gift. I'm not sure if he knew we were still working for Frank. Maybe not. He gave nothing away, poker-style. I offered him half what he is demanding. He laughed in my face. I have forty-eight hours to consider, then I can expect mass arrests and the Corsicans to take our place.

Friday, August 17th
It had to be done. We visited a club owned by the Corsican boys in Leamington Street and left our calling card. Fairly typical, they talk tough, but when it comes to action, up goes the white flag. The customers fled. Our foreign friends insisted we had misunderstood their intentions. Donald could be getting a good order for glasses and crockery, most of which were smashed. I think they have got the message.

Saturday, August 18th
It has taken all my powers of persuasion to get Cécile to agree to my plan. She insists jail is preferable to risking her child's life. We argued for hours. I'm convinced Nadine is in absolutely no danger and the way things have been organised, it is highly unlikely Frank will ever know what we are up to.

I have reached an agreement with Sweet. Half the down payment he was demanding, but the full monthly payout to be honoured by October. This way we should be able to maintain Frank's takings as the competition is gradually culled.

Donald was easy to bring on board. My major worry was Leo Joseph, the dodgy lawyer. Enter Inspector Sweet, who paid him a visit. I imagine, like the rest of us caught up in this web of intrigue, he is frightened by, rather than having any loyalty to, Frank. Sweet maintains the police have enough on Leo to send him down for a long stretch. Smiling, he assured me the solicitor was firmly in our camp. I hope so.

Thursday, September 27th
We are now over a month into our agreement with

Sweet. The down payment was difficult for us, as Frank would have been suspicious about a drop in the takings. Cécile and I took money out of our own accounts to pay the police. Cécile obviously has some capital tucked away, and I was able to make a contribution. I hope that smarmy bugger Sweet is not going to do the dirty on us. So far only a couple of girls have been arrested and the Corsicans continue to operate. We are going to have a real struggle making the first payment. Cécile is in nagging mode. I know she is worried, but she is driving me mad.

The drop-off of the cash will be varied each month. Different times, places and personnel will be involved. I just hope we can afford it, but I have agreed not to make any more direct contact with Sweet. Doubts and worries are crowding in on me.

Monday, October 8th
At last! What a relief. Massive police activity today, with dozens of arrests. Cécile still hysterically nervous. Our relationship has regressed. She irritates the hell out of me. We argue and bicker. That's marriage for you! I'm still in the spare room. That's not!

For the moment I'm a nursemaid. Most of my day is taken up with looking after Nadine, but I get no thanks for it. A new nanny from a local agency starts next week. She's fat, fifty and French.

Thursday, October 16th
I can't see the new nanny lasting long, although I rather like her. She is a wonderful cook, but generally disorganised. Cécile constantly carps. She is a dreadful employer.

Saturday, October 19th
My birthday. Cards and presents from Cécile and Nadine. Nanny made me a cake. I'm rather touched. Cards, too, from Winnie, Gaynor and Esther.

Friday, October 26th
The money is beginning to flow. Each week I deposit the surplus in two deposit boxes at Harvey's Bank. At this rate, I reckon in two or three years I will be able to disappear and reinvent myself. Getting a new identity will be difficult and expensive, but not impossible. Australia beckons.

I bumped into Father Tony in Berwick Street market today. I feel rather guilty; I've been ignoring him. We have agreed to meet for lunch next week.

Monday, November 5th
We all went to see a firework display in Hyde Park. Very spectacular, but freezing cold. Walking home, we bought bags of roasted chestnuts. It was a real family occasion. Cécile is being friendly to me again. I lust after her, but she has shown no sign of interest. My visits to Doreen continue. Sad man!

Friday, November 9th
My meeting with Father Tony was really relaxed. We went to see his parents again. Ate a massive fry-up. Wonderful at the time; galloping indigestion later. He told me Cécile was a regular visitor to the church for weekday Mass. I had no idea.

Tuesday, November 13th
Completion on Maida Vale properties today. I have

never had so much money. I have convinced myself that money will provide my escape route. Let's hope I'm right.

Nanny has given in her notice. I don't blame her. Nadine unwell tonight. We called the doctor. She's got chickenpox.

Monday, November 26th
Although I was in a deep sleep I was vaguely conscious of movement in the next-door bedroom. Cécile has been getting up most nights to check on Nadine, although she is much better now. Gradually I was aware of someone drawing back the blankets and a warm body next to mine. I recognised the perfume. Neither of us spoke. She had not given the slightest indication that this was about to happen. Our lovemaking was frantic, greedy and not altogether satisfactory. Then she was gone. I called after her, but I heard her door close and the lock clicking. This morning at breakfast neither of us mentioned what had happened.

Thursday, November 29th
I have finally been admitted to my wife's bedroom. Nadine is much better, so the three of us breakfasted in bed. Nadine seems to think that the situation is natural enough. We are no great love match, Cécile and I, but we are friends and more importantly allies. Sex does help. We are both more relaxed. Do we have a future together?

Saturday, December 8th
Cécile remains totally secretive about her background after her childhood. She talks openly about growing

213

up in Normandy. The rest is a void. I'm pretty sure she was once 'on the game'. I imagine she doesn't want her child to know, hence the mystery. We all live with secrets, but I would like to know who Nadine's father is.

Tuesday, December 11th
Doreen is miffed that I don't visit her now I'm a respectable married man. She's surely not jealous? I notice she avoids criticising Cécile.

Friday, December 14th
A special treat today. We went to a late-night performance by Noel Coward at the Café Royal. He was fantastic, so witty and seemingly 'off the cuff'. I don't think Cécile really understood how clever his lyrics are. She didn't think much of the food. Typical bloody French reaction.

Monday, December 24th
Cécile joined me for midnight Mass at St Patrick's. Rather embarrassing. We were shown to the front pew. Pride of place with half of Soho there. I get the impression that Cécile was once quite a devout Catholic. Now, of course, she is denied the sacraments. Father Tony greeted us warmly enough.

Tuesday, December 25th
A difficult day introducing Cécile to my father and Uncle Robert. They had both been invited to our wedding. I was pleased at the time that they had declined; Robert by choice, father due to declining health. We had rehearsed our lines. The catering business

was flourishing. I don't think they approve of Cécile, but Nadine carried the day. Uncle Robert only icily polite. Dad looks dreadful. He refuses to see a doctor.

Monday, December 31st
I find New Year a melancholy time. I worry about what lies ahead. Cécile reads my mood. As midnight sounded we clung to each other with a real intensity. I would never admit it to her, but I know we are skating on pretty thin ice.

Meeting the Ace Reporter

By 1984 I was already a familiar face on British television. My rise had been meteoric. I first appeared on a children's programme, recruited for my ability to produce instant sketched portraits. A studio audience of youngsters voted on a famous celebrity whom I had to sketch within a three-minute timeframe. This had to be done without reference to photographs. Fortunately I knew the short list prior to the programme. I found producing a likeness of a pop star or footballer really easy, but it wasn't my artistic ability that caught the attention of leading producers. I was at ease in front of the cameras. I was declared a natural. I quickly built up a young fan base. I moved on, introducing a series of inane game shows. Then another change of direction. Using my knowledge of art, I fronted six programmes on the Pre-Raphaelites.

Star status beckoned. I grew my hair and wore trendy clothes. The lady readers of the *Sun* voted me 'top male totty' of the year. It was about then that I started my daily radio programme, which, of course, is still running, as well as a weekly chat show on BBC1.

I can't honestly remember why I attended the farewell party for David Fane, the TV critic for the *Daily Record*. I had only met him a couple of times, but as he had consistently given me good reviews over the years, I suppose I felt he would appreciate my support. He did. It was a relatively low-key affair held at a restaurant in Conduit Street. There was the usual mix of television executives, PRs, hacks and minor celebrities. The drink flowed, press photographers snapped, and I sought to make an early exit without appearing too rude. Trying to extricate myself from a pushy author, who was insisting her readers would love to see her interviewed on my show, I was alerted by a snippet of conversation from a group standing next to us. Rudely turning my back on the romantic novelist, I realised that the conversation was concerning David Fane. Not the TV critic, but in a previous incarnation as a crime reporter for the *Sunday Record*. He had been quite famous, an ageing hack confirmed, writing under his real name – Desmond Bailey.

I think he was flattered by my invitation to lunch at Inigo Jones in Covent Garden. Even more so, at my insistence on sending a car to pick him up from his home in Colindale. I knew he didn't drive any more. His rather crumpled appearance was in stark contrast to the smart restaurant. Clothes obviously held little interest for him. His tweed jacket had leather patches at the elbow, and his trousers, secured by a plastic belt, were several sizes too large for him. Yet his appearance was obviously still of some importance to him, his slicked-back hair dyed an unconvincing black.

I led him gently, unsure how he would react to my revelations. We gossiped. Outwardly he was rather prim, but scurrilous none the less, each rumour seemingly uttered as if he had been caught off guard and quickly partially retracted. He was performing, wanting to be overheard.

I waited for coffee to be poured before I explained the real reason for our meeting. His reaction was that of a poor actor trying to register devastating news. He didn't speak. He didn't have to. In quick succession, his mouth dropped open, the colour drained from his face and sweat broke out on his forehead. Alarmingly the dye from his hair formed two rivulets, which meandered towards his nose. Instinctively, he brushed a hand across his face, then his napkin. For a moment I thought he was going to cry. I repeated. 'I am Derek Emm's son.' He still didn't speak. I explained my father had left diaries and that he had featured in them. No response. He continued to stare, as if too scared to move. I assured him I was only trying to find out as much as possible about my father from surviving contemporaries and I didn't want to upset him.

Regaining some composure, he asked to be excused. He needed to collect his thoughts. I watched the rather sad figure weave his way through the crowded room towards the gents. Ten minutes later I asked a waiter to go and check that he was all right. He had left, informing the driver waiting for him that he was taking the Tube home.

I didn't give up. Each day I rang. Each day he hung up. I called at the house. He didn't answer the door. I wrote repeatedly. He didn't reply. I couldn't force him to talk to me. I resigned myself to the fact that here was one part of the jigsaw that would remain empty.

With no prior warning, I received a letter from him in July 1989. It read:

Dear James,

Your revelation to me about things that happened all those years ago came as a nasty shock. So why should I decide to break my silence now? Simple. I'm ill and what seemed ghastly, embarrassing and threatening then is now of little consequence to me.

218

I don't know what you want to hear. I suppose that your father was essentially a good man who found himself ensnared into a life of violence and corruption. Forget it! He was a cold, scheming bastard, who for a time ruined my life. Anyone who can stoop to blackmail to further their own ends is beyond contempt.

Thinking about you in retrospect I could see a likeness. Just. He was a handsome man. Not a word that is used much now. Although of only average height, he had a commanding presence. Slightly sinister might be more accurate. I assume he always dressed in black to create that impression. Pathetic really. Besides, his clothes were at odds with his BBC accent. Unlike you, his hair was always tidy. His military background no doubt. I think he may have been short-sighted. He gave the impression of constantly staring into sunlight, which created a permanent smile. Very irritating, but an expression that broadened when under duress. I think this added to his reputation for invincibility. A man who smiles in the face of danger is not to be trifled with. During my investigations for the Sunday Record *I found rumours of his wartime exploits had been massaged and exaggerated. He was respected and feared by many in the criminal fraternity.*

The whores and prostitutes liked him. Pathetically, some seemed to almost hero-worship him. At the time I interviewed over thirty of them and not one had a bad word to say. Annoyingly they seemed in awe of him. It was a class thing, I concluded. They all came from poor, deprived backgrounds and instinctively looked up to him. Stupid women who looked on him as someone who was protecting, rather then exploiting, them.

He changed my life. Perhaps I should thank him,

but as you know he set me up in the vilest way. He sensed a weakness in me and played on it. Money and the discharging of body fluids are the most corrupting elements in our sad lives.

It's confession time, James. I was delighted when the Captain was arrested. He was a fraud. He abused the advantages he had been given. I followed his trial with an increasing sense of glee. On the morning of his execution, I tried to imagine the rope tightening around his throat and I drank a toast to his demise. Normally I don't drink and certainly not at nine o'clock in the morning.

I assume you are collating information in order to write a book or possibly create a television programme. Well, I dare you to use this little contribution. A myth has grown up around your father's memory. It's false. He was the lowest of the low.

The signature was shaky and indecipherable. Desmond Bailey died ten days after I received his letter.

The Seventh Diary – January–June 1952

Thursday, January 3rd
The only outward concession I ever make to the winter elements is the wearing of black leather gloves. Initially this was supposed to convey a message to everyone of my toughness. I've been frozen all day, even though unseen I sport long johns and a thick vest. I'm a total fraud!

Wednesday, January 9th
The cold weather appears to be reducing the ardour of the male population. Turnover is flaccid and, despite reduced competition, this may be a difficult period. Last year, hordes descended on London for the Festival of Britain. That gave a glimpse of what the future might hold, but meantime the country remains in the grip of austerity.

I have arranged a meeting with Leo Joseph. I intend forming a number of new companies to enable me to obtain additional mortgages. My idea is to buy another large house and, after evicting the tenants, to split the property into separate units which I will then get valued individually. The rental income will be sufficient to pay off the mortgages over twenty years and provide me with some income. Jam today, jam tomorrow! I try not to think about the actual evictions. A horrible messy business with which I don't have any direct contact.

Sunday, January 13th
Life on the home front has settled into an acceptable routine. I take and collect Nadine from school most

days, which is time-consuming. She has settled in well and has made friends with Caroline, who lives in the next block. Cécile continues to work long hours. She is still given to bouts of sheer fear that Frank will find out what we are up to. He has been very quiet lately.

We now have a daily help. Ethel keeps the place spotless, and she is very good with Nadine. Like everyone else she refers to me as Captain. I'm obviously stuck with the title. I often wish I had been a corporal or a trooper. I have been denied my own name even by Cécile. We also have a cook, who comes in three times a week. I think Mrs Banks is a perfectly good plain cook. Cécile thinks otherwise. She is terrible with staff, always hectoring and criticising.

This afternoon we went to feed the ducks on the Serpentine. What a weird life! On one level we flirt with middle-class normality. Later this evening we are going to a drinks party, given by Caroline's parents. As far as they are concerned, we run a small catering supply business, but the dark shadows of reality seldom leave me.

Wednesday, January 30th
There was a serious fight last night between various Chinese factions. It started in Wheelers kitchen, but spilled out onto the street. Knives, machetes and meat hooks were wielded. Gaynor said there was blood and bodies all over the place. Miraculously, they all staggered away when they heard the police cars arriving.

Monday, February 4th
I have bought a huge Victorian house in Kilburn. I think it's a bargain. Leo Joseph doesn't agree; he

advised against it. The place is full of Irishmen. I don't see that as a problem. Alex will be in his element. I think we could convert it into six or possibly even seven units.

Wednesday, February 6th
The King has died. I feel shocked and saddened. I know he was really only a figurehead, but in his way I felt he was a brave man, catapulted into a rotten job that he never sought. Princess Elizabeth and Philip are flying back from Kenya. How strange to be entering a second Elizabethan age. Let's hope it's as good for the country as the first one was.

Saturday, February 9th
It's an ill wind ... London is bound to be crowded with mourners for the funeral on Friday.

Friday, February 15th
I stood on The Mall to watch the funeral procession. Many people had slept on the pavement overnight. I still had a wonderful view. I found the experience very moving. The Brits are superb at staging state events. The troops immaculate; just the sound of their boots and a single drumbeat. The crowd silent except for a child's cry. The Duke of Windsor looked old and ill. Prince Philip young and handsome. I noticed several people crying.

Cécile is cross with me for going. Miffed also that Nadine's school has closed for the day and that she has had to look after her. Although the mood in the country is sombre, I sense opportunity and change. We have a new government and soon a young and beautiful queen will be crowned. Cécile is oblivious to all this. I hardly warranted a greeting when I arrived home. She was off to check up on the girls. 'Some of us have to work,' she said pointedly.

Bloody French! They have no soul.

Thursday, February 21st
It lashed down with rain all day. I was absolutely soaked. I relented. I bought a raincoat. Black, of course!

Saturday, April 5th
The Kilburn house is now mine. I went over this morning unannounced. I think I could have made a big mistake, encouraged by the low purchase price. When I first viewed the property I was accompanied by the estate agent. The tenants were seemingly OK and outwardly friendly. The place was rather untidy but otherwise fine. I've been conned. It's little more than a rooming house, teeming with Irishmen who arrive in shifts. They bundled me out when they found I was their new landlord. The place is filthy and reeks of rancid cooking and stale booze. I think Alex and Ted may have their work cut out here.

Monday, April 7th
A phone call from Uncle Robert. Dad has suffered a stroke. Having just put the phone down, Frank rang issuing guarded threats. He caught me at the wrong moment. I exploded, ranting at him before hanging up. Attack is the best form of defence. Does he know anything or is he just suspicious? I won't tell Cécile he has been on. I can't stand any more of her histrionics.

Saturday, April 12th
Dad died today. I have sat by his bedside for the past week, sleeping in an adjoining alcove. This afternoon he seemed slightly better, so I decided to have a short walk in the spring sunshine. He was dead when I returned twenty minutes later. No doctor or nurse had been in to check on him. He died alone. My first emotion was guilt. Quite a common reaction, I understand. I hadn't lived up to his expectations. Well not latterly anyway. I hadn't paid him enough attention either, selfishly obsessed by my own problems.

This evening sorrow and sadness moved in. Cécile tried to be supportive, but only managed to annoy me with her concern. Even Nadine irritated me, constantly seeking attention. After supper I left them and went for a long walk, alone with my melancholy thoughts. I returned at about ten o'clock. Unusually, Cécile was already in bed. There was a note on the kitchen table. Alex is in hospital. He has been attacked by a group of my Irish tenants in Kilburn. I sat up into the early hours drinking whisky. It brought me no relief. Cécile had locked the bedroom door. I went to the spare room and cried like a baby. I must have wakened Nadine. She and her teddy joined me on the narrow bed. She hugged me and wiped my eyes with the sleeves of her nightdress. She called me Papa and I clung to her as if my life depended on it. Why shouldn't I? She is my only shaft of light.

Sunday, April 13th
I went to visit Alex in St Mary's Hospital. What a state he's in. He looks quite grotesque. His face is swollen and bruised. He's had over twenty stitches, and his front

225

teeth are missing. He reckons most of the damage was done by a chair. He speaks with a lisp. I tell him he sounds like a queer. He didn't think that was very funny. Two of his assailants are in the next ward. The nurses are showing him little sympathy. The matron puts the fear of God into him. I have never seen him fazed by a man, but the rustle of Matron's starched uniform has him curling up in a ball under the blankets. There is no escape though. He is on the end of another tirade, as I unwrap the grapes I have brought. He is taking up valuable bed space due to his own stupidity. She casts me a cutting stare. I'm glad I'm not one of her patients.

Alex is keen to go back and sort the Paddies out when he's discharged. I think other tactics are called for. He reckons there are over fifty of them in the building at any one time.

Friday, April 18th
I hate funerals. Only a handful attended. A few distant relatives, a couple of old colleagues and the glamorous widow. She has chucked the doctor but still shows no interest in Uncle Robert. He didn't even invite any of us back to the house after the ceremony. We went instead to a rather dismal pub.

Cécile came supposedly to show support, but only succeeded in annoying me. She kept nagging for us to leave, whilst I was still talking to an old friend of father's who had travelled all the way down from Sunderland. It struck me that away from our normal environment, Cécile looks like a tart. True she wore black, but she has reverted to caked makeup. I became increasingly grumpy and upset. We had a huge row. Tonight I'm back in the spare room.

Friday, April 25th
We have been struck by a rarely discussed occupational hazard. Candice, who has been operating from St Anne's Court since before the war, has syphilis. I was horrified to learn she was diagnosed over three months ago. She must be almost sixty and looks older. I gave her enough money to get her back to France. Cécile is furious with me. She reckons Candice has substantial savings. I can't think why she is getting so excited; I didn't ask her for a contribution. How many more of the girls have a similar problem? I want to set up a system whereby they will have regular checkups. Cécile says we can't afford it and that the girls should be left to make their own arrangements.

Wednesday, May 7th
My life has taken a turn for the worse. Cécile is being foul. She accuses me of leaving her to run the whole show, which is untrue. In fact I am left doing all the mundane things that she has little interest in. I have certainly been preoccupied with the problems in Kilburn. I have still received no rent, in spite of repeated promises. I decided to take the lawful route. Solicitor's letters have gone unanswered and the bailiffs are unwilling to act. The house is a no-go area. We have tried our usual tactics of illegally cutting off services. This has no effect. The property is stuffed with builders, plumbers and electricians. Alex and Ted are willing to have another go with the help of friends, but I don't want them to attract unnecessary publicity. I have another idea. The last throw of the dice before acknowledging defeat.

Tuesday, May 13th

I contacted Rufus White, one of the West Indians who occupied Paddington to such effect. I have offered him a similar deal if he can oust the Irish. He knows that it will be a difficult task. He has gone away to think about it. I stand to lose a fortune on the deal. Local estate agents tell me I paid far too much for the property, which at the time I was convinced was dirt cheap. I still obviously have a lot to learn.

Monday, May 26th

Utter mayhem! I have backed another loser. Rufus and his boys tried their best, but they were outnumbered. The Irish showed great solidarity, reinforcements appearing as if by magic. There was a massive punch-up and the St Mary's wards are testament to the ferocity of the fight. When the police arrived everyone closed ranks. I seem to have been responsible for the forming of a new alliance. They lie side by side bandaged and stitched, the best of friends. I think Matron has my number. Her withering stare had me running for cover. This little episode has added to my losses. I've had to pay Rufus and his friends a bundle for their troubles. At least no one was arrested.

Wednesday, May 28th

I went to the house in Kilburn today. The place is a tip. Not just untidy, but filthy. The spokesman for the tenants was Dermot Casey who is all beer belly and charm. Again he promised to pay the rent, but suggested I may be interested in selling. Whoever said the Irish are stupid?

228

Cécile is continuing to be difficult. She is full of irrational fears. She thinks Nadine should have a full-time bodyguard. I should be more sympathetic. We all have demons lurking. I know. For the past couple of nights I have woken screaming with fear. Cécile is convinced I share her concerns. She is unable to accept that I am reliving a part of my past that refuses to die.

Wednesday, June 11th
I've had an offer on Kilburn for barely half that I paid for it. The estate agent recommended I accept, in view of the tenant problem. I'm going to hang on.

Tuesday, June 17th
I took Cécile for supper at the Ivy in an attempt to mend fences. I have persuaded her to tone down her makeup. She looked great. She liked the restaurant. I think it was the clientele rather than the food that appealed. We spent the evening stargazing. Errol Flynn was at the next table with an unidentified Indian girl of incredible beauty. Later Douglas Fairbanks arrived with Danny Kaye and the Oliviers. Vivien Leigh kept looking over to our table and smiling. Cécile was convinced she was flirting with me. If only!

Back home over cognacs, our conversation reverted, as it often does, as to how we can escape from Frank's hold over us. Cécile now seems to assume that whatever happens we are bound together. Although we are married this comes as something of a surprise. When I dream of the future Cécile doesn't figure. Tonight, though, we were as one. Loving, supportive and passionate.

Saturday, June 28th

Today I took Nadine to the zoo. Cécile didn't come – working as usual. She packed us an excellent picnic, so she obviously approved. Nadine was wide-eyed. Everything had to be seen. She was frightened by the lions, excited by the tigers and fascinated by the masturbating monkeys. She had rides on a camel and an elephant, but the highlight was the feeding of the polar bears. The child is so affectionate that everyone assumes I am her father. She never disillusions them, and I feel a strange sense of pride. I have always struggled with the perception of love. It comes in so many forms; love for parents and on a different level for friends. Then, if you are lucky (which I'm not), in a romantic guise. This little girl I find captivating. Perhaps it helps that she is so pretty, but I love being with her. She's cheeky, funny and wise beyond her years; I feel proud and protective towards her. Is that love? If not, it's the nearest to it I have in my life right now.

Monday, June 30th

A cash offer for Kilburn. The same price as the one I received a couple of weeks ago. Reluctantly I accepted. Your first loss is your best loss so the saying goes. It is only later that I learn the purchaser is none other than Dermot Casey. I've been fleeced. How to lose money without even trying!

Tonight I couldn't sleep, so I sat up reading the *Caine Mutiny*. Brilliant! Just after midnight the phone rang. Cécile's sister is coming to stay. Horror as opposed to joy was my wife's reaction.

The Eighth Diary – July–December 1952

Friday, July 4th
Cécile is embarrassed by her sister, and I can understand why. She insists Minette stays at a hotel, as she doesn't want her mixing with Nadine. Every family has its skeletons. I must say Minette is an extremely shapely one. She makes no secret of how she earns her living, and Cécile feels tainted by association.

Minette is attractive and provocative. Younger, blonder and sexier than her elder sister. She speaks no English and yet she flirts with me outrageously. I get the impression her visit is not solely for a vacation. Cécile is very preoccupied. I wish she would be more open with me. The name Xavier crops up constantly in conversation. Cécile refuses point-blank to tell me where he fits into the scheme of things.

Tuesday, July 8th
Minette left for France today. I took her and Cécile to the Caprice for dinner last night. A mistake! Minette made no concession to the elegant surroundings. She looked every inch the hooker, in a low-cut imitation leopard-skin dress and high heels. She is more at home in the bars of Soho.

My mood tonight is bleak. Cécile finds it impossible to be open with me. My property deals have turned sour and I'm fed up with the life I'm living. Nadine is the one chink of light. She is growing up fast. She is outward-going, cute yet vulnerable, and I love her in a way that complicates my life further. If I did, or could, break away from all this, I would miss her dreadfully.

231

Friday, July 11th

I received a letter from Mrs de B. in Majorca. She is full of angst about Claudia, who is due to start at university in Madrid in the autumn. She is going to read law. I feel certain that generations of the de Bonos have taken a keen interest in the subject, but Claudia will be the first to help administer it. Mrs de B. wants me to visit them. We could do with a break, but Cécile won't hear of it. She's far too busy. She suggested that I go alone, as I obviously haven't enough on to fill my time. I just might. We are getting on each other's nerves at the moment.

Wednesday, July 16th

Frank rang. I have to admit I do hold my breath when I hear his voice (guilty conscience). For once he wasn't aggressive or hectoring. Rather the reverse, hesitant and unsure of himself. He wanted to know if there had been any rumours circulating about him in London. I have no idea what he was talking about. I think he might have been drinking.

Thursday, July 17th

Had a massive row with Cécile. She accuses me of not giving her any help. It's true, I have been devoting more time lately to the shop, as I'm still licking my wounds after my latest plunge into the property market. She drives me mad. If I try to help her, she accuses me of interfering. She is quite irrational.

I went to see the girls in Greek Street. What a welcome! Esther cooked me a superb lasagne, whilst Winnie and Gaynor left clients literally hanging around, as we talked over old times. They wish I was back living with them. So do I.

Alex is not very popular. He is a tidiness freak. Also he makes it clear he can't abide blacks. Winnie says the feeling is mutual.

Every time I see Winnie I feel incredibly randy. Unfortunately Esther watches me like a hawk. The feeling stayed with me. Doreen was thrilled to see me. I was full of guilt afterwards. I hope Cécile doesn't find out.

Wednesday, July 23rd
I have booked a flight to Palma. Cécile is furious. I don't care. She's being a real pain. It does occur to me that the invitation may be a smokescreen. Is this branch of the family going to demand money from me as well?

Sunday, August 3rd
Claudia met me at the airport. Gone is the attractive schoolgirl. Enter the self-possessed and sophisticated stunner. She is darker than I remember. Her skin tanned by the constant sun and her hair jet black. Her face is dominated by thick eyebrows, and although her individual features are not classic, the overall effect is memorable. The expensive casual clothes and heady perfume helps to complete the image, as did the parked Fiat sports car. Her attitude towards me was wary. More accurately, off-hand.

The de Bonos' house is spectacular. Set a couple of blocks back from the sea in the old town, it provides a refuge from the midday sun. The entrance is approached through massive iron gates and a shaded cobbled courtyard. Inside, the marble floors make the house feel quite cold. First impressions are of festooned flowers and heavy old-fashioned furniture. Mrs de B. has aged, but seemed pleased to see me. Claudia told me in the car that her mother had rediscovered God. Pictures of Christ and saints dominate the living areas.

Lunch was delicious and served in the courtyard against the hum of the city traffic in the background. The conversation was safe, non-provocative, but I have an idea that there is an agenda which hasn't been explained to me yet.

This afternoon I was left to explore the beautiful old town. Later, supper was served in the vast gloomy dining room. Mrs de B. had invited some neighbours, a retired accountant and his wife. Claudia was out with friends. The evening was pleasant enough, but I am beginning to wonder why I am here.

Tuesday, August 5th

Yesterday it all came pouring out. Mrs de B. was transformed from a conventional hostess to a hysterical bereaved wife. I felt really sorry for her. Harry had been killed, murdered. She knew this as a fact, but was powerless. The brothers had a violent argument. There had been a power struggle. Harry lost. The car crash was no accident.

How was she sure? I queried. Because Frank had told her openly. He insisted Harry had been double-crossing him. He had offered her a deal. Retirement away from Paris and London. He would allow her to keep the money Harry had left, although he maintained much of it rightfully belonged to him. The punch line was familiar: any prevarication or deviation from his orders and Claudia would be targeted.

As I listened to her, I began to form a different

opinion. My assessment of Frank is that he is full of bluster and threats, but I doubted what the poor woman was telling me. Assuming Harry's accident was genuine, Frank's putting the fear of God into Mrs de B. was an easy way for him to take total control. By targeting Claudia, he was using the same tactic he was employing with Cécile by threatening *her* child.

I didn't tell Mrs de B. about my doubts and promised to give serious thought to her suggestion that I should sever my connection with Frank.

I was wrong to suspect that I had been invited in order to winkle some money out of me. She informed me she was still wealthy and now she was able to put the money to good use, supporting numerous charities. I think she is in denial as to how her money was obtained.

Claudia continues to act as if she wished I wasn't here. What a shame. I feel quite hurt by her attitude.

Wednesday, August 6th
Claudia's reaction to me is even more marked when I am with her mother. Embarrassingly, they had a row in front of me and Claudia was forced to apologise for her rudeness. Under duress, she has agreed to show me some of the island later in the week.

Sunday, August 10th
I'm not sure that today was life-changing, but it is certainly one that I will never forget. The de Bonos went to early Mass, and then, after a hurried breakfast, Claudia and I set off in the open-topped Fiat for the north-west of the island. It was an exhilarating drive once we left Palma and weaved our way into the

mountains. There was no traffic on the roads except for the occasional donkey, either laden or ridden by an old woman dressed in black. We drove up what were little more than tracks, through lemon and orange groves. It was as if the wind in her hair transformed Claudia from a spoilt, pouting teenager into a ravishing carefree temptress. The radio blared. We sang, our voices drowned out by the warm wind buffeting the car and the growl of the engine as we headed upwards. She flirted. I was flattered. I flirted, too. Outrageously. I had a feeling of euphoria. The dramatic scenery, the beautiful girl. Grubby London and my troubles were forgotten.

We approached Deya along the stunning coastal road, before leaving the sea on our left and turning inland. We had coffee in a bar on the main street before heading back towards the sea again, down an unmade road. Parking in the shadow of overhanging trees, we continued on foot down a rocky track. After about ten minutes, we reached a gorge and beyond I could make out a small secluded beach. Perched on rocks above was a shack from where we could pick up the tantalising waft of grilled fish. We climbed rickety wooden steps and joined a party of perhaps a dozen diners. Their motor boat was anchored just off-shore.

Sitting opposite each other, we gazed out over a calm blue sea and sipped a cool white wine. It was a magic spot. Quite idyllic. We feasted on grilled tuna and salad. I felt like a teenager on a first date. We lingered long over the meal. The other diners left without my realising it. If happiness could be bottled, this was the moment.

We talked easily. Of trivial things. Our meeting, school and of her going to university.

Risking a complete change of atmosphere, I mentioned my conversation with Mrs de B. and her insistence that her father's death had been no accident. Claudia just laughed. Of course, it was an accident. Her mother was being ridiculous. Attention-seeking. There was no way her Uncle Frank would harm his brother.

The patron bid us goodbye, his business finished for the day, and set off home, leaving us sitting on the balcony of the open-sided building. It had turned four o'clock when Claudia suggested we took a swim. We ambled down to the deserted beach. I stripped to my underpants and paddled in the water, waiting as she undressed. As I looked out to sea she ran past me, not stopping until the water was waist-high. She was naked. I was shocked. She shouted that we should have a race to a huge rock, about a hundred yards out to sea, where some young boys had been diving earlier. I set off after her. She was a strong swimmer and she clambered up before me. Congratulating her, I splashed about below. Lying on her stomach she reached out for me, helping me onto the flat surface of the rock. Gently she pushed me beneath her. Nothing was said as she straddled me. I was aware of barnacles scouring my back. Her wet hair obscured the sun. She smelt of musk and sea water. I had forgotten the feel of young flesh. I roared from a mixture of ecstasy and pain, as my back was lacerated by her rocking motion. The sun was low in the sky, when we slipped back into the water and made our way back to the shore.

Collecting our clothes, we scampered into the under-growth. We found some lush cover amongst the olive trees. This time our lovemaking was more measured. Dreamy, almost trancelike. Somewhere nearby a goat grazed, a bell at its throat. I didn't know why this was happening. I didn't want to know. For the moment, life was wonderful. This may not have been love, but then neither was it just sex. At least, not the sex that I had become used to. She told me she had always dreamt of this moment since we first met. Amazing!

We were quieter on the way home, locked into our own thoughts. By the same time tomorrow I will be back in London. To my crazy, deeply flawed life. My mood veered from delirium to deep depression.

Mrs de B. welcomed us warmly. A young man was waiting to take Claudia out. He was deferential towards me. Polite, well brought up. An older man may have sensed something. He was oblivious. Claudia resumed her slightly antagonistic attitude towards me. She is devious. Twenty minutes later having changed, she bid me goodbye. A firm handshake and she was gone, on the arm of the young man. I can't believe that making love to a de Bono woman won't have repercussions.

Monday, August 11th
An uncomfortable flight back to London wedged between two large ladies burnt alarming shades of pink. Nadine was very pleased to see me and the flamenco doll I bought back from Palma. Cécile arrived home very late. She said she needed to speak to me urgently, but it would have to wait for the morning as she was exhausted. Not too tired, though, to comment on the state of my back. Terrible things, barnacles!

238

Wednesday, August 13th
As I suspected, Cécile's worries relate to Frank. He has been issuing threats again, always directed at Nadine. Cécile is paranoid, worse than Mrs de Bono and, I'm convinced, just as deluded. Frank is a bully who preys on fears. Increasingly, I feel tempted to call his bluff. In the meantime I have an idea. It's Nadine's birthday next week. A dog will offer a sense of security. And what a dog!

Thursday, August 21st
Cécile is horrified. Nadine beside herself with joy. Clancy is huge. She weighs more than me. She is a three-year-old Irish wolfhound who looks ferocious but is as soft as butter. She was advertised in the *Evening Standard* as needing a good home. The owners live in a prefab in Chelmsford. Hardly a suitable environment, particularly as the couple were out at work all day. Bored, the dog had become destructive. I lied, telling them I lived in the country, with acres of ground. Fifty pounds secured the deal.

Cécile thinks I'm irresponsible, but I'm trying to convince her that Clancy will be a superb guard dog. I plan to take her to the park each morning. Running alongside my bike on a lead should keep her fit.

Sunday, September 7th
Although Clancy was a present for Nadine, she is really my dog. I love her. She is a sheer delight. She welcomes me by leaping up and putting her paws on my shoulders and wagging her tail violently. Today I had her tail cauterised. The glazier comes tomorrow to fix the china cabinet.

239

Each morning I take her to the park and she lopes alongside me on my daily three-mile run. People exercising their dogs run for cover. She looks so frightening but is actually really friendly. She is also easy to train. She has become part of the Soho scenery. She walks sedately at my side, as pedestrians instinctively dive into the gutter to avoid her. In a pub or bar she just lies at my feet, bushy eyebrows jumping as she watches what is going on. Now and again she barks, and the effect on people is really comical to see. If I tell her to stay, she waits patiently for my return. Last week I called in to see Father Tony at St Patrick's. I left Clancy sitting by the entrance. When we walked outside, there were four or five people standing on the pavement, too afraid to push past.

Cécile is still very boot-faced about the new arrival, but at least she concedes that Clancy is amazingly gentle with Nadine.

Saturday, September 13th
I was introduced to Sir Piers Leveridge at a drinks party last night. He is an MP for some remote constituency in Cumberland. He told me he has just inherited a row of houses in Wandsworth with sitting tenants. He wants rid of them. Not the rest of his inheritance, a sprawling estate in Suffolk. Why don't I have a rich daddy? Life would have been so much easier.

Friday, September 19th
Piers Leveridge is not as stupid as he looks. He's demanding top-dollar prices for his houses. Further negotiations required.

Sunday, September 28th

A couple of weeks ago I was approached in Lisle Street by a man who introduced himself as Douglas Glass. Apparently he is a well-known photographer. He told me he was taking a series of shots of 'Soho characters'. I didn't think anything of it. Today I am plastered all over the *Observer*, under the caption 'The Captain and Clancy'. It doesn't explain to its readers which of us is which or, luckily, why I am a 'Soho character'. Although the photograph flatters me, I don't welcome the publicity.

Friday, October 3rd

Piers Leveridge has agreed to sell me three of his Wandsworth houses. I took him for supper to the Gay Hussar by way of securing the deal. Although not much older than me, he's overweight and out of condition. Not a great human specimen. His thinning hair still manages to produce dandruff in alarming quantities and he sweats profusely. He spent some years in the Scots Guards, of which he speaks with pride. He is now a stockbroker in the family firm. He married last year, a good match, to the daughter of a leading brewer. There must be *some* good-looking girls in the upper echelons of society. Poor old Piers hasn't found one. Let's hope they don't have children!

He was like a dog on heat as we made our way over to the Gargoyle Club. I've been vague about my business interests, but I think he has a fair idea. Over our meal I banged on about liberalising the laws relating to censorship and live entertainment. He didn't respond but gave me a funny look. The man is the most outright racist I have ever met. He wants a ban on all immigration from the West Indies.

241

Racist he may be, but he almost managed to get himself run over when Winnie appeared outside the house in Greek Street. Sensing an opportunity I introduced him, explaining that Winnie had been a neighbour when I had first arrived in London. He appeared embarrassed, but I noticed his sweat factor rocketed. Later over a drink, I explained the specialist nature of the services provided by Winnie and Gaynor. He feigned no particular interest and the conversation moved on.

Thursday, October 16th
Cécile has the annoying habit of periodically opening my mail. With a steely look, she handed me a letter that had arrived from Claudia. I'm sure I looked guilty. She caught me off guard. Luckily it just said how she was loving law school. Good girl, no reference to Deya. I swear Cécile suspects something. Women seem to have some inbuilt radar system. 'How is your back?' Cécile enquired. I pretended I didn't understand what she was getting at.

Thursday, November 6th
Amazing news. Cécile insists that Frank and Zoe have been arrested in Paris. We certainly haven't heard from them lately. She won't tell me how she found out, but she is excited and animated. I must make enquiries.

Tuesday, November 11th
A visit this morning from Chief Inspector Sweet. The smooth bastard has been promoted again. He's so smug and pleased with himself. It's true Frank and Zoe have been arrested and he can guarantee that they will not be bothering us for a good few years. It's time he says

242

to renegotiate our agreement. I protest. He insists. I stall. I have to check this out. I have arranged to meet him next week.

Saturday, November 15th
Cécile is adamant that she doesn't want me to go to Paris. It's not my safety she is worried about, rather I suspect that I might find out too much. Her behaviour is really curious. I'm going anyway. Out of spite, she insists Clancy is sent to a boarding kennel.

Tuesday, November 18th
I have been here two days, without getting very far. Frank and Zoe have been in custody for two weeks and investigations continue. It is very difficult for me to get information. My French is poor, which doesn't help, but nobody wants to talk to me. My hotel is right in the middle of the red-light district and it is used by some of Frank's girls, but they all appear either too frightened to talk to me or imagine that I am some mad English punter.

Wednesday, November 19th
This afternoon after protracted negotiations and a massive bribe, I managed to get the concierge to let me into Frank's apartment. They obviously left in a hurry. The remains of a meal were still on the kitchen table, their huge double bed unmade. The place had a musty, sickly-sweet smell. It was obvious the apartment had been searched by the police. Drawers and cupboards had been left open. I should have realised. What could I hope to find? All the relevant items will have been taken as evidence.

Suddenly the door behind me opened. I relaxed. I recognised the figure. Xavier, the man who had accompanied Cécile to the restaurant when I first met her. He is thickset and tough-looking. Although wary, he extended his hand in welcome. His grip was strong. He showed neither surprise nor anger at my arrival. His English is no better than my French. Opening windows, he pointed to the sofa. I sat down and waited. 'We need to talk,' he said. I agreed.

Friday, November 21st
So now I know the full story. Well, maybe an abridged version, but one that I'm inclined to believe. I sat up for most of the night with Xavier, drinking the last of Frank's vintage calvados.

Xavier is a printer. He is married and lives in a suburb to the west of Paris. He has struggled over the years producing calendars and hotel brochures. Just prior to meeting the de Bonos he had landed a contract producing a glamour magazine. This was absolutely tame, featuring young bikini-clad girls frolicking on the beach. His profit margin was paper-thin. Bankruptcy loomed. Enter Harry de Bono. He commissioned a specialist nudist publication. Very discreet, except the girls featured didn't wear bikinis. The print run was large, requiring the payment of overtime to his staff and large orders to his paper suppliers. His desperate pleas for payment fell on deaf ears. Harry didn't even return his calls. The bank gave him forty-eight hours. His business, which his father had founded, was doomed.

The day before the bank's foreclosure, Frank arrived at his premises, brandishing a cheque for payment in full. There was one condition: Xavier was required to print another magazine. This was explicit, shocking and illegal. The magazine was to have international distribution. Reluctantly, Xavier accepted. Each publication that followed was more shocking and debauched than the last. Because of the extreme nature of the photographs, most of the female models tended to be prostitutes, who were drawn from the local Paris trade. Unlike London, no one figure dominated in Paris, but the largest operator was Michel Jaume. It was he who supplied the girls. Most of the coordination was carried out by a slim, serious young woman. Cécile. Initially she was very cool towards Xavier. He felt she was embarrassed by the unsavoury business she was engaged in.

Over the months they began to see themselves as kindred spirits. Both controlled by unscrupulous men. They had a brief affair. Hurried meetings. Unsatisfactory, leading nowhere. Until, that is, Cécile found she was pregnant. Xavier was horrified, particularly as Cécile insisted on keeping the baby. His marriage was good; his affair with Cécile a stupid mistake. Eventually they came to an agreement. As his finances were now in better shape, he agreed to support the child, providing Cécile didn't contact his wife.

Cécile would never tell Xavier what hold Jaume and the de Bonos held over her. It was months after the baby was born that Minette explained that Cécile had once appeared in a particularly gruesome film.

Minette was quite vitriolic about her sister. 'She may seem grand now, but she's a tart just like the rest of us. She was the wild child. It was her who got me into all this. She's a bitch and you are a sucker.'

For whatever reason, Cécile had somehow risen

through the ranks. She handled Jaume's girls brilliantly. The de Bonos didn't miss a trick.

They saw an opportunity to use her skills once they had been expelled from London. Jaume was bought out and retired to Monte Carlo. Cécile was installed in Soho.

Now with Frank and Zoe in custody, everything was about to change again. They were being held on a raft of charges, including demanding money with menaces, illegal gun possession, distributing hardcore pornography and living off immoral earnings. Xavier reckons that Frank will get up to eight years and Zoe maybe four or five.

Xavier leaves for Spain tomorrow with his wife, otherwise he is convinced he will also end up inside.

All of us have been caught up in the de Bono web. Now we have a chance to break free. Cécile and I need to have a serious talk.

Sunday, November 23rd

I tried to talk to Cécile about my Paris trip and my meeting with Xavier. She went crazy. She accused him of being a pathological liar. Then she subsided from eye-bulging fury to icy calm, but refused to discuss her past, which she says has nothing to do with me. I think she is embarrassed and is desperate to keep the truth from Nadine (not that I would ever tell her). I think she feels she has also lost face with me. I suppose a former blue film star isn't the ideal background for my wife, but I gave up being shocked by human behaviour years ago. She has suggested we divorce and that we go our separate ways, as it now appears we are finally out of the de Bonos' clutches.

246

I've decided to let her cool down. We both have to give the future careful thought. There are rich pickings to be had.

Saturday, November 29th
It has taken all this time for us to talk rationally. Cécile craves respectability, a normal life. I have promised not to pry into her past any more. She is mortified by what she has done. I sympathise, so am I. Still ashamed and troubled.

Assuming money can buy independence and happiness, we are set fair. We now have a chance to amass a fortune. Even with the 'Sweet cop' taking his extra piece of silver, we should generate untold wealth. We talked of the future. Of educating Nadine and branching out into legitimate businesses. I dare not tell Cécile that I see pornography as a huge area of potential expansion. I'm obviously tainted now. My thoughts remain in the gutter. We talk of the future, but now my instinct is to live for the day. Cécile longs for retirement. Of a comfortable life in the country. In discussion I don't disagree with her, but in reality I can see an exciting future. I'm going to enjoy myself.

With Frank out of the equation, Cécile is, at last, much more relaxed. She even allowed Clancy to sleep in Nadine's bedroom tonight.

Friday, December 5th
I took Cécile to see *Limelight* tonight, starring Charlie Chaplin. I thought it trite, but Cécile loved it. We were planning a late supper, but it was freezing and horribly foggy when we left the cinema, so we took a taxi home.

247

You could barely see a few yards ahead and there were huge traffic jams. We abandoned the cab and walked back from Barkers.

Sunday, December 7th

The fog is worse than ever. The papers are calling it 'smog'. It's quite possible to get lost as soon as you step outside. It's so cold that everyone in London is lighting coal fires. This is causing cold air filled with smog to be trapped between a layer of warm air, which is sitting a few hundred yards above. There isn't a breath of wind to shift the foul stuff. A shroud of stagnant yellowy, black coal smoke envelops everything. Last night theatres had to close because it was impossible to see the stage. Public transport is at a standstill. So is our business. A freelance girl was murdered on Friday, in an alley off Beak Street. Her throat had been cut. None of the girls want to venture out. I don't blame them.

Monday, December 8th

I had a phone call informing me that Esther had collapsed with severe bronchitis. It took over an hour for the ambulance to turn up. I set off on foot to visit her at Middlesex Hospital, but it was impossible. The pea-souper is getting worse. I'm reduced to wearing a scarf round my nose and mouth to act as a mask. It's already blackened and soiled. People are dying in their hundreds. Our local undertaker is stacking coffins like tins in a grocer's shop. The smog is all pervasive. Even with the windows shut there is no escape. It forms a heavy mist in the flat. It attacks your lungs and stings the eyes. Utterly foul!

Tuesday, December 9th

It has gone. Quite suddenly. This morning it seemed certain we were going to have to endure another breathless day, staggering through the gloom. Then, as if by magic, a westerly breeze stiffened into a full wind and the smoke particles were blown away.

It's reckoned that up to 5,000 people have died as a direct result of the smog over the past few days. Esther is home from hospital and insists on wearing a mask, even though the day is now as clear as a bell.

Monday, December 15th

Poor Father Tony is so depressed. He has officiated over more funerals in the last week than in the previous six months. Very sadly, one of our youngest girls died of an asthmatic attack last week. Theresa was only nineteen. She came over from Cork in the summer. Her family arrived yesterday in time for the funeral. She had told them she was in the chorus of a West End show. They must have thought it was a pretty funny chorus line: our girls come in all shapes and sizes. Many tears shed. I was introduced to her parents as the show's producer. I've become an accomplished liar. Father Tony didn't let the side down, referring to Theresa's talent for living life to the full. Buckets of Guinness consumed at the Nelly Dean.

Although I hardly knew the girl, I found the service very moving. I was quite maudlin by the time I arrived home. Cécile seemed embarrassed to find me sobbing. Delayed reaction, I think, to my relative self-control at Dad's funeral. I miss him terribly.

Monday, December 22nd
If you have money, flaunt it! And right now I have. I took Cécile and Nadine to the Ritz for lunch. They both had new outfits. I had the impression that we were judged to be that much-loathed species, the nouveau riche, by the head waiter. Why is it that so many waiters and servants are such snobs? This man had refined condescension to an art form. I had my revenge by sending back two bottles of wine. Actually there was nothing wrong with them, but I knew he wouldn't argue. The food was nothing to write home about, but the dining room has to be the most spectacular in London. I gave the waiter a ridiculously large tip. Money is going to be dangerous in my hands, but it amuses me to see initial aloofness turned into grovelling obsequiousness.

Thursday, December 25th
We didn't go to midnight Mass this year. Nadine joined us for the eleven o'clock morning service. St Patrick's still has an emotional hold over me. I can sense God, or at least a feeling of goodness. Perhaps holiness is a better description, but I find I can't be a part of it. Cécile prays with a fervour that to me is a touch too theatrical. She obviously worries about what God has in store for her. So should I.

It was a lovely family day. A leisurely lunch (French style), extravagant presents, listening to the radio and playing Monopoly. At such times I do realise that the simple things in life are the most rewarding, and yet I know that I am now set on a course dedicated to building up some real wealth. Why? I already have enough to relaunch my life. Since I arrived in London this is all I sought. Now, perversely, I need more. I kid myself that it is the challenge that appeals to me. That's rubbish. Money and power are seductive.

Tuesday, December 30th
Cécile is a Shakespeare fan. I am not. (Too much shoved down my throat at school.) She took me to see Paul Schofield in *Richard II*. I thought I would hate it. I didn't. He was amazing, as was Eric Porter. We went for drinks at Jimmy's on the way home. Not a good idea. Cécile hates the place. The wine tasted like paint stripper. Everyone drunk and not making much sense by the time we arrived. We left after a couple. I think Cécile felt I had rather ruined the evening.

Wednesday, December 31st
Felt lousy all day. I think I may have flu. At least I'm not going through my usual year-end retrospection. It's not even nine o'clock yet and I'm going to sleep. Happy New Year!

PART 6

THE ROAD TO PENTONVILLE

The Ninth Diary – January–June, 1953

Friday, January 2nd
New Year, new order, new ideas. I have arranged a formal management meeting for next week. Cécile is impressed. We need to reappraise our situation. I am astonished by the amount of money that is flowing in. The prospects are amazing, particularly with the Coronation coming up later in the year. It is estimated that over a million people will be visiting London. Legions of sex-starved men looking for Soho fun. Our coffers should overflow, but we need to plan in order to make the best of our opportunities.

Wednesday, January 7th
The series of meetings I held yesterday went well. I hired a suite at the Piccadilly Hotel, looking down on Regent Street. We sat round a huge mahogany table, each place set with a blotting pad, writing blocks and pencil. Cécile sported a new dress, whilst Alex and Ted wore their best suits.

Earlier I had interviewed Donald in his latest ginger creation. We reviewed the progress of the catering business. It obviously needs an injection of capital, which I agreed. He is also to employ an assistant. He was so delighted that I swear I saw a hint of colour come to his normally pasty cheeks. I invited him to join us later for lunch.

It was strange sitting in such formal surroundings discussing a typed agenda. Alex and Ted were awarded hefty pay increases. Cécile had been against this when we had discussed the matter last week, but I overrode her objections. It would be a false economy not to share our success with key staff. We also agreed to form a number of new companies to accommodate our expanding interests. Alex and Ted were formally appointed to their boards. They beamed their approval.

I proposed starting a new bookshop venture. We have direct access to pornography from the Continent. Although Cécile was against this, we voted to go ahead, providing Sweet didn't object. Unlike existing outlets, ours was not to be a hole-in-the-corner operation. The shop would be bright, well-fitted and contain material attractively displayed and, although breaking the current laws, would not cause real offence. It was agreed that I should seek a suitable property. I would also increase the lobbying of politicians for a relaxation of laws covering our industry. I want to see not just bookshops but legalised adult cinemas and clubs. These could offer live shows. Tasteful but risqué.

To accelerate our bargaining power, we decided that Ted should set up a series of cameras. Seven of our girls who tended to attract the most upper-crust punters were highlighted. The girls concerned will be offered better terms, as will their maids who will be doing the snapping. Films will be developed on a regular basis and vetted for the famous and influential. We know that many of Winnie and Gaynor's clients feature in Debrett.

Over the next couple of days Cécile and Alex will be interviewing all our girls at the Charing Cross Hotel. Each will be set new targets, but will also be allowed to keep a larger percentage of their earnings. We are also extending their holiday entitlement and improving our dress exchange scheme. Ted will have responsibility for this and for recruiting up to twenty more girls in readiness for the Coronation boom. I am to work with estate agents and existing landlords to establish suitable flats in the area.

Donald joined us for an excellent buffet lunch. We toasted each other in champagne. I'm convinced that by offering such good terms to all our team, we can look forward to a year of considerable expansion.

God, I'm beginning to sound like a company chairman presenting his annual accounts!

Tuesday, January 13th

I have a new confidence. It's infectious. Cécile is impressed by my businesslike approach. Alex and Ted are remotivated. Donald is a changed man. He keeps reps waiting and snaps at suppliers down the phone. Despite the foul weather, business booms on all fronts. Our first couple of cameras have been installed. How low can I sink? I liken it to adultery. I've already done it once, so who cares? Anyway, the photographs are only a form of insurance for the future. They may never be used. At the very least, they should make amusing viewing.

Wednesday, January 14th

Piers Leveridge invited me to a drinks party at his splendid town house overlooking Regent's Park. He obviously feels that I add a certain frisson to the occasion. Not that the rest of the group are exactly out of the top drawer. No sign of his lady wife, just an odd bunch of rather louche-looking men. Most of the ladies wouldn't have looked out of place in my set-up, although they did have pukka accents. I didn't stay long.

Tuesday, January 20th

One invitation leads to another. I'm being drawn into the social swim. I had a call from Quentin Hoggard, a chap I met at Piers' place last week. He's another MP. Labour this time. Not that you would know it. He farms hundreds of acres up in Bedfordshire. I've been talked into supporting one of his pet schemes, a boxing club for delinquent kids in Hoxton. The main requirement for entry into this somewhat seedy sector of the great and the good is obviously money. That and a passable social manner and you are in.

Rich men it seems have wives whose eyes tend to wander. I have forgotten the art of flirting. They must think me incredibly unsophisticated. Even though Cécile doesn't want to attend these gatherings, I explain that I am married. This only seems to increase my attraction. More importantly, I am making some influential contacts. I'm playing the long game.

Wednesday, January 21st

The first group of photos have revealed nothing. Well, that's obviously not true. It's just that identifying men without clothes on is difficult. We have to be more discriminating. I have no interest in copulating businessmen. I suppose it is unreasonable to expect our girls to know politicians and judges from the local greengrocer. My enthusiasm for this scheme is evaporating.

Friday, January 23rd

Our formal, more businesslike approach is in danger of running out of control. Cécile has had forms printed that each girl is required to fill in on a daily basis.

258

Entries have to be countersigned by their maid. Each form has a column for time spent, the service offered and the price charged. Whilst I'm sure the information, if collated, would be of great interest to sociologists, if it fell into the wrong hands we could all land up in jail. Cécile belittles my concerns. She is convinced this is another safeguard against us being short-changed. The time and motion expert complete with stopwatch beckons!

The girls are now being convened in small groups by Cécile, and they discuss ploys for increasing their turnover. Marketing has reached the sex industry. I find the whole idea hilarious. The punter is offered a basic service at a set price, plus a bewildering array of extras. The table d'hôte, sir, or would you prefer the à la carte menu? Cécile is furious at my light-hearted attitude. Meanwhile the money continues to roll in.

Thursday, January 29th
Tonight Cécile wanted to discuss Nadine's education. The child has only just started school, but she is adamant plans must be made. She is in favour of the international school here in Kensington. I am inclined to the more traditional values of an English public school. The desire for respectability is obviously still very much on our minds.

Increasingly, I find that I present myself in different modes depending on whom I'm speaking to. To Soho locals I don't have to pretend, but as I spread my social wings, I am constantly having to reinvent myself. My new-found wealth is helping me to move up the social ladder again. I am already on two charitable committees, and I've been invited to become a governor of Nadine's school.

Clancy is being tiresome. She is on heat. Judging by last week's record takings, so is the entire male population of London!

Tuesday, February 10th
Buying freehold properties in Soho is impossible, but I have managed to secure a number of leases, including a double-fronted shop in Dean Street. This will be our bookshop. Nothing too offensive, but pushing against the current restrictive laws. This is one of the few properties that we are renting which doesn't have any connection with Harold Jacobson. He appears to have set up a bewildering array of companies. All my enquiries only lead me to frontmen, who are obviously under instructions to keep Mr Jacobson as a shady background figure.

Wednesday, February 18th
I swear Cécile is obsessed. She now spends even longer hours huddled over her paperwork. It is now left to me to read Nadine a bedtime story before tucking her up for the night. That's no hardship; I enjoy it. Last night after a solitary supper, I settled down with a bottle of whisky and indulged in a bout of self-analysis. This is a profound weakness, which should be confined to teenage years.

I concluded that life has as much to do with chance as talent or hard work. It is a confusing mix of opportunities and dangers, a large proportion of which are outside our control. We fail to appreciate many of the opportunities and, as in my case, are drawn inexorably towards the dangers. We all thrash around trying to find happiness, but it is illusive and ever changing. Love and money are dominating forces. Love of our parents and close friends, we tend to take for granted. True romantic love it seems is the rarest gift. I don't know, never having experienced it. I so wish I had. And what of money? When I had none, it seemed as if this would be the answer to all my problems. No, not true. Observation of the rich indicates that most are miserable and discontent. Now each week I bank more cash than many earn in an entire year. What am I to do with it? Invest wisely and make more. Then what?

My relationship with Cécile, whilst not volatile, is decidedly cool. She resents my socialising. She knows these people are not really friends, and I am cultivating them for a purpose. It makes no difference. Although she refuses to come with me, I sense she is jealous. They are a strange group, bound together by their wealth, or at least the impression of it. The men tend to be significantly older than their wives or the other women who congregate around them. Most of the women are attractive. Predominantly blonde, slim and outwardly glamorous. Mixing with the famous is an added aphrodisiac for them. The unmarried ones hover on the fringes, seemingly happy to be picked up by fat, ugly, old men, just as long as there are expensive gifts, meals and the occasional holiday on offer. They are a separate breed, these peroxide girls. Vacuous on the surface, but as hard as nails. They play the same game as our street girls, but for higher stakes.

All this is leading to a confession: I wish I was a Catholic. Three Hail Marys, and life continues. OK here goes! I was unfaithful yesterday. Well, I have been before with Doreen, but somehow she doesn't count. I met Cassandra (I bet that's not her real name) at a charity lunch last week. Like an idiot I was flattered by her attention. She fits the part perfectly. Outwardly sophisticated, slim, with long blonde hair (perhaps I'm still missing Mary). She speaks terribly slowly, as if she doesn't trust her self-imposed accent. The experience didn't leave me exhilarated or even feeling guilty. Empty would be a truer description. I played the game and paid the price. We went shopping afterwards, for the baubles which are important to her. A bracelet from Garrards. Pecking me on the cheek, she hailed a taxi to take her back to her mews flat. We agreed to keep in touch. No chance. We both knew I was not about to become her new meal ticket. I wasn't even any good in bed.

So if money is not going to bring me happiness, what will? I'm not so stupid to realise that our present arrangement with the police can't go on for ever. The trick is to know when to get out unscathed. I know in my heart this is not going to happen. My depression deepens.

Clancy can read my moods. She climbed onto my lap and licked my face. She's a Pekinese issued with the wrong body. She weighs a ton, but I didn't attempt to move her. We were both asleep when Cécile arrived home.

Tuesday, February 24th
I had a visit from Sergeant Miller, a sidekick of the 'Sweet cop'. I was expecting him. Last night two of our girls were involved in a scrap. Skin and teeth all

over the place! One was a new girl from Liverpool, who had only been with us for a couple of days. As usual it was about territory. Glenys, who is one of our old hands, reckoned the new girl was invading her pitch. The police don't want any more trouble. I will have a quiet word.

Monday, March 9th
My reputation as a 'do-gooder' grows. Today I am pictured in the *Evening News* presenting a cheque to the treasurer of Great Ormond Street Hospital. I am referred to as a leading entrepreneur. Well, I suppose that's one way of putting it!

The papers are full of news of the death of Stalin.

Tuesday, March 17th
Dad will be doing headstands in his grave. He belonged to an era of self-restraint. The mention of money was considered bad form and conspicuous spending of it showed a total lack of breeding. Sorry, father. Now I have it, I am spraying the stuff around with great abandon. Waiters jostle to serve me. Shop managers ease assistants aside. I have spent a fortune on clothes. Still all black, of course, but now I sport crocodile shoes and cashmere jackets. I shower Nadine with gifts. She loves it. Her mother is furious. I am still banking fist-loads of cash. Even my property deals are looking good. The new bookshop opens tomorrow.

Thursday, March 19th
So far the police have shown no interest in our new venture. We have appointed a friend of Ted's as manager. I am distancing myself from the shop in case things

go wrong. Cécile is a prude. She doesn't approve. It offends her. More than a little hypocrisy being shown here, I think.

Sunday, March 22nd
Lunch with the girls in Greek Street. Marvellous, just like old times. I took them all presents and a couple of bottles of champagne. Esther cooked a traditional roast in my honour. The beef was rare. Quite superb.

Our efforts at photography had produced very little until last week. Mainly amusement value only. Then, within two days, we have captured a leading member of the shadow cabinet, a bishop who broadcasts regularly and the ambassador of one of our major allies. They have been filed away for possible future reference.

Wednesday, March 25th
Old Queen Mary died last night. She always looked a miserable old bird. This adds to my theory about money not bringing contentment. Obviously adding privilege doesn't do the trick either. What the hell does?

Saturday, March 28th
I'm trying to rebuild bridges with Cécile. I arranged to take her to the theatre and then on for a late supper. She was pleased enough, until she learnt we were off to the Palladium to see Johnnie Ray, the new singing sensation from America. It was the opening night and the theatre was packed with screaming teenagers. He simpers and cries whilst making love to the microphone. Complete uproar. The girls go mad, screaming in adulation. Cécile muttered through the entire show. I thought he was wonderful. A breath of fresh air.

We sat right next to Noel Coward and a lovely lady, who I think was Gladys Cooper. He greeted me as if he knew me, but his voice was drowned out by the general pandemonium. I think tonight underlines change. It's everywhere and it is perhaps symbolic that old stagers like Joe Stalin and Queen Mary have departed the world recently. The young are asserting themselves. People are no longer willing to be pigeon-holed. These are exciting times. Cécile doesn't agree. She likes stability. Change unsettles her.

Saturday, April 4th
Most evenings are now spent watching television. Like most of the country, we have bought one in order to watch the Coronation. The standard of the programmes is rather uninspiring, but we tend to sit glued until the epilogue.

Tuesday, April 7th
Clancy was attacked this morning by a ferocious Jack Russell bitch in Hyde Park. Off to the vet for stitches. Why are small dogs, like their human counterparts, always so bloody aggressive?

Sunday, April 12th
I went to eleven o'clock Mass with Cécile and Nadine. I wish I hadn't. My feelings of guilt and futility came crashing into my consciousness again. I have treated Cécile very shoddily recently.

Saturday, April 18th
This has been a week where we have made a great effort to inject some real meaning into our marriage.

Tonight that collapsed under a hail of recrimination. It was prompted as usual by what Cécile reckons to be my cavalier attitude to money. Then it lurched on to my recent infidelities. I had no idea Cécile knew what I had been up to, or that she would be jealous. I tried to placate her, which only accelerated her fury. Eventually I stormed out, feeling an unwarranted sense of grievance.

I was determined not to give her the satisfaction of returning home and apologising. It was already late when I went to Doreen's flat. I sat in the kitchen with her maid, whilst she sorted out her last couple of punters. Later, I think she was quite grateful that it wasn't sex I was after. We sat up talking and drinking coffee until four o'clock. She is also desperately unhappy with her life and dreams of escaping. I am so selfish – this has never occurred to me.

Wednesday, April 22nd
Had a strange phone call from a chap calling himself Charles Brewer (English name, but with the suspicion of a foreign accent). He said he had an interesting proposition to put to me. His attitude was extremely patronising. He is staying at the Grosvenor House, and he suggested I called in. He seemed to think I should drop everything. I told him he knew where to contact me if he wanted a meeting and hung up.

Friday, April 24th
I was in the middle of my weekly meeting with Donald this morning when Margaret, his assistant, came in to inform me my chauffeur was waiting. Going out to investigate, I was informed that he had been instructed

266

to take me to the Grosvenor House Hotel to meet Mr Charles Brewer. I sent him packing. This Charles Brewer obviously has a screw loose. He can get lost.

Saturday, April 25th
I am gradually convincing Cécile that a cup of tea is the best way to start the day. She was going through her usual routine of mock disgust when the phone rang. I recognised the voice at once. The car would pick me up at nine o'clock, he said. Just that. Then the line went dead. No thank you.

It was a lovely day and I proposed we took Nadine to Whipsnade Zoo. I hustled and harried them. We left the flat at a quarter to nine.

Whipsnade Zoo was a great success. We walked for miles and were all tired by the time we arrived home. As I opened the door, the phone rang. 'You are beginning to annoy me, Captain.' The voice was familiar now. 'Tomorrow, my hotel at ten. You can take a taxi, but be there. We need to talk.'

I don't normally write my diary at three o'clock in the morning, but I can't sleep. Cécile knows I'm uneasy. She is suspicious. So am I.

Sunday, April 26th
Charles Brewer lives well. He had taken a suite. No ordinary suite, but one normally reserved for visiting heads of state or film stars. I was escorted in a separate lift to the top floor, by an under manager. I was let into a vast living room by a man whom I recognised as the chauffeur. No uniform today. A smart double-breasted suit and leather gloves. Never trust a man who wears gloves on a lovely spring morning. He is

heavily built, but light on his feet. He glides. He's no youngster, probably in his late fifties. Without asking he poured me a coffee. His movements belie his girth, they are precise and studied. His face is expressionless. In fact, I notice it is completely unlined. The face of a clown, but this man isn't funny.

Enter Charles Brewer, immaculate, diminutive. Something about his features stirred a memory at the back of my mind. Mr Gloves is dismissed with the wave of a hand. I was on my guard, but not really concerned. Brewer sat down without shaking hands or even acknowledging me. I reckoned him to be in his mid-thirties. Dark skinned with receding hair, nearer to five foot tall than six. Everything about him was tiny except his hands, which are quite out of all proportion. Huge spatula-shaped fingers, the backs covered in coarse, sprouting black hair.

Leaning forward, he handed me his business card. I hardly glanced at it. 'Well, what's so important?' I enquired rather rudely. He didn't answer. I realised his eyes were still fixed firmly on the card he had handed me. I read it. My stomach lurched. No address or telephone number. Just a name. Carlo de Bono.

Wednesday, April 29th
It's three days since our meeting and I'm still in shock. The little man manages to convey a certain menace. I tend to believe he is the de Bonos' kid brother, but is he a real threat or a sham? Something about him doesn't add up. I'm spending big money having him checked out in Paris and Milan.

His manner was calm, placid, almost effeminate. His

demands were not. Cécile and I stand accused of systematically robbing his family. He insisted we were, and remain, employees. He calmly informed me that he intends taking over control from July 1st. I laughed. He ignored me. What's more he demanded payment of thousands of pounds from our deposit accounts. He reeled off a series of numbers. I have no idea if these are a figment of his imagination or not. The guy is mad. I told him it would only take a couple of phone calls to have him deported.

He was unfazed. He issued his own threats. These were pure de Bono. He wouldn't target me directly, but those close to me. My old problem. Temper. I was boiling with rage. How dare this weed threaten me! Lunging forward, I grabbed him by the throat. I lifted him off the floor until his face was opposite mine. He didn't resist, but there was no fear in his eyes either. I tossed him aside like an unwanted gift. Mr Leather Gloves looked on. His hand rested inside his jacket. Carlo shook his head. The hand was removed. The clown's face registered no emotion.

More threats from little Carlo. I would regret my actions ... I could either arrange an orderly handover or...

'Creep!' I shouted as I made for the door. This annoyed him. He ran down the corridor. Pulling at my sleeve. Roughly I brushed him aside. As I pressed the button for the lift, he stood halfway down the corridor, a tiny comic figure.

'I can't understand what she saw in you.' I jammed my foot in the door of the elevator.

'Who?' I queried.

'Claudia.' He spat the name out. He was close to tears. 'You took advantage of her, you bastard.'

'Creep,' I repeated. He rushed towards me, his huge hands raised in anger. The doors closed. He looked so ridiculous I was still laughing when I reached reception. Will I still be able to laugh in the months to come?

Monday, May 4th

I haven't told Cécile about Carlo. If I did it would be panic stations. I'm fairly convinced that the little man doesn't really pose a threat. Enquiries in Milan and Paris have drawn a blank. Despite rumours to the contrary, he is totally unknown in Italy and he hasn't tried to pick up the pieces in Paris since Frank and Zoe were jailed. The man is a bluff.

Wednesday, May 6th

My suspicions about Carlo have been confirmed. The Grosvenor House contacted me today. Charles Brewer had slipped out of the hotel without paying. He left a note saying I would settle the account. Sorry, no chance!

Nobody has any idea where our friend has gone. Who cares? It's back to business as usual.

Tuesday, May 12th

Donald was killed yesterday in a tragic accident. He would insist on riding on a hydraulic platform, used for taking stock to the basement below the shop. The lift travels very slowly, allowing him to release a catch and push open a metal hatch onto the pavement. I have warned him dozens of times about how dangerous this is. Disastrously, heavy cartons from a supplier had

270

been moved onto the trap door at the insistence of a policeman. He had complained they were causing an obstruction. The driver ran down the stairs to warn Donald. Too late. He suffered a horrendous death. The whole episode has really upset me. I had grown fond of Donald. I have left a message of complaint for Inspector Sweet.

Wednesday, May 13th
Sweet rang. He insists that no constable was near Greek Street at the time of the accident. Liars! They constantly cover up for each other.

Thursday, May 21st
I attended Donald's cremation at Golders Green. The inquest recorded accidental death. Despite the missing policeman, it never occurred to me that this was not the case. Until, that is, I read a card on a wreath outside the chapel. It read simply, 'July 1st'.

Friday, May 22nd
I rang Mrs de B. in Palma. What could she tell me about Carlo? I expected the normal de Bono reticence. Quite the opposite. She was effusive in his praise. He was the youngest and most brilliant of the brothers. He was a qualified accountant, had a business degree from Cornell University and was a talented linguist. Proudly she proclaimed he was also deeply religious and had taken on the mantle of head of the family. She depended on his advice and he was taking a protective interest in Claudia. She wanted to know why I was enquiring about him. I decided to be honest. She derided the suggestion that he would be interested

271

in her husband's former business. Can I be sure? Can I believe her? Sadly, can I trust anyone?

Sunday, May 24th

I took longer over my run in the park today, mulling over recent developments. Clancy kept barking in an attempt to get me moving at my normal speed. Arriving home, I found Cécile in a blue funk. She shivered violently, as if in shock. She appeared unable to speak. She handed me a typewritten card. The message was simple: 'Talk to your stupid husband. By the way, how is Nadine?' There was no signature.

Monday, May 25th

I have briefed Alex and Ted. Find that slimy little sod. I sense he's still in London. Luckily we have good contacts. Someone will know where he is. Cécile is over-reacting, refusing to let Nadine out of her sight. Young Carlo needs teaching a lesson.

Wednesday, May 27th

A very worried Inspector Sweet visited me today. We had agreed never to meet in public, but he's badly rattled. He's heard a rumour that he is about to be suspended and that his new boss is going to target me. He wants to know what's going on. I wish I knew. I had asked for his help in tracking down Carlo. No sign, he has gone to ground.

Friday, May 29th

I finally managed to get Cécile and Nadine outside today. London is filling up and everywhere is bedecked with flags and bunting. We ended up in the ice-cream parlour at Harrods.

Saturday, May 30th

This evening Carlo rang. He was polite but extremely irritating. I don't handle him well. I should have arranged a meeting. Instead, I told him to bugger off. He said I would regret my response and hung up. I still have no idea where he is. Neither the police nor our own enquiries have given us a lead. It's like trying to fight an invisible enemy.

Cécile is so worried, she is in favour of standing down. I tell her she is crazy. Why should we pack up because of some vague threat?

Sunday, May 31st

A black day. Last week I promoted Margaret to take charge of the catering business. As promised, I took her to Wheelers for a celebration lunch. As the restaurant was fully booked, we left Clancy in her basket in the stockroom below the shop. When we returned a couple of hours later she was dead. Chunks of poisoned meat had been scattered on the floor. I was distraught that anyone could be so callous. Margaret took me next door where Esther made us a strong cup of tea. I know it's stupid to become so attached to a dog, but I feel her death as much as when Dad died.

This evening another phone call. I was furious, but tried to keep calm. Did I accept his terms? I stalled and suggested a meeting. He's not having that. He insists our rule is over. Capitulate or we will suffer greater distress nearer home. The bastard. I screamed abuse at him. He hung up leaving me feeling distressed, angry and impotent.

Monday, June 1st

Ted rang to inform me that Inspector Sweet has been

suspended. Certainly, for whatever reason, the net seems to be closing. Cécile has decided to throw in the towel. I am tempted, providing I can negotiate for us to keep the money we have secreted away. Surely this will be possible?

Clancy's killing has really rattled me. Was Donald's death an accident? I don't know. When Carlo rings next, we will have to reach some sort of compromise. The very thought of being able to start a new life suddenly has great appeal. I feel almost demob happy. I don't know if Cécile and I will stay together. Probably to start with. I would miss Nadine terribly if we did decide to go our separate ways.

So I must wait for Carlo's phone call and in the meantime look forward to tomorrow. I have been offered fantastic seats in Whitehall to view the Coronation procession. Cécile is so frightened that she wants us to stay at home and watch it on television. Nadine will be so disappointed. I think we should go, to witness a snippet of history. It could be symbolic. A new era for the country and a fresh start for us.

Picking up the Pieces

My father's diaries end abruptly on the eve of Coronation Day. Tracking down the leading characters he mentions so many years after his death proved more difficult than I had imagined. Apart from Mary, his first wife, his landlady and Beatrix, they had all disappeared from the scene. Either death had claimed them, they had moved or pointedly refused to speak to me. The obituary list included Frank de Bono, who had suffered a massive heart attack whilst serving his sentence. I eventually tracked Zoe down in 1989. She was in a mental hospital just outside Saumur. God knows what had happened to her. She sat in a corner, gently rocking herself backwards and forwards. For a whole day I tried to prise some sense from her. I had a wasted journey. Harry's wife had died in the early sixties. I visited Palma in a vain attempt to track down Claudia. No trace. Latterly I have even employed local detective agencies in Spain and Malta. No leads, just large bills.

My enquiries concerning Winnie and Gaynor were met with blank stares in Soho. Their house of correction has long been forgotten. Their basement, by the mid-eighties, had become a wine bar. Leo Joseph retired to Bournemouth and died choking on a chicken bone in 1981. Ted had simply disappeared. I was unable to trace any relatives. He left no trail. It was as if he had never existed. Surely I would be able to trace someone as visible as Alex. He, at least, was remembered. It was reckoned he had returned to Belfast after my father's arrest. Naively, I visited the Shankhill in search of the Captain's right-hand man. Not a clever move.

Strangers asking questions are unwelcome. It was a frightening experience.

My enquiries continued to draw blanks. I convinced myself there was a conspiracy of silence. Father Tony had joined a missionary order and was based in Tanzania. Each time I tracked him down, he appeared to have moved on. My letters went unanswered.

My most urgent search centred on my half-sister, Nadine. I knew that she and Xavier were alive because I had glimpsed them at my mother's funeral. I remember being very hurt that she didn't make contact with me. The solicitors must have known of her whereabouts but said they were not at liberty to reveal them. Another closed trail.

Inspector Sweet had been jailed after my father's trial. Years later he was living in obscurity in a semi-detached bungalow in Rustington. He also ignored my letters and shut the door in my face when I called.

For the time being, I had to content myself with newspaper reports of my father's trial. Even here the coverage was surprisingly sparse. Possibly it was because he refused to 'play the game'. He confined himself to a simple statement at the time of his arrest. He pleaded guilty but refused to answer any further questions, thereby infuriating his own legal team and the British public. Lord Justice Hanson used his summing up to launch an attack on a man who, he asserted, had enjoyed many advantages in life. A superb education, followed by distinguished war service, all of which he cast aside pursuing a squalid life of shame. That this had ended in cold-blooded murder underlined the fact that Captain Derek Emms was an utter disgrace to his family and class. So saying, he donned the black cap and sentenced my father to be hanged by the neck until he be dead.

It was over a year after my mother's funeral that I received a letter from Nadine, written in spidery capital letters. She suggested that perhaps the time was right for me to visit her. Frustratingly, the notepaper was not headed. For reasons best known to herself, she was teasing me. Then a couple of days later I received a telephone call. I recognised the high-pitched voice immediately. Xavier. He picked me up the following day. Sitting next to him in the familiar blue Bentley, he no longer appeared threatening. Just old and world-weary. We drove south across Hammersmith Bridge, heading through the suburbs towards Banstead. The nursing home was approached down a rather grand drive. In contrast, the buildings comprised a series of ugly modern units.

My meeting with Nadine was both awkward and emotional. I was shocked by her frailty. She was totally paralysed from the waist down. Her legs were pipe-cleaner thin and wasted in contrast to her upper body, which had ballooned. This was not the enchanting child that my father constantly referred to. And yet her face, although coarsened, presumably by drugs, still bore a resemblance to our mother's. The staggering blue eyes and long lashes remained, but her body had been overwhelmed by the consequences of that appalling day in her life. It was soon obvious to me that she also continued to suffer mental stress. We struggled to find common ground. She refused to talk about the past. Mention of my mother reduced her to tears. Xavier was no more forthcoming. He had been totally against us meeting. I had so many questions. His only

277

interest, he emphasised, was Nadine's well-being. Over the years I dutifully visited my sister, but our conversation never rose above the safe and mundane. Her life revolved around watching television, and, as my celebrity status grew, so did her affection for me. After Xavier died, I took over the financial responsibility for her. I started taking her on outings. The highlight was when I arranged for her to be my guest at some TV award ceremonies. Sadly, she died last year. We had spent a huge amount of time in each other's company and yet I never managed to penetrate the triviality of our relationship. This was what she wanted. It was her way of coping.

Belatedly, Alex came into my life. After a busy day filming, I arrived home exhausted and had fallen asleep in front of the television. Reaching for the remote control, I found myself confronted by an old ruddy-faced Ulsterman who was being interviewed whilst serving a life sentence in a Cape Town jail. He was a huge powerful man and even before his name was flashed up on the screen, I knew, as if by instinct, it was Alex. The programme featured British citizens serving prison terms abroad, comparing their treatment. The clip of Alex was short, but the next day I rang the programme-makers. With their help I was able to make contact with Alex and so started a correspondence that lasted some months.

His recollections of my father were selective. The Soho years were largely ignored. It was his war service that he turned to most often. In so doing, he highlighted an incident that caused my father the nightmares he periodically referred to in his diaries. He and Alex had been part of a commando raid that had gone badly wrong. The mission had been to land in a small craft on the French coast near Dieppe. They were to capture and bring back German prisoners for interrogation in a snatch operation, prior to the first major Allied landing of the war. Alex explained that they were spotted as they came ashore. It was pitch dark and the air was thick with burning cordite. The landing party did manage to grab a number of Germans from outside the local garrison. Their hands were secured so tightly behind their backs with electrical wire that if they struggled it was likely to sever their thumbs. Amidst the confusion and panic it was obvious the mission would have to be aborted. As the prisoners were marched towards the shore, a counter order was issued. They were instructed to shoot their captives. The Germans were forced to kneel and were executed amidst the general mayhem. Although this was later officially denied, Alex was adamant this outrage had taken place. The man whom my father had tied up spoke perfect English. Seeing his comrades being murdered, he begged him to extract a photograph of his family from his tunic pocket. Why? Hoping that this would save him? It didn't. Derek Emms shot the man in cold blood. Obeying orders certainly, but the image of that German soldier haunted him for the rest of his life. He told Alex that one day he wanted to track down the family, to explain and apologise. He never did. I still have the photo of an unknown wife and her beautiful blonde child, smiling across time from an alpine mountainside.

So for many years I learnt no more. I had accepted that my search for the truth about the Captain had closed in on me. Then just over a year ago a message on my answerphone asked me to contact a Sister

Evangeline. She urged me to come straightaway to a convent in Hendon, where a Father Boldini wanted to see me urgently. Father Tony. The convent is set back from the busy main road leading to the M1. It's a tranquil oasis, nestled behind substantial walls and surrounded by towering Scots pines. The main house is of high gothic design, utilised now as a hospital for sick priests. A young novice led me up a grand staircase to a huge dark room on the first floor. His body was marooned in a massive old-fashioned bed. A picture of Christ looked down on the old man, whose breathing was shallow and irregular. I pulled up a chair. So here at last was the handsome young priest my father had mentioned so often, now old and ill. Reduced to a jaundiced, skeletal parody of himself in his prime.

It was almost an hour before he woke. He reached for my hand. His touch was cold, but clammy. 'Jamie,' he whispered. Old age can be cruel. His head seemed too large for his body. Loose skin hung from his sticklike arms. I didn't answer, but squeezed his hand. He kept closing his eyes, as if the act of speaking required all his strength. In a voice that I had to strain to hear, he told me of his love for my father, who was not the ghastly man many had supposed. He had been weak and impetuous, but in the end he had found some comfort in God. I somehow doubted that. The old priest had tears in his eyes, as if he was desperate for me to accept what he was telling me. I nodded. He appeared to relax. I wanted to ask him why he hadn't replied to my numerous letters, but I was alarmed that his breath was now coming in gasps, as if being dredged from his unwilling lungs. Tears were rolling down his cheeks.

I rang a bell on his bedside table. An older nun who I took to be Sister Evangeline came in and said I should leave. She told the priest that he was very silly getting himself in such a state. He became even more distressed. With a huge effort he raised himself on one elbow. 'The drawer!' he gasped. Gently I opened the drawer to his bedside table. Amongst the bottles of tablets lay a battered brown envelope. I held it in front of him. He nodded. 'Take it,' he whispered. 'God be with you.' He made an approximate sign of the cross.

The nun hustled me to the door. I visited him twice more, but by then he was in a coma. He struggled on for another ten days. The nuns marvelled at his constitution. I went to his funeral. And for perhaps the first time in my life I prayed. For him and my father. The priest had supplied the final explanation of what happened on that fateful Coronation Day, back in 1953.

The Final Notebook – HMP Pentonville, 1953

This is not a confession. A reflection certainly and a considered one. I have had plenty of time to play that day through in my mind.

It is ironic that as Coronation Day approached, Cécile and I had decided to quit. I still had doubts about the threat Carlo posed, but I reckoned it was only a matter of time before some hoodlum decided to challenge us. Worried, too, that the police support was tenuous. We were vulnerable. It was astonishing how much wealth we had accumulated in such a short time. Of course, wealth is relative, but we had ample to enable us to plan ahead with confidence. On the eve of the Coronation I think we both experienced a real feeling of relief. We talked tentatively of the future. A new life to be spent together? Possibly? But probably not in the long term.

In the morning, the papers proclaimed the conquering of Everest, by Hillary and Tenzing. Contrived timing no doubt, but overall the outlook for the country appeared positive.

Cécile still favoured watching the day's events on television, but I had managed to obtain three prime seats in one of the temporary stands erected in Whitehall. Rather grudgingly she agreed to come. We set off in a steady drizzle.

Central London should have been a blaze of colour, but the bunting was bedraggled and flags hung limply to their poles. Nadine, like most of the children, carried a small Union Jack. Cécile had managed to unearth a far larger tricolour, which I felt inappropriate, but I knew better than to argue with her over such matters.

Like others we took up our position hours in advance. Ever practical, Cécile had brought sandwiches and a huge thermos of coffee, which was most welcome.

The streets were lined as far as the eye could see with crowds standing as much as ten deep. In front, at regular intervals, members of the forces stood at ease, sometimes exchanging banter with the boisterous crowd. All three services lined the route. Our section was manned by immaculate ratings from the Royal Navy. Eventually the sound of distant music heralded the arrival of the procession. Guardsmen, mounted cavalry, Scottish regiments with skirling pipes, interspersed with Gurkhas and exotic representatives of the Commonwealth and Empire. Even the foul weather couldn't dampen the spirits of the cheering crowds. Then the Cinderella-like coach, gleaming gold and drawn by horses of jet black. A glimpse of the new Queen and other members of the Royal Family. I pointed out Winston Churchill to Nadine, but she was more interested in the horses and the marching troops.

And then they were all gone. A couple of council trucks drove slowly along the route, whilst offending horse droppings were cleared. We now waited and ate our sandwiches before the newly crowned Queen returned to Buckingham Palace. Bored, I scanned the crowd with binoculars. Turning towards Trafalgar Square, I spotted a familiar figure on a balcony of an office building. Annoyingly I had continued scanning further down the street. By the time I had located the balcony again it was empty. A sign above confirmed my sighting. Leveridge and Leveridge. I refocused the binoculars, trying to penetrate into the room where a crowd of guests were drinking from fluted glasses. No sign of Piers. I panned in the opposite direction. What a commotion. A group from the crowd had broken away and had formed a giant, swaying conga. They were singing and cheering. Carnival time, in rainy old London!

As the long column of troops continued to march by on their return from the Abbey, I suddenly remembered Piers Leveridge. I trained my glasses over to the balcony, which was now full of guests who rushed forward to get a better view. Next to Piers, another familiar figure, Carlo de Bono. I said nothing to Cécile.

Later that afternoon, we walked down The Mall and stood in a vast crowd, waiting for the Queen to appear on the balcony. Nadine sat on my shoulder waving her flag. We cheered. The crowd sang the national anthem. Cécile declared that the British were mad, but she too waved her tricolour.

The mood was sustained on the crowded Tube train. Nadine was still chattering excitedly as we entered our apartment block. Fleetingly I registered something wasn't quite right. Not normal. I was too slow to react. Everything happened so quickly, but now those few seconds remain with me. I fight to remove them from my mind, but they return constantly and in hideous detail.

The doorman to our apartment was a familiar figure. He had been on duty the very first time I had arrived, hot and sweaty, to see Harry. The door was held open for us as usual. We were talking animatedly. The figure was familiar, but out of context. This was not our doorman, although he wore the uniform. Turning, I shouted a warning. The lift doors opened. An elderly neighbour greeted Cécile, distracting her attention. The woman was about to take her dachshund for a walk.

Fritz wagged his tail and Nadine bent to stroke him. As I shouted, the clown-faced man I had met at the Grosvenor House fired two shots in quick succession. Nadine toppled forward. Silently, not a sound. Fritz howled, one of his hindlegs shattered. For a moment no one moved, united in shock.

Clown-face looked appalled. 'Why did she move?' Nobody answered him. He turned and rushed for the door, dropping the gun which clattered onto the tiled floor. That broke the spell.

Cécile screamed. Our neighbour shouted. Fritz howled. Nadine was silent, motionless. My military training deserted me. I was frozen by indecision. Should I run after the gunman or attend to Nadine? I did neither. Just staring uncomprehendingly. Nadine lay in the foetal position, her legs tucked up to her chest. She was deathly pale. A scorch mark on her coat marked the bullet's point of entry. There was surprisingly little blood. 'She's dead, dear God, she's dead,' Cécile screamed. Our neighbour, still in shock, stood hands to mouth. Fritz ran around dementedly squealing, his shattered leg hanging uselessly.

It was cowardice that finally sent me in pursuit of the gunman. The scene was one from hell. I couldn't cope. I ran away. Snatching the fallen gun, I stumbled out onto the street. There was no sign of the clown. Passing cars sounded their horns, Union Jacks waved from their windows. I should have gone back to help Nadine. I didn't. A feeling of rage and hatred consumed me. I saw a taxi offloading a couple of passengers fifty yards ahead. He was pulling away, as sprinting I drew level with the cab. He told me he wasn't for hire. I ran in front of him. He slammed on his brakes. He

285

wasn't impressed. He was going home. I offered him ten pounds to take me to Whitehall. He didn't want to know. I drew out the gun. 'Take me!' I demanded. He didn't blanch. 'Fucking nutter,' he replied smiling. I was beside myself. I explained my daughter had been shot. He suggested I should call the police, before calmly pulling away and leaving me waving the gun in my frustration. What does it take to shock Londoners? Several saw me with the gun. None reacted. There were no more cabs to be seen. I ran towards the Tube station.

The crowds had gone from Whitehall. The street was deserted, apart from workers shovelling mountains of litter. The drizzle had intensified into a steady rain. I was soaked. It was a long shot that the Leveridge party was still going on, but worth a try. I had rung his home number from Charing Cross Station. No reply. I walked along the street, staring upwards looking for the identifying sign. Many of the buildings had similar balconies. Eventually I located the door to Leveridge and Leveridge. Locked. In despair I rang a bell next to the double-fronted doors. The reception desk was deserted. I kept pressing, sobbing at my impotence.

The caretaker thought I was drunk. I continued ringing the bell even after he opened the door. I was in a daze. I pushed a bundle of notes into his hand and pleaded with him to tell me where I could find Piers Leveridge. He said I could keep my money. He seemed quite offended. He told me Leveridge and his guests had gone to a celebration dinner at the Savoy. Gratefully, I tried pressing the money on him again. 'Piss off,' he said, closing the door in my face.

Running back to the station, I tried ringing home. No reply. I rang three hospitals. Three thinly manned switchboards. Long waits. I hung up in frustration. Finally I rang the police. They were unable to give any information regarding incidents over the phone. It was suggested I called in at my local police station with proof of identity. Pure rage!

I tried to compose myself as I walked up the Strand towards the Savoy. My anger was being replaced by an eerie feeling of calm. A sense of purpose. My emotion and grief were replaced by a cold, calculated loathing. There was a job to be done. Maybe the intention had only been to wing Nadine. Certainly she had bent to stroke the dog at the moment the gun was fired. Carlo had employed an inefficient hit-man. But what sort of person could target a child? I assumed that Carlo would still be with the Leveridge party, providing him with an alibi. I also knew what I was about to do and the consequences.

As I entered the foyer to the hotel I caught sight of myself in a mirror. Dishevelled, soaked and at odds with the plush surroundings. The attendant in the lavatory took my raincoat and brushed my jacket. I rinsed my face in cold water and applied splashes of cologne. I brushed my wet hair back from my face. The bristles were gentle on my scalp. Calming, soothing. My mind had turned in on itself, almost trancelike. The attendant had hung my raincoat amongst the sea of others. Black and dripping, it stood out amongst the line of gabardine. I realised I had left the gun in the pocket. He handed me the coat across the counter. He must have seen the revolver, as I slipped it into my waistband. Perhaps he didn't. Anyway he didn't react. I handed him a pound note. Bowing slightly, he opened the door for me.

There were several celebration dinners taking place in the hotel. Eventually I was directed towards the River Room. As I studied the table plan, I was conscious of a female vocalist, accompanied by an impressive band. She sang well. A love song. 'Jealousy' I think it was, adding to my sense of unreality. Charles Brewer was listed as sitting next to Piers' wife on table eight right next to the bandstand.

The door attendant wouldn't let me in. I had no tie. It was dinner jacket only. I explained I was delivering a message. A waiter would pass the message on for me. Come on! I know the game he's playing. A final confirmation that money does open most doors. Two crisp white fivers. I was in.

The noise was immense. Music, the babble of conversation. I walked slowly. No one gave me a second glance. Waiters squeezed between tightly packed tables, swaying like dancers. Cigar smoke, raised glasses, glittering jewels, fashionable gowns, deep cleavages and the hubbub of animated chatter.

The carpeted aisle was soft beneath my feet. It was Piers who noticed me first. He raised his hand in recognition, lowering it quickly. I wasn't welcome. He whispered something to Carlo, who was sitting with his back to me. He turned. His expression told me he knew. Rising clumsily, he knocked his chair over and caught the elbow of an elegant lady at the next table. Her claret splashed down the bodice of her expensive dress. Rudely pushing his way between tables, Carlo sought an escape route. I was conscious that the vocalist was singing 'Time on My Hands'. Not for you Carlo, old chap! He broke into a trot, wildly searching out his options. The closely packed tables were making it difficult for him. He opted for the bandstand.

Pushing the peroxided singer aside, he knocked the drummer's cymbals crashing to the floor. Only a few of the diners appeared to notice. The musician continued unabashed. Obviously true pros. He disappeared behind heavy velvet curtains which formed a backdrop to the stage. I vaulted onto the bandstand, ignoring the steps. Carlo was unlucky. It was reasonable for him to expect there would be an exit from the small dressing room. The door was locked. He didn't cower. He decided to brazen it out. He even held out a hand in greeting. I told him quite calmly that he had killed my daughter. He seemed genuinely concerned. Not, I think, out of compassion, but annoyance at a job botched. I pointed the gun. Not so self-composed now. He talked, jabbered. It had been a mistake. A ghastly mistake. We should go into partnership together. I stopped listening, but I let him continue. Eventually be stopped. He was grinning foolishly. A smile of friendship. I led him gently by the arm. I felt him relax. He was being taken back to the safety of the crowded room.

The cymbals were back in place. The vocalist had a deep voice for one so slender. Below us a sea of faces. Few seemed to notice us except Piers. He was standing, smiling, presumably desperate to avoid any embarrassment. Unlucky Piers.

Why the sense of theatre? What possible reason did I have for ruining such a momentous day for so many people? Perhaps a perverse sense of wanting them to share just a little of the pain and bewilderment I was suffering.

I held Carlo firmly. He didn't resist. I'm sure he thought he was safe. The band leader was giving me anxious looks, but he carried on to the end of the number. As they finished, I went forward to the microphone. Taking out the gun, I forced Carlo to kneel in supplication. I imagine most of the audience assumed we were part of some cabaret act, but not for long.

Gradually the whole room went quiet. I told them that this man had hired the gunman who, this afternoon, had shot my five-year-old daughter. A faint rumble of shocked whispering, drowned out by Carlo protesting his innocence. I pushed his head between his knees. I noticed a thickset man in dinner dress walking slowly between the tables towards me.

For a moment I hesitated. The last time I had been in this position, bullets had screamed over my head. I held the gun to Carlo's temple and fired. His body convulsed and crumpled at my feet. There was a single woman's cry. Slowly I walked down the steps from the stage. Many people sat transfixed, others dived under the tables. I faced the thickset man. Reaching into his breast pocket, he produced a red silk handkerchief which he held out in front of me. We didn't speak. I raised the gun. His face showed no fear, just a hint of compassion. I remember giving a slight nod of my head, before placing the gun in the handkerchief. I was grabbed from behind and frogmarched from the room. Commissioner Banks of Scotland Yard had been a guest at the dinner. He is a brave man.

That night I gave them a short terse statement. Later, I was advised Nadine was alive. Just. Cécile visited me regularly. I had expected her to be full of recrimination.

If we had stayed at home that day and watched the Coronation on television, this whole ghastly tragedy may have been avoided. She had warned of the threats to Nadine from the moment we met. I hadn't believed her. Astoundingly she refused to point the finger. I am shamed by her loyalty, but still overwhelmed with remorse. Not about Carlo's death, but that I had allowed him to ruin our lives.

The trial was just that! I refused to give evidence or details of any extenuating circumstances. I am guilty. My defence team were frustrated, the prosecution, too, at being denied the opportunity to dissect me in the dock. The judge despised me. He's not alone.

I find the thought of Nadine being crippled for life unbearable. For a few days after my arrest the prognosis was relatively hopeful. Then news and confirmation that she would never be able to walk again. I feel so helpless. I can't sleep, constantly reliving the moments leading up to her shooting.

Cécile's reaction has been staggering. She offers a loyalty I don't deserve. I underestimated the evil intent of the de Bonos. My act of revenge was utterly selfish. Action ill thought out and leaving Cécile to face the consequences. And what consequences! Today Cécile told me she is pregnant. I don't know how to react. Am I thrilled or horrified? I just hope the child will bring some joy to Cécile – she deserves that.

Poor Father Tony! He visits me daily. I'm convinced he hopes I will be an eleventh-hour convert to Catholicism. I feel so sorry for him. He tries to make excuses for me. There are none. I have been weak all my adult life, assuming superficial glamour and wealth would guarantee happiness. I was wrong on both counts.

Ten more days. Boredom, memories and sleeplessness combining to dull my brain. Endless games of draughts. None of the warders can play chess. Presumably these men have been hand-picked, but by God they are dull. It would be wrong to say that I am not worried about my forthcoming appointment. Worried, but I will be relieved, too, when it's all over. I haven't met the hangman, but I know he watches me at exercise. I am weighed regularly. That is important. I remember reading the hangman's task required a specific skill, for an instantaneous dispatch. I hope I will be brave. In truth what the hell does it matter? No one cares – except me.

Epilogue – The Captain's Club

The book I published on my father's life caused something of a sensation, as did the documentary that followed on Channel 4. Opinion was divided as to whether I had been wise to reveal my secret. Some felt it would damage my career; others that it was wrong for me to benefit, albeit indirectly from crime. I silenced these critics by donating the proceeds to charity.

During my research I had met Marcia Jacobson, the acknowledged 'Queen of Sex', in London. She was the daughter of the late Harold Jacobson, the property developer my father had met back in 1950. It appeared that he had implemented the very idea my father had discussed with him all those years ago. He had branched out into the sex industry as restrictions were eased in the sixties. By the time of his death he owned cabaret clubs, cinemas and a stable of soft-porn magazines. The business had come of age and gained a certain respectability. Then last September I received a letter from Marcia Jacobson inviting me to the opening of a new revue club in Denman Street. My initial reaction was to refuse, until I noticed the name of the enterprise. I had to go.

Indulging myself, I joined early diners who were taking a pre-theatre supper at the address in Greek Street where my father had lived, over fifty years before. I sensed it was going to be a nostalgic evening, and although I had often walked past the building I had never been inside. The problem with being constantly on television is that you sometimes feel you have become public property. People seeking autographs interrupt conversations with friends or family in restaurants. It becomes a real bore. That's why I usually only eat at restaurants that pointedly preserve my privacy.

The restaurant in Greek Street is fairly upmarket, specialising in dishes from the Alsace region of France. The owner spotted me as soon as I came through the door and wanted to seat me at a table overlooking the street. I opted for one tucked away at the back of the room. I had signed three autographs by the time the waiter brought my kir. Calling the owner over I explained the relevance of the building and very kindly he took me on a guided tour. The basement where Winnie and Gaynor had plied their trade was now the kitchen. (I couldn't help noticing that none of the chefs were French.) Upstairs he was only able to show me one room, as the others were let. Looking down on the traffic below, I wondered if this had been the room my father described in his diaries. It gave me a strange feeling, consciously trying to reach out to him in my mind.

Downstairs I picked at the food. What had he really been like? Until I had read his last journal I had imagined him to be a victim of circumstance. Nothing planned. Rather like me, just drifting, accepting what turns up and trying to make the best of it. His description of his killing Carlo had rather ruined that impression. Whatever the provocation, there had been a ruthless, cold-hearted edge to the man. But then how would we react if someone purposely targeted one of our children? Perhaps Father Tony had been right. He couldn't cope. He was looking for a way out.

Leaving the restaurant, I sauntered through the streets where my parents had operated. As always when I visit

Soho, I felt uneasy. Perhaps rather like walking through a deserted graveyard at night, half expecting ghosts to appear. Now there are no street girls standing on corners, just signs in doorways. A new generation of ruthless operators, controlling girls ghosted in from Eastern Europe. Now the Albanians, not the Maltese, hold sway.

The one remaining link was provided by Marcia. She is still the largest property owner in the area, with an amazing portfolio of sex shops, clubs, flats and tenements, built up over the years by her father.

I headed down Shaftesbury Avenue, towards Denman Street. I wasn't sure what to expect. Standing opposite the double-fronted building, I stared at a neon sign which was now illuminated as darkness fell. A huge photograph of a girl stood with her back to the street, her head turned. She was winking suggestively. Her hat was worn at a rakish angle and from the waist down she was naked, except for very high heeled shoes. Her khaki tunic fascinated me. Unbuttoned, it had three pips on the epaulettes. The sign flashed 'Welcome to the Captain's Club'.

A cluster of men stood outside the entrance. It was still an hour to the official opening. I eased my way through the crowd. I was obviously expected. A tough looking doorman let me in. A demurely dressed young woman then escorted me to the lift, which whisked us to the top floor. Pressing a security buzzer, she led me into a rather plush suite. Refectory tables were laden with an amazing selection of fish, cold meats and salads. A waiter offered me a drink. From behind the bar, a photograph of Harold Jacobson stared down, his expression wary, with a hint of haughtiness. Rows of racks had been set out, displaying the numerous titillating titles from the Jacobson publishing empire. Top shelf material generating huge profits. Presumably there was going to be a press reception. Marcia didn't miss a trick.

I didn't hear her come into the room. She looked fantastic. Not beautiful, but outstanding. Dressed simply but expensively in a crisp white blouse and long black skirt, she exuded that added allure so common in powerful, successful women. Although we had only met fleetingly she brushed my cheek with the faintest kiss. We didn't speak. She linked arms and led me through an adjoining room. Two huge roulette wheels waited to be initiated. Baize tables had been set up for baccarat and blackjack. The croupiers rose as one; she ignored them. We passed through offices with computers and banks of surveillance equipment. Staff offered greetings. There was no response from Marcia, as she led me onto a balcony overlooking a sizeable theatre-like room. There was a traditional raised stage, but the auditorium was set out with a series of round tables of differing sizes. A horseshoe bar was situated to the side of the entrance.

A murmur of chatter was cut short, as the staff saw us looking down on them. Marcia gave an imperious wave of the hand. The curtain to the stage parted. Standing to attention were perhaps a dozen girls wearing G-strings and open-topped khaki tunics. Marcia squeezed my hand. Each girl stepped forward to collect a glass of champagne. I noticed Marcia incline her hand slightly towards the stage. A smaller curtain parted. On a screen a photograph of my father was projected. It was one I had never seen before. I was struck again by his good looks. 'The Captain!' the girls chimed and downed their drinks with military precision. It was a strange tribute, but one which I think would have amused him. In spite of myself, I felt a surge of emotion.

Back in Marcia's office, we were also handed champagne. We raised our glasses. 'To the *Vice* Captain,' I said with emphasis. She smiled and holding my hand we went to welcome the new members of the club.